psych's

Guide to Crime Fighting
for the Totally Unqualified

ch's

Guide to Crime Fighting
for the Totally Unqualified[1]

SHAWN SPENCER WITH BURTON GUSTER
AND Chad Gervich

G|C

**GRAND CENTRAL
PUBLISHING**

NEW YORK   BOSTON

---

[1] Or, *The Unlicensed Detective's Guide to Crime Solving*[a]

[a] Or, *Mark of Genius: Conversations with Shawn Spencer*[b]

[b] Or, *Eat, Love, Play* Street Fighter[c]

[c] Or, *The New(er) Testament*[d]

[d] Or, *Postmodern Representations of the Phallus in Pre-Neoclassicism*[e]

[e] Or, *Why I'm No Longer Loaning Gus My iPad*

All illustrations are by Steven Parke unless otherwise indicated. All photos are courtesy of NBCUniversal unless otherwise indicated. All Shutterstock.com images are copyrighted 2013 and under license from Shutterstock.com. See page 290 for additional copyright information.

Designed by Timothy Shaner, NightandDayDesign.biz

Grand Central Publishing
Hachette Book Group
1290 Avenue of the Americas
New York, NY 10104
HachetteBookGroup.com

Printed in the United States of America

LSC-C

First Edition: May 2013

20 19 18 17

Grand Central Publishing is a division of Hachette Book Group, Inc.
The Grand Central Publishing name and logo is a trademark of Hachette Book Group, Inc.

The Hachette Speakers Bureau provides a wide range of authors for speaking events. To find out more, go to www.hachettespeakersbureau.com or call (866) 376-6591.

The publisher is not responsible for websites (or their content) that are not owned by the publisher.

Library of Congress Cataloging-in-Publication Data

Spencer, Shawn.
   Psych's guide to crime fighting for the totally unqualified / Shawn Spencer ; with Burton Guster. —First edition.
      pages cm
   ISBN 978-1-4555-1286-7 (trade pbk.) — ISBN 978-1-4555-1285-0 (ebook)
   1. Psych (Television program) I. Title.
PN1992.77.P75S64 2013
791.45'72—dc23
                                                              2012045969

To a man whose steadfast and passionate dedication to all things good has remained an infinite source of enlightenment and inspiration.

This one's for you, Billy Zane.

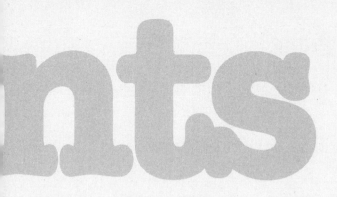

Forew

I thought I'd start by telling you would-be sleuths you're in good hands. Shawn Spencer is nothing if not a hell of a detective. And I'm not only saying this because he's mounted my exercise bike and refuses to get off, I'm saying it because it is so.

It wasn't long after we first met that I happened upon him unexpectedly between tunes at a Tears for Fears show at the Santa Barbara Civic. I was swapping out one bass guitar for another (as one does) only to discover my instrument being handed to me not by my longtime guitar tech, Ivan, but by Shawn! He explained he'd been hired by the venue's management to investigate some suspicious goings-on with their security staff. Then he asked me to autograph the back of his neck with a Sharpie, but I had a set to finish.

He turned up again at the after-party, where I witnessed him dress down a trio of nefarious characters—all of whom were arrested—while chatting up our road manager and scarfing down no fewer than forty-five mint Oreos. I've never seen anything like it. And I'm a legendary rock icon. I've seen things.

I have since crossed paths with him numerous times, in some very surprising places (the produce department at Whole Foods, the TFF tour bus,

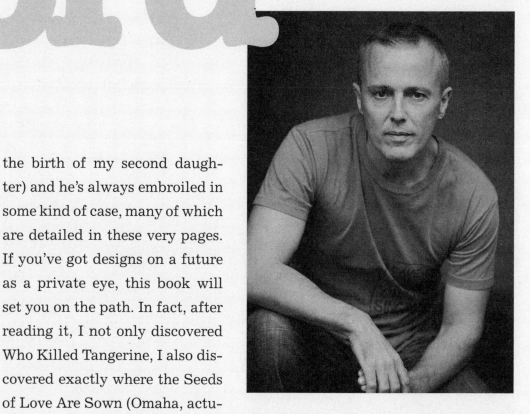

the birth of my second daughter) and he's always embroiled in some kind of case, many of which are detailed in these very pages. If you've got designs on a future as a private eye, this book will set you on the path. In fact, after reading it, I not only discovered Who Killed Tangerine, I also discovered exactly where the Seeds of Love Are Sown (Omaha, actually). I've wondered about that stuff for longer than I care to remember.

Enjoy the book. It's not just going to make you a better detective, it's going to make you a better person. Shawn may be more than a few bricks short of a full load, but he knows what he's doing. If only he'd get off my exercise bike.

—Curt Smith
Los Angeles, CA
www.legendaryrockicon.com

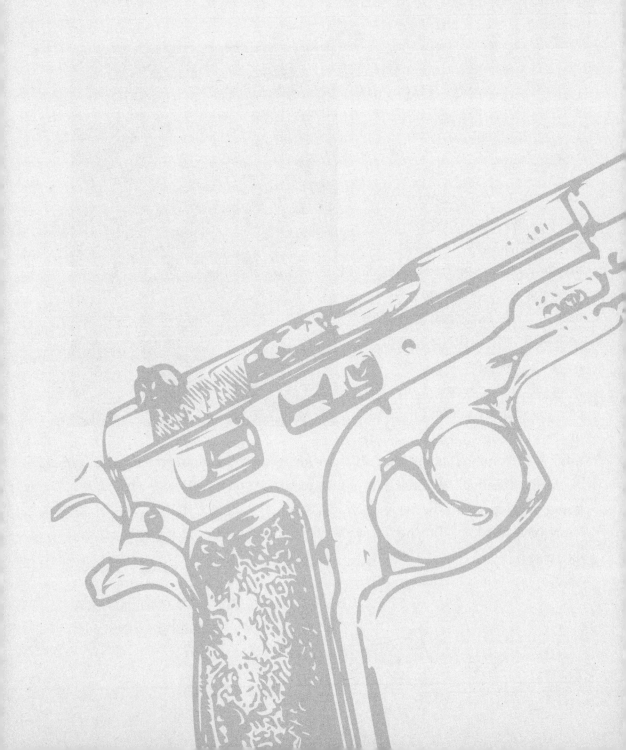

Author's Note

Because Grand Central Publishing was too cheap to provide an actual editor, this book was edited primarily by friends and colleagues, so everything on these pages has been quadruple fact-checked by actual cops, a pharmaceutical salesman, and a retiree who's read *The Pelican Brief* seventeen times.

If there are any mistakes, factual or otherwise, blame them.

Here you are. Page one. You're a detective, Jack! In fact I think you should say it:

"I'm a detective."

Feels pretty good, right? It should, because you just made a declaration. But it also pains me to report that these first sentences, your first little baby steps into the world of detectiving, were a test, and you failed. Remember, a real detective *never* does what another detective says. There, you've learned something already. Congratulations. I say we celebrate with a bowl of Kix.

Now, we all know you haven't been graced by the fates with my gift. It's a good thing, believe me. Being a psychic detective is a little like being Morrissey. People love you and look to you for guidance and solutions, hanging on your every word and admiring your twee English manner. It can be hell sometimes, and were it not for the occasional milk shake, it would be. But remember, we're not setting out to make you a psychic detective. That parking spot's already taken, Kingfisher.

The purpose of these pages is to harness your special talent. Whether you're a brain, an athlete, a basket case, a princess, or a criminal, you can be a detective, and this book is going to take you there like a little blue Toyota.

So there. You're a detective. You just said you are, and thus it is so. Say it again. And again. In fact, tell everyone you encounter today and let them show their support, and if they don't, they probably have something to hide. Consider investigating them.

1

Chapter 1

Setting Up Shop

Introduction

All right, I lied.

You know how in the introduction, just a few pages ago, I said all that stuff about how "now you're a detective," and "just say it," and "say it again," and "thus it is so," etc.?

Yeah, well—that wasn't exactly true.

I mean, philosophically, sure, now you're a detective, but come on. An aspiring shoe salesman doesn't just say, "Now I am a shoe salesman," and BAM, he's suddenly got a storefront and a bunch of shoes to sell.

Well, the same is true for detectives.

You can *think* like you're a detective. You can *feel* like you're a detective, but until you get some specific detective things, *you ain't no detective.*

This chapter is designed to help you get those specific things: an office, a catchy sign, the right massage chair, a badass detective-mobile, a well-stocked kitchen of healthful and delicious snacks and beverages.

Once you do everything in this chapter, *then* you'll be a detective. (Actually, that's not true, either. Once you solve a case, *then* you'll be a detective.)

Wait, no—I take it back. If a shoe salesman opens a store but doesn't sell any shoes the first day, he's still a shoe salesman. He just hasn't made his first sale. Big deal. So maybe you don't have to solve a case to be a detective, but you *do* need to get some basic stuff: the office, the sign, blah blah blah.

So just to recap...

Saying you're a detective: *not a detective.*

Saying you're a detective and having the basic stuff: *detective.*

Saying you're a detective, having the basic stuff, and solving a case:
   more of a detective than the guy who just says he's a detective and has the basic stuff...even though that guy's technically still a detective.

* * * * * FOR IMMEDIATE RELEASE * * * * * *

PSYCHIC SLEUTH AND LANGUAGE PIONEER SHAWN SPENCER BRINGS DETECTIVE NAMES INTO THE TWENTY-FIRST CENTURY

SANTA BARBARA, CA—JANUARY 21, 2013 In a dramatic move bound to have a lasting effect in the private law enforcement community as well as the worlds of literature and film, Santa Barbara psychic detective Shawn Spencer has proposed a list of new names for detectives. "It's the twenty-first century, and our people, the detectives, are still saddled with some colossally lame names. Gumshoe? What does that even mean? It's bugsome is what it is."

Spencer made no effort to conceal his ire for "legendary noir novelist and all around fuddy-duddy Raymond Chandler," as well as "every hat with a press card in the fifties," for outdated terms like *bloodhound* and *flatfoot*, as well as the roundly reviled *dick*, which remains a commonly used detective descriptor.

"Seriously, other professions aren't treated like this. Accountants and insurance agents are always respected," Spencer said. "Teachers have their job descriptions built right into their names. And God knows no one sits around thinking up names for cops. Wait. Okay, bad example."

The award-winning sleuth (who approves of *sleuth* as a name, citing the term's "timeless coolness") was on hand yesterday speaking to a small gathering of tastemakers in a local park, where he unveiled his proposed list of new names by which detectives will be known now and forever. "As of this moment, *slewfoot* and *peeper* are gone forever."

* * * * * FOR IMMEDIATE RELEASE * * * * * *

SHAWN SPENCER'S ALL NEW LIST OF NAMES FOR DETECTIVES

ASSASSINTRUDER

INVESTIGAMER

RICO SOLVÉ

ROXFORD

SAMURAI

SHERLOCK HOMEBOY

SIR

SOULEYE

AGENT SMITH

MR. ANDERSON

KILLHEART

WILLIAM WALLACE

KILLHEART SAMURAI

Spencer then encouraged the gathering to "go forth and propagate. Spread the word like your seed."

The enthusiastic crowd roared, eager to embrace Spencer's message.

"It's about time somebody stood up for the rights of detectives—I mean Mr. Andersons," said Norma Davis, an aspiring William Wallace.

And Douglas Weaver, a local plumber, added, "Uh, I don't really know what a souleye is, but yeah—I guess I can call him that if he wants."

Even as Spencer called the crowd to arms, he kept the message positive. "We need to end this stilted era of detective naming. It's time, my friends," the Killheart Samurai said.

* * * * * * FOR IMMEDIATE RELEASE * * * * * *

What Kind of Detective Are You?

Y ou're still reading—outstanding. Considering we're on page 8, you have an attention span 61.3 percent longer than most kids today.

I'm also going to assume (and thereby make an "ass" out of "u" and "me") you believe you've got what it takes to be a detective. Well, that's great and I dig your confidence, but I'm afraid you're still a few *Luftballons* short of the required ninety-nine. You've failed to consider a crucial piece of the puzzle: *What kind of detective are you going to be?*

It's a deceptively simple question. After all, one might just surmise (as I did in my nascent years), "Hey, I'm a hepcat with a strong hairline, so that's the kind of detective I'll be," and to some degree, you'd be right. But to a greater, deal-breaking, do-or-die degree, you're dead wrong.

If you're going to succeed as a detective, you're going to have to make a choice.

The Six Types

A n exhaustive empirical study into the neurological processes of *Homo roxfordus*—conducted by yours truly and my (occasionally) trusty sidekick, Gus, but mostly yours truly—revealed some surprising findings. Most notably, we, but mostly I, determined that there are six distinct detective "personalities." Each has its own attitude and methodology, and each occupies its own place in the public consciousness. You need to identify which type you are. It will determine how you spend your money, who you accept as clients, and perhaps most importantly, how your public sees you.

So think hard and search the faces of the gods, because this matters...but once completed, you'll be one massive step closer to legit detectiving.

Which one will you be?

The Hangdog

Real Fictional Example: COLUMBO

You show up late to the crime scene, wearing the same gear you had on yesterday, which disarms the suspect, lowering his guard such that he's nailed when you ask the essential question—like, "By the way, McDermott, if your brother wasn't going with you, where's his hacky sack?"—on your way out the door.

Necessary Tools: rumpled trench coat; disheveled, asymmetrical hairstyle; glass eye

1.

The Old Guy

Real Fictional Example: LENNIE BRISCOE (and the late Lanie Briscoe, had she lived to be a detective)

NOTE TO ALL OLD-GUY DETECTIVES, ESPECIALLY THOSE IN SANTA BARBARA WHO RETIRE, THEN UNRETIRE, THEN RE-RETIRE: Lennie Briscoe is a shining example of how old-man cops should act. Calm and levelheaded with zingers so subtle you don't notice they're zingers. How old-man cops should *not* act: Wandering around in old Tommy Bahama shirts, butting their noses into their kids' business. (Another Briscoe plus is he's an alcoholic. Sure, alcoholism has its downsides, but at least he had a hobby that kept him out of his kids' hair.)

Necessary Tools: crisply pressed suit, short-fused partner, Johnny Castle as a potential son-in-law

2.

The Other Dude

Real Fictional Example: N/A

You're always at the side of your dashing entrepreneurial partner, who started an agency and gave you a job out of the goodness of his heart and because you make a grilled cheese that's the perfect amount of crunchy versus melty. Also, while your deep reserves of scientific "knowledge" are often totally false (like claiming humans are both "carbon based" *and* made mostly of water, which is totally contradictory), you occasionally have some tidbit of truth which actually proves useful (like knowing how to defeat the giant baby in *The Son of Dr. Tongue*). You also have a car and are reimbursed for mileage at the more-than-generous rate of 6.3 cents per mile (7.8 cents if you refrain from listening to Wilson Phillips CDs), which is helpful, but by no means the only reason you're still around. Oh, and your Jade East cologne smells amazing. Not even kidding.

Necessary Tools: African Americanness; an attractive, magical head

3.

The Hack

Real Fictional Example: PATRICK JANE

With almost no real investigative skills of your own, you crib techniques from other detectives who happen to be on slightly smaller cable networks. Still, you manage to be fairly successful, which is a comment less on your own skills than on the skills of other people who paved your way.

Necessary Tools: incredible good looks…like, seriously, a gorgeous face and amazing hair, almost like you're some kind of Greek god or perfectly chiseled sculpture (I can give credit where credit's due)

4.

Liam Neeson

Real Nonfictional Example: LIAM NEESON

You somehow manage to convince people you're an action hero, even though you're so tall and gangly you look funny when sneaking around or fighting people. Also, you don't use your detective skills wisely. Say, for instance, you're in that movie *Taken*, trying to save that girl from *Lost*, and you have to break into an apartment building. Why would you scale the wall instead of just picking the lock? The truth is, you're a lover, not a fighter (you're great when you're a noble Nazi or a single widower helping his son hit on some tween chick), but the rest of the world thinks you're a tough guy, which just goes to show how *not* intuitive the rest of the world is.

Necessary Tools: the ability to convincingly deliver lines like "What I do have are a very particular set of skills…Skills that make me a nightmare for people like you," even if these "skills" never prove to be very cool or original

5.

The Pinkerton

Real Fictional Example: CYRUS KENILSWORTH III

A master of old-school skills like looking through magnifying glasses, finding fingerprints, and running across the tops of trains, you also wear a lot of suspenders and bowler hats. You may have a mustache, and you probably say things like "By the pinch of the game," "Verily," or "I think he's got the hump." You're also a great shot with a musket.

Necessary Tools: monacle, pocket watch, musket

Assessing Business Potential: Is There Enough Crime in Your Area to Support Your New Profession?

Before getting too far into this detective agency thing, you need to stop and ask yourself one very important question, *Are you prepared to die for all you consider just and holy?*

If the answer is yes, you should probably join the military or become some kind of missionary—being a PI is clearly not the right path for you. If, however, the answer is no, you need to ask yourself an even more important question, *What's love got to do, got to do with it?*

And then, *Does your community support enough crime to warrant its own detective agency?*

After all, there's only one reason to become a private detective: to pick up chicks. And to make money. And to have cool business cards, earn the respect of baristas, and be able to write off your *Spenser: For Hire* box set.

But being a successful detective means having enough crimes to solve, and unfortunately, not everywhere in this world is as crime ridden as we might like. So it's important—before plunking down a bunch of money for an office and an air hockey table—to assess exactly how much crime you have. (It is also important *not*—let me repeat, NOT—to promote crime in your area just so you can become a detective. I realize that in the beginning you may have to swipe a Twix a day from the local Munchie Mart so Mr. Mulligan, the manager, will hire you, but you should at least leave the money in the tip jar.)

There are several statistical ways of calculating your neighborhood's criminal activity, but here are the ones used by most official law enforcement agencies.[1]

Dead Body Rate (DBR)

One way of assessing business potential is by looking at an area's Dead Body Rate (the number of dead bodies that appear each week). Not every dead body is a murder (although most are since homicide is America's sixteenth leading cause of death), so you need a DBR high enough to ensure strong business traffic. Every neighborhood is different, but I usually analyze the DBR this way:

3–6 bodies/week—You may not get rich, but there's enough murder to sustain a fun hobby.

7–15 bodies/week—A good solid number. As long as you also have a healthy dose of burglaries and extortions, you should be fine.

16–23 bodies/week—Damn, it's like you're living in the Bermuda Triangle of dead bodies! (Actually, the reverse Bermuda Triangle since bodies keep appearing, not disappearing.) If you can handle the workload, you should soon be a wealthy investigamer.

Over 23 bodies/week—Get out. Now. Seriously. This is not natural. *Are you even listening to me? The killer's probably in your house* <u>*right now*</u>!

---

[1] Most of the statistics below come directly from the U.S. Department of Justice. Not all, but most. So if you find any flaws or inaccuracies, don't cry to me—take it up with the DOJ.

Popular Criminal Hangouts

Certain businesses and organizations tend to attract unsavory crowds, so many detectives gauge business potential by looking at what's already in the area. If you live in a community packed with knitting stores and pet spas, you probably don't have a lot of crunchy criminal goodness…or a social life (although opening a pet spa should be a crime in and of itself). Other types of enterprises, however, may signal a more vibrant criminal community, which—for you—spells jackpot. According to a study from the Pew Center for Stuff, here are the establishments most likely to attract the denizens of the underworld:

- Opium den
- Brothel
- Applebee's
- Blacksmith shoppe
- Zumba studio
- Anywhere that presents historically themed dinners, usually with knights or pirates
- Political campaign headquarters
- Orphanages
- Hotels that seem to make a big deal of advertising they have "Color TV"

The Mustache Factor

It's a well-known fact that people with mustaches can't be trusted. Look at the evidence: John Wayne Gacy, Dr. Phil, Jeff Foxworthy, Yanni. This is why the FBI has long used mustaches as the basis for warrants, arrests, and even prosecutions, so there's no reason you can't use them to determine the viability of setting up a detective agency. If you walk around the block and see more than 2.3 men (or women) with mustaches, you're in a pretty crime-heavy part of town. If you see more than 6.9 people with mustaches, *get out*. Especially if any of those people are under five. This is worse than a Dead Body Rate over twenty-three…*Escape while you still can.*

The Secret 'Stache

Don't believe a mustache is the doorway to evil? Check out these mustached photos of four of America's sweethearts, and tell me you wouldn't cross the street if you saw them coming your way.

Does this look like lovable Paul Rudd? Hells to the no. This is a Paul Rudd who's been pushed to the edge. A dangerous Paul Rudd. Put him in one more movie like *Dinner for Schmucks*, and this is what he'll turn into.

When she sings "We Are Never Ever Getting Back Together," I have a pretty good idea what she means: *you're frickin' dead*. (Also, if you've ever seen this video, could you please explain why Taylor Swift has a bunch of furries bouncing around her living room?)

Say what you will about Zac Efron, Corbin Bleu is the dreamiest guy in *High School Musical*. Even with a mustache that screams, "I will gut you slowly, peel off your skin, and wear it like a coat," he's pretty dreamy.

I don't know what's scarier—the thought of this thing being inside of you for nine months or the thought of this thing coming out of you, living in your house, and growing up to borrow your car.

Houses with Things Burglars Want to Steal

Just as certain business establishments attract crooks, so do certain types of homes. Nobody wants to rob a double-wide trailer filled with Kenny Rogers eight-tracks and old TV dinners. If a thief's gonna thieve something, he wants to hit the house that has money, stereos, or anything autographed by Tom Brady. So hide in some bushes and peer in people's windows. What do you see? Make a list of things you spot that people may want to steal: cash, jewels, big-screen TVs, those famous paintings made up of all the little dots, or any unopened packages of Starbucks Holiday Blend. If multiple homes in your area have at least three of these items—or one Addams Family pinball machine—you're probably in a crime-rich, detective-friendly area.

Seriously, Jules? Your job was to edit the manuscript, not fingerprint-doodle all over it.

Juliet: Sorry. You know it's a weird compulsion.

I don't mind you doing fingerprint doodles. I just mind you doing Donald Trump. You know I've been boycotting him ever since he ignored my application for Celebrity Apprentice.

Surveying the Territory

Assuming you've found a neighborhood with an acceptable number of murders, kidnappings, and armed robberies, the next step is to find an actual place to take advantage of them. I know this seems like it should be simple. After all, I know virtually nothing about real estate, and I scored an office only steps from an awesome Santa Barbara beach.

It's important to recognize, however, that my incredibly sweet office is situated atop an ancient Indian burial ground, and this can dampen the appeal. (To be fair, it's not a *Native American* burial ground; it's an actual *Indian* burial ground. Some guy from Mumbai was run over by a bus a few years ago. Fortunately, Mumbaians don't have a high rate of hauntings or possessions, although someone keeps leaving my Strawberry Yoo-hoos unrefrigerated.)

While you may not be able to find an office on a Southern California beach, you can still use some simple tips to score the best location wherever you are.

Finding a Location

Knowledge of local geography is invaluable when choosing an office site. You obviously want to be close enough to the criminal element that crime victims can find you, but far enough away so you're not burgled or assaulted by the same people who victimized the victims who want to hire you. Ask around. Try and figure out the ratio of criminals to noncriminals and go from there.

Above: Great for an office.

*Left: Also great for an office,
depending on the rent.*

Once you've found a building, it's time to consider other factors. What's the parking situation? Utilities included? Are there food vendors nearby, as well as other food vendors nearby the aforementioned food vendors? And what kind of food are we talking here? Casual dining? Fast food? Tapas? Consider all this before making your decision, unless you see readily available strombolis, calzone, and/or horchata, in which case, you should move your ass in immediately.

A reasonable proximity to a local police precinct is also a plus. You'll be doing a lot of work there, and it's not a terrible idea, once you're settled, to pay them a visit, tell them who you are, and then ask for a parking space. If you're refused, don't sweat it. You can always head back when they're closed on Saturday and stencil one yourself.

The Office

Your office is like your calling card. So if you actually have a calling card, your office is like the calling card where you keep your calling cards. In other words, it's your primary interface with clients (or as Gus and I call them, "people who need us to solve crimes for them"), and you need it to say everything you want clients to know about you. Then you should go ahead and *tell* them everything you want them to know about you, because sometimes clients can be obtuse, especially if a family member or associate has just been murdered.

The interior of your office should appear comfortable yet professional, smart but not snotty. It should also be inviting but still slightly intimidating in an I'm-a-nice-guy-but-I-could-snap-your-neck-like-Steven-Seagal-if-I-needed-to kind of way. This can be taken even further by a smart color scheme. Gus and I selected a variety of warm browns and sagey greens as a means of putting clients at ease while conveying our clear superiority. It's been working for us.

I understand all this might just be pie in the sky for some of you, and I get it. Newbie snoops don't often have the cake, but that doesn't mean you can't be a detective. It just means you're going to have to improvise when it comes to your digs.

Below is a list of frequently considered locations for upstart detective agencies, as well as the pros and cons of each.

	Pros	Cons
Bowling Alley	Arcade, $3 shoes	Noise, beehive hairdos
Movie Theater	Movies, popcorn, discount Tuesdays	Clients often want to talk during the movie.
Moretti's Italian Café	Large tables, great penne alla vodka, terrific service	Mr. Moretti always strokes your cheek and calls you "bambino."
Hospital	Open 24 hours, cool X-ray machines, plenty of beds	The cries of the dying
Spa	Hot tub	Cucumbers in the water, New Age music, lotions, patchouli, candles, getting wrapped in seaweed
The Gap	Affordable clothes, great jeans, sweaters that nicely accentuate my pectorals	Not much room for foosball tables, no food service
Detroit	Inexpensive office space, low tax rates, Tigers games	High probability of getting shot
Public Library	Lots of books make you look smart; librarians have a "dirty-me-up" sexiness about them.	20-minute limit at computers, homeless people in bathrooms
Police Station	Vending machines, donuts, hot junior detectives	Donuts are always stale, police actually expect you to "work" (primarily head detectives and old-man cops who keep finding reasons to come out of retirement).
Chili's	Nachos, Big Mouth Burgers, Awesome Blossoms (which, despite being slandered and discontinued as one of the unhealthiest dishes in America, still freaking rock)	None
Club Labyrinth	Super-loud music, girls in age-inappropriate clothing, killer mojitos	An unhealthy predilection for the work of ABBA and Lady Gaga, drinks with umbrellas

How to Make Your Office Bitchin'

So you found an office location—whoop-de-do. I mean, I'm happy for you and all, but come on, it's not enough just to have an office location. It's not enough to have an office *space*. It's not even enough to have an office filled with officey-type things like air hockey tables and inflatable wall pencils.

No, your office must be *bitchin'* like the apartment in *My Two Dads*, and admitting that doesn't make you gay. (Come on, the place had a *giant car chair!*)

Take the Santa Barbara Police Department. It's got desks, copy machines, staplers, phones; one guy even has a goldfish in a hamster ball. But so what? The whole place is still a minefield of roughly textured jujumagumbo. Look at Lassiter's attitude or Buzz McNab's total inability to become a detective. They're both due to the fact that their work spaces *aren't bitchin'*. And that Lassiter had a bad childhood.

So put some thought into your home base. Do you want something sleek and minimalist like the Fortress of Solitude? Something ultra–high tech like the headquarters in *Alias*? Or a more mysterious, underground feel like the city of NIMH?[1]

Bitchin'-ness sometimes takes a while to perfect, so here are some tried-and-true suggestions that have helped make the Psych office a maelstrom of bitchin'-ness:

- ■ Have at least one secret compartment under the floorboards. This can either hide valuables or lead to an underwater lair.

- ■ Get a cryogenically frozen head (or piece of head). This shouldn't be hard. There have been enough cryogenically frozen people—Walt Disney, Ted Williams, Gary Busey—that you can probably find it at Walmart.

- ■ Have a live zebonkey or grolar bear as your mascot. →

- ■ Helicopter pad

---

[1] GUS: Actually, Shawn, NIMH was the government laboratory where the rats were created, not the city where they lived.[a]

　[a] All right, readers, I hadn't planned on doing this till chapter 1.2, but since he's insisting on correcting every little thing I say, I might as well introduce my trusty black sidekick, Emile Coriander. (Then again, it's appropriate that I introduce him in a footnote, since—by the very nature of being a sidekick—he's already kind of a footnote.)[b]

　　[b] GUS: Thank you, Shawn. And I'm not your sidekick *or* footnote. We're partners, remember?[c]

　　　[c] See, Emile, there you go again, correcting everything. Frankly, this is why you can't find a woman.

■ Set all office ringtones to "Tubthumping" by Chumbawamba.

■ Install a fireman's pole between floors.

■ Solar power is so 2012. Today's bitchin'-est offices use electric eels. They're environmentally friendly and look supercool.

■ Install a moat and drawbridge, preferably with a troll underneath.

■ Do not give family members your address or phone number.

■ Wednesday = Ladies Night

■ Keep Chow Yun Fat and Gina Carano in a cage, and make them fight whenever you get bored.

Other Acceptable Mascots If You Can't Get a Zebonkey or Grolar Bear

HAGFISH: Remember playing with Slime in the '80s? Well, imagine being an underwater worm and shooting that out of your body. Like what you see? Then a hagfish may be the right mascot for you.

FOSSA: No one's really sure what this thing is. Is it a cat? Is it a mongoose? What the hell is a mongoose anyway? At any rate, the fossa's a creepy-looking thing that lives in Africa and eats lemurs, which makes it a pretty bitchin' mascot.

EUPITHECIA ORICHLORIS: A carnivorous caterpillar that eats you if you touch its back legs. (Well, not *you*. Other insects. It's a caterpillar; it's not going to eat a human. Unless that human is very, very tiny.)

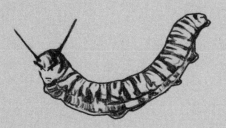

NORTHERN SNAKEHEAD FISH: These fish are so mean that they were named after another even *meaner* animal. They can also walk on land and survive out of water for almost three weeks! Supposedly, the Chinese breed them for eating, so that should tell you how evil these things are. Choose one of these as your mascot, and you're sending criminals a definite message. A message that says, "I am a hideous freak of nature, but a hideous freak of nature that will *tear your ass up*." I like it.

YETI: This could be the Arctic yeti (a peaceful, social animal that subsists mostly on seaweed and berries), the Himalayan yeti (a reclusive beast that lives mostly on the flesh of other animals), or Bumble (a bouncy mammal that hates Christmas and survives on a liquid diet due to lack of teeth).

Money Management for the Professional Detective

Since I'm psychic and because we're only in chapter 1, I know there are still many of you who think a detective can get by purely on charm and wit and sophistication and hair and face and hair. It's not even remotely true, not even in my case, although I have written a lot of checks my face and hair eventually cashed.

A detective needs a head for business. Columns need to balance. Ends need to meet. You might have come to this for the justice, but it's cake that's going to keep you in business, so you've got to be smart with it, because nobody is going to bring a case to a guy wearing a barrel, even back in the cartoon days, when people wore them all the time.

Now, I've been running an award-winning detective agency since you were in diapers, and it all boils down to a few essential economic principles.

It's most definitely a foregone conclusion, but it bears mention because, despite its obvious resemblance to something that sucks, budgeting is necessary. But it's a *have to*. So we're going to start there. Here's how it goes...

FIRST RULE OF ECONOMICS

THERE ARE TWO TYPES OF INCOME: GUARANTEED AND NONGUARANTEED.

GUARANTEED income includes any regularly scheduled money you know will be coming in. For instance, Grandma Spencer sends me fifty dollars every year on my birthday—that's guaranteed income. I also receive a six-dollar monthly rebate from DirecTV because I once complained about my DVR fee—more guaranteed income.

NONGUARANTEED income is money you *can't* count on every month, which basically is all your detective cases. Never include nonguaranteed income in your budget calculations, because, well, that's what *nonguaranteed* means—you can't count on it. Plus, this means all the money you make from actual detectiving is just 100 percent *profit*.

Here's a chart of my monthly guaranteed income:

Source of Income	Amount	Comments
Grandma Spencer's birthday check	$4.17	The birthday check comes only once a year, so I amortize the $50 over 12 months.
DirecTV rebate	$6	I'm thinking of calling next week to complain about *MTV*2.
Blood donation	$8.33	Semiannual, also amortized
Friday night pizza	$8	Every Friday, Gus and I order Rocky's Pizza and watch *Kitchen Nightmares*. The great thing is there's a $2 coupon in the *Penny Saver* each week, so it's basically like an extra $8 a month.
TOTAL	**$26.50**	

So if our total guaranteed monthly income is $26.50, we need to spend *less* than $26.50 per month in order to stay profitable. After all, we can't spend more than we bring in, and we're only guaranteed to bring in $26.50. Impossible, you say? Think again, Garfunkel; this is where it gets good.

I give you part two of the First Rule of Economics:

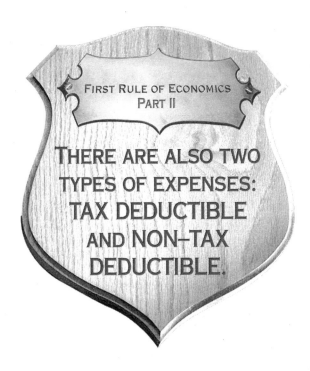

FIRST RULE OF ECONOMICS
PART II

THERE ARE ALSO TWO
TYPES OF EXPENSES:
TAX DEDUCTIBLE
AND NON-TAX
DEDUCTIBLE.

TAX DEDUCTIBLE expenses are expenses the government lets you subtract from your annual taxes. It's Uncle Sam's way of saying, "We're giving you a little help to apologize for creating an economy in which it's impossible to start your own business without getting immediately Stratemeyered by Walmart or Costco."

In order to qualify as tax deductible, an expense must relate *directly* to your business: rent, utilities, puffy pens, Slankets, etc.

Anything that *doesn't* relate directly to your business is *non*–tax deductible, like, say, taking your girlfriend to dinner. Unless your girlfriend happens to be a junior detective on the local police force, in which case—BAM—tax deductible![2] You also can't deduct things like—oh, I don't know—your dad's Christmas present, unless your dad happens to be *head of the consultants at the local PD.* BAM—another tax deduction!

See how this works? It's not about tax loopholes or creative accounting; it's about arranging your life so you only hang out with people who offer some type of financial advantage.

Here's a chart of last month's tax deductible expenses. I've included each item's original cost and its "actual" cost once you calculate its tax deduction.

> **WORD OF THE MINUTE**
>
> # STRATEMEYERED
>
> **S**o, apparently, this is a huge newsflash, but did you know that the Hardy Boys and Nancy Drew weren't actually written by Franklin W. Dixon or Carolyn Keene? They were created by this other dude, Edward Stratemeyer. I had no idea, and frankly, couldn't have cared less, but Gus seems to think this is some kind of big deal.[1] Anyway, we've now started using the verb *Stratemeyer* to mean "getting lied to, crushed, or screwed over by corporate America."

---

[1] GUS: It *is* a big deal, Shawn! They lied to me. Preyed on my innocence! I went through my entire childhood writing letters to Franklin W. Dixon and Carolyn Keene. Now all I can do is picture this Stratemeyer guy sitting there, laughing over my letters, wondering what this idiot kid in California looked like. Would it have been that hard to put the real guy's name on the cover?[a]

[a] GUS: And by the way, Shawn, Stratemeyer didn't even write the books himself. He hired *other* people to write the books for him! Plus, I looked him up on the Internet, and he looks exactly like Snidely Whiplash. *Exactly.* You don't think that's a bit weird?

[2] This is why I recommend dating a cop. They're cute, they carry a gun, and the tax benefits are amazing.

Tax Deductible Expense	What You Paid for It	Secret Cost (when you factor in tax deductibility)	Comments
OFFICE EXPENSES			
USB drive shaped like Wayne Gretzky	$12.95	$4.29	Essential for computer backup and cool thumb-drive collection
Golden Crisp cereal (5 boxes)	$15.62	$2.68	Quite possibly the greatest creation in the history of mankind
Pocket towel	$10.50	$6.73	Seriously—a towel that fits in your pocket? Tell me that isn't awesome.
Kashi Autumn Wheat cereal (3 boxes)	$12.83	$12.82	For Gus (it helps his menopause)
Dark City on Blu-ray	$14.99	$5.42	Because Kiefer Sutherland rocks
Remote-control robotic arm	$150.95	$1.74	I've heard some offices *don't* have remote-control robotic arms, so how do they get any work done?
Star Wars ice cube trays	$5.95	$2.00	Because warm soda is just wrong
Monster Beats Beatbox and iPod Dock by Dr. Dre	$399.99	$12.86	Because he's peepin' and he's creepin' and he damn near got caught 'cause his beeper kept beepin'
DETECTIVE TOOLS			
NASA space pen	$11.00	$2.83	For all those times you have to write upside down or underwater
Electronic drum kit	$450.00	$2.56	Real drum kits are so 2009.

DETECTIVE TOOLS (continued)			
TightWire iPhone app	$0.99	$0.05	If you're gonna be stuck on a stakeout for 6 hours, you might as well laugh at a fat guy on a tightrope.
Astronaut ice cream variety pack (vanilla, chocolate, pistachio, peach, strawberry, coffee)	$25.00	$4.79	Normally, I wouldn't buy an entire variety pack, but they were out of Neapolitan.
ADVERTISING & MARKETING			
Promotional skywriting	$1,550.29	$9.45	Wrote "Happy Birthday, Robert Palmer" over Butterfly Beach
INVESTIGATIVE RESEARCH			
2 tickets to Monster Jam	$110.75	$11.48	Scoping out potential investigative/combat vehicles
Original KISS comic with blood in the ink	$75.00	$23.20	When you see one of these on eBay, you don't pass it up.
Java Monster energy drink (2 48-packs)	$150.00	$68.90	A guy's gotta eat.
Wireless electric skateboard	$289.99	$12.93	"#1 form of transportation" —*Modern Detective* magazine
Supertramp's *Breakfast in America* (on vinyl)	$10.84	$2.26	Only 14 records to go before completing my Wall of Awesome Album Covers (anyone know where I can get David Bowie's *Heathen* on vinyl?)
Mockingjay on audiobook	$12.58	$3.84	Please tell me Katniss and Peeta end up together. No, wait, don't. Just give me a hint. Actually, no—I don't want to know. Okay, blink once if they make it, two if they don't.
TOTAL	**$3,310.22**	**$190.83**	

And just to compare, here's a chart of last month's *non*–tax deductible expenses.

Non-Tax Deductible Expense	Amount	Comments
Birthday card for Aunt Millie	$1.75	
TOTAL	**$1.75**	

Now, I'm sure you've noticed that last month's expenses ($3,310.22) are *considerably* more than last month's guaranteed income ($26.50). To be specific, $3,283.72 more, which means we have a serious cash flow problem. Like, a going-out-of-business cash flow problem.

That is, unless someone knows the (totally legal) secrets of tax deduction-ology, *which I do*.

Look at each expense's *actual* cost, or what the expense cost after factoring in its tax deductibility. Suddenly, each expense costs considerably less than it originally did. In fact, once you factor in tax deductibility, our total expenses come to only $190.83!

Calculating tax deductibility is an incredibly complicated formula using lots of x's, y's, and π's. I don't understand much of it myself, but I assure you, it's 110 percent legal, and any good accountant will know how to do it.

Of course, $190.83 is still more than $26.50, the amount of our guaranteed income, which means we're still spending more than we're making. So how do you get rid of the extra $164.33?

Welcome, my friend, to the world of "dependents" and "charitable donations."

The IRS gives people tax breaks for dependents, children or adults you're responsible for because they can't otherwise take care of themselves. It also gives deductions for donations to charities and nonprofits. Here's a look at the money I spent last month on dependents and charitable donations.

DEPENDENTS		
Name of Dependent	**Deduction Value**	**Comments**
Gus	$54.71	Not all sidekicks count as dependents, but Gus qualified because he clearly can't care for himself on his own.

CHARITABLE DONATIONS		
Name of Charity	**Deduction Value**	**Comments**
Sausage of the Month Club	$37.68	The spicy lamb is amazing, and don't miss the veal-garlic artichoke!
The Eric B. & Rakim Foundation	$49.49	Working tirelessly to reunite the greatest hip-hop duo of all time.
Save the Slap Bracelet	$72.38	Finally, someone has taken a stand against the persecution of America's most underrated fad.
The Haggis & Coddle Society	$28.93	Need to make good with your girlfriend (because you accused her of treating her cats better than you, even if it's true)? Give some money to her family's favorite Scottish-Irish charity.
TOTAL	**$243.19**	

Follow the math? I was $164.33 in the hole until I spent $243.19 on charitable donations and dependents.

Which means I'm not only *not* in the hole—*I've made a profit of $78.86* (which more than covers Aunt Millie's birthday card).

That's right, folks, I made $78.86 last month by doing nothing but *buying stuff*.

And that was *before* solving any cases. Check out our docket, and you'll see we closed five cases last month—Why Mr. Ingelsby Was Coming Home Late Every Night, The Mystery of the Missing Mailman, The Clue on the Stairs, The Case of the Bloody Claw, and Where Gus Keeps His Peanut Butter

Oreos—which amounted to twelve days of work, which (at $1,200 per day) equals $14,400 of pure profit.

Add in the $78.86 we made from doing nothing, and last month's profit comes to $14,478.86. Not bad for twelve days' work and just being a savvy shopper.

So there you go—the keys to managing a detective agency budget.

And if it seems shady, it's not. This is how most Fortune 500 companies and the federal government do their books every year.

Legal Disclaimer

The material in this piece is for informational purposes only, not for the purpose of providing actual legal advice. Shawn Spencer is neither an accountant nor a lawyer, and he barely passed high school calculus. He also returned TurboTax after trying it for less than five minutes. Mr. Spencer bears no responsibility should the advice in this piece lead to insolvency, criminal prosecution, or incarceration.

—Adam Hornstock, legal counsel to Shawn Spencer.

Recommended Reading List for Aspiring Detectives

As a budding young sleuth, you've obviously shown a certain aptitude for the detectiving arts. This doesn't mean, however, that you're fully cooked, and a true detective never stops learning.

Here's a short list of recommended reading material every PI should keep on his or her shelf. I've referred to these tomes many times over the years, and they always prove to be illuminating, helpful guides to crime solving.

CRYPTONOMICON by Neal Stephenson: Obviously, Gus put this on here, which means I'm never going to read it, and it's probably about dragons or math or subatomic particles. I have to admit, however, that it *does* make you look supersmart when it's sitting on your shelf.

THE MYSTERY OF CABIN ISLAND by Franklin W. Dixon: Not only the best Hardy Boys book, but possibly the *best book ever written*.

CRAZY FROM THE HEAT by David Lee Roth: Brilliant and profound. When I'm weary, feeling small, when tears are in my eyes, this is the book I turn to.

THE GOONIES (a novelization by James Kahn): It's hard to imagine anything better than *The Goonies*, but as people always say, the book *is* better than the movie. With amazing characterizations and a rich, textured world, this instant classic is destined to live for years alongside *Huckleberry Finn* and *Story of O*.

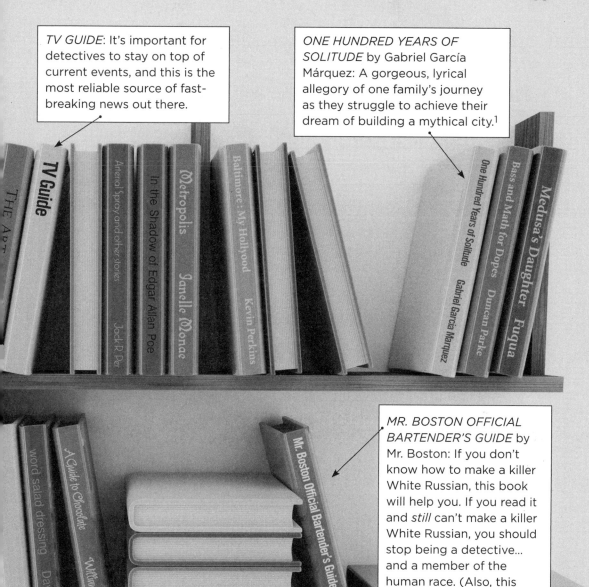

TV GUIDE: It's important for detectives to stay on top of current events, and this is the most reliable source of fast-breaking news out there.

ONE HUNDRED YEARS OF SOLITUDE by Gabriel García Márquez: A gorgeous, lyrical allegory of one family's journey as they struggle to achieve their dream of building a mythical city.[1]

MR. BOSTON OFFICIAL BARTENDER'S GUIDE by Mr. Boston: If you don't know how to make a killer White Russian, this book will help you. If you read it and *still* can't make a killer White Russian, you should stop being a detective... and a member of the human race. (Also, this is written by the *real* Mr. Boston, not that idiot from VH1 a few years ago.)

[1] I have no idea what this book is about. I literally copied that description off Amazon. (Thank you, TKBabe94.) This book has the most boring title of any book in the world, which is partly why I've never read it, but when your girlfriend gives you a gift—and goes on about how it's a first-edition hardcover—you'd better put it on your shelf.

Books *Never* to Have on Your Shelf

- *BRIDGET JONES'S DIARY* by Who Cares: No book screams "I am a chick" or "I have terrible taste in *everything*" louder than this. Never allow this book near your bookshelf. If it's already there, or even in the vicinity, burn it immediately, shower, exfoliate, and watch *The Bridge on the River Kwai* at least twice.

- *HELTER SKELTER* by Vincent Bugliosi and Curt Gentry: I know it's a true story and a crime story, but this book just *looks* so creepy I wouldn't want it on my shelf. I'm pretty sure it's a secret portal for the undead.

- Anything by Ayn Rand: First of all, having anything by Ayn Rand on your bookshelf will make you look like a political nutjob. Second of all, these are not books. They are not stories. They are one-thousand–page bludgeonings of your frontal lobe. I had to read *ATLAS SHRUGGED* in high school and wanted to shoot myself after ten pages. I am guessing this chick never got asked to prom in a serious way.

Selling Your Business, But Not Your Soul... Okay, Maybe Your Soul

And now, my tomodachi, it's time to learn a painful lesson: Even with a bitchin' office and foolproof business plan, people aren't just gonna walk in your door and hand you mysteries to solve. Even if your detective agency has a cool name like Spandex Luau or Suzannimation.[1]

No, you gotta get out there and pound the pavement, shake the trees, and spread the word that Spandex Luau is ready to crack some cases and bust some skulls.

In other words, you's gots to market yourself.

The good news: marketing doesn't have to be expensive. I mean, look at the Gap. Their whole marketing plan consists of getting people to buy sweatshirts that already say "the Gap" on them. I mean, people are basically paying the Gap for the privilege of being walking billboards. Which is a brilliant move by the Gap's marketing department, because not only are customers paying all their expenses, but the marketing execs get to just sit back drinking Long Islands and playing badminton all day.

---

[1] JULIET: Uh...Shawn?...I think you mixed up your Detective Agency Name List with your Cool Band Name List.[a]

[a] True dat. But you gotta admit, Suzannimation would be a pretty great name for a chick band.

Now, because I'm an ethical person, I've never felt comfortable hawking Psych T-shirts on every corner in town.[1] But here are some of the more successful marketing campaigns Gus and I have used, and since we, like Goldman Sachs, have reached a level of success that no longer requires us to market ourselves, I bequeath them to you. Don't screw 'em up.

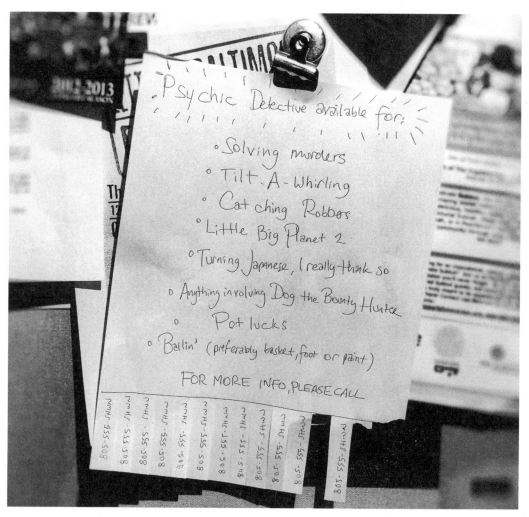

Psychic Detective available for:

- Solving murders
- Tilt-A-Whirling
- Catching Robbers
- Little Big Planet 2
- Turning Japanese, I really think so
- Anything involving Dog the Bounty Hunter
- Pot lucks
- Ballin' (preferably basket, foot or paint)

FOR MORE INFO, PLEASE CALL

Above: Great in theory, but we kept getting hired as guitar teachers and babysitters.

[1] GUS: Maybe, Shawn, that's because you insisted on going with some cheap silk-screener who printed "PSUCH" on all the T-shirts and then refused to give your money back.

Above: Not only a fun way to spread the name of your business, but also the best organic, yeast-free, flax-and-barley bread you'll ever eat! (I'm kidding. No way am I gonna eat that crap.)

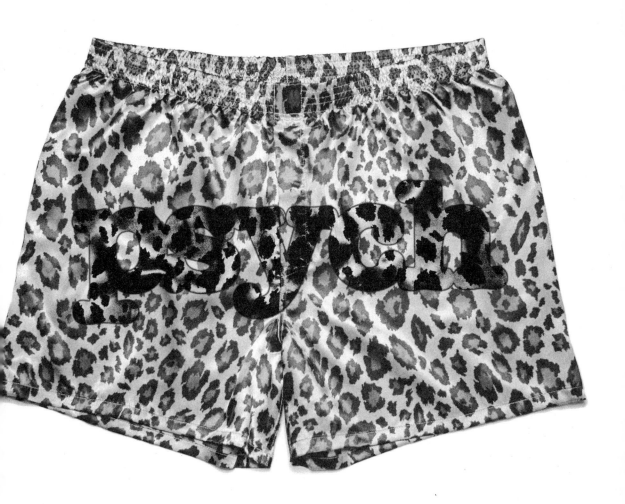

Above: Personally, I hate these. I don't want my name or the name of my business anywhere near a stranger's crotch. But CheapThreads.net was having a bulk sale, so what the hell. Also, they're surprisingly comfy.

Left: Most tramp stamps look terrible, which is why Gus had his removed. Still, I found these surprisingly alluring. Unfortunately, the health department shut down the whole campaign after our tattoo artist gave his first three customers hepatitis C.

Right: Psych: All the crime solving, none of the scruff.

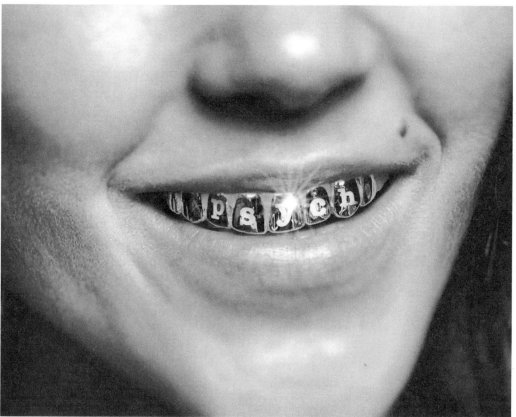

Above: There ain't no crime in the Dirty South, when you're walkin' 'round with Psych in your mouth.

Above: I thought Psych sutures were a great idea, but Gus passed out every time he saw them.

Below: Not quite as effective as our animal-branding campaign.

Right: Psych: Our aim is true.

Grand Opening!

Congratulations, the doors of your detective agency are now open, and to celebrate, we're going to have a party, complete with drinking games, sorority chicks, and a musical appearance by both Gallagher brothers, who reunited just for this event.

Except by *party*, I mean, "pop quiz," and by *drinking games, sorority chicks,* and *Gallagher brothers*, I mean, "grading on a curve."

I would've told you up front, but I figured if I said, "To celebrate, we're going to have a quiz," you wouldn't show up.

And like it or not, it's time to take this detective thing seriously. After all, this is not a game. This is not a joke. This is not finger painting or shark diving or Wiffle ball.

You are on the path to becoming a private detective, one of the most difficult, dangerous career paths that exists.

(I know I've been saying pretty much the exact opposite, that anyone can become a detective, that all it takes is a semifunctioning brain, etc., but the truth is…okay, the truth is, yeah, a monkey could do this. Maybe not any monkey, but definitely that monkey from *Rise of the Planet of the Apes* and probably even *Dunston Checks In*.)

And as your teacher, your sensei, your Patches O'Houlihan, I have only one goal in life: to make you the best private investigator possible. And, of course, to see the Lions go to a Super Bowl. And maybe to play Mr. Blonde in a remake of *Reservoir Dogs*. And to watch the sun rise over the Andes at Tres Cruces de Oro. And to have the original Guns N' Roses play my birthday party. But after those, definitely to make you the best private investigator possible.

So if I feel a quiz is what it takes to make you the next Jessica Fletcher, or even to save your life someday, then dammit—we're gonna have a quiz. Come on. It's only five questions.

You have ten seconds per question. No looking back at the chapter for answers. Although if you do, I won't know about it. (But you will, and if you can live with that kind of guilt—well, good luck to you, my friend.)

Questions

1 Which of the following would NOT make a suitable location for a detective agency?

    A. an empty office at your local police station

    B. an abandoned slaughterhouse

    C. Gymboree

    D. your mother's basement

    E. Library of Congress

2 How many Indiana Jones movies are there?

    A. one

    B. three

    C. four

    D. thirty-five

3 According to a recent FBI study, violent crime fell 5 percent in 2009. This drop in crime was due mostly to:

    A. more cops on the street

    B. fewer cops on the street

    C. more private detectives, like yourself, working hard to keep America safe

    D. man-eating tigers

    E. murder and assault are no longer considered "violent" crimes

4 How do you know when it's love?

_____

_____

5 At tax time, the IRS allows private detectives to write off which of the following expenditures?

   A. home office space

   B. frappuccinos

   C. ninja weapons (foot spikes, shuriken, makibishi, etc.)

   D. Lakers tickets

   E. aquarium toilet

Answers

1. Trick question—BOOM! Right out of the gate! The correct answer is *none of the above.* I suppose Gymboree is slightly better than an abandoned slaughterhouse, and the Library of Congress would be cool because it's the Library of Congress, but you definitely don't want to be stuck in the police station or your mother's basement.

2. D—thirty-five. This includes the original trilogy, plus twenty-eight episodes and four TV movies of *Young Indiana Jones,* all of which were better than *Kingdom of the Crystal Skull,* which I don't even count.

3. First of all, if you said D (man-eating tigers), you're an idiot. Police departments don't use man-eating tigers, and if they did, how would the tiger distinguish between a criminal and a normal citizen? It wouldn't; it would eat everything in its path and cause mass chaos throughout the country. The correct answer is that the FBI can only count so high, so violent crime may have actually *risen*—we can't be sure. Now, I realize this answer wasn't technically listed, so let's go with the closest *other* answer, E (many crimes are no longer considered violent).

4. I can't tell you, but it lasts forever.

5. All answers acceptable

If You Scored...

5 *Correct Answers*: Mazel tov, bubeleh, you clearly have the gift deep within your bones. Take a night off, load up on mai tais and Mike and Ikes, and I'll see you on the morrow.

4 *Correct Answers*: Close enough. Go back, erase your one wrong answer, and consider yourself passed.

3 *Correct Answers*: Three out of five ain't bad—it's a better average than the Death Wish movies. In fact, watching the original *Death Wish* probably isn't a terrible idea right now. Do it, and consider yourself passed.

2 *Correct Answers*: Hey, you could've done worse, right? The good news is detectiving isn't an exact science. The bad news is I don't want some unprepared half-wit out there saying I was their teacher. So do me a favor—take a cold shower, eat a Strawberry Toaster Strudel, and take another stab at the three questions you got wrong. Remember, you still have two lifelines: Phone a Friend and Ask the Audience.

1 *Correct Answer*: If you got the Indiana Jones question right, give yourself an A and proceed to the next chapter. If your one right answer was something else—well, I'm not really sure how you screwed this up. You probably chose the wrong detective personality. Are you sure you're not a Liam Neeson? Or maybe the *actual* Liam Neeson? (Wait, if you *are* Liam Neeson, *that is so cool that you're reading this book*! And for the record, I'm a big fan of yours, although *Clash of the Titans* sucked. And so did *Taken*. But I always cry at the end of *Love Actually*.) Go back, reevaluate your detective personality, and then take this quiz again. Or don't. Just choose a different personality. I'm betting it'll make a difference.

0 *Correct Answers*: Seriously, dude? Half these questions weren't even real questions, and you *still* couldn't get any right? Flog yourself for ten minutes like that guy in *The Da Vinci Code*, listen to at least half of *Credo* by the Human League, and try again.

Chapter 1.2

Sidekicks...and Why You Need One

Introduction

One of the most important aspects of being a professional detective is having a reliable sidekick. Most people underestimate the importance of selecting and grooming the right person; they think a sidekick is either a partner, a buddy, or some kind of tagalong.

These couldn't be further from the truth.

First of all, a sidekick is not a partner. The word *partner* implies equality, and you and your sidekick are not equals. Was Tattoo equal to Mr. Roarke? Was McMahon equal to Carson? Woodstock equal to Snoopy? If sidekicks were our equals, they wouldn't be sidekicks—*they'd be doing what we do.* They'd be called "frontkicks" or "main guys" or "*el jefe*" or something. But they *can't* do what we do, which is why they're sidekicks.

This doesn't mean, however, that they're not valuable.

A good sidekick is like a Swiss army knife, an extension of yourself, small enough to stay out of sight when not needed, but packed with hidden skills (some useful, like intimate knowledge of pharmaceuticals; others not so useful, like speaking Fremen to girls in bars).

Sidekicks are, in many ways, like obedient puppies; they desperately want to please their master, but they rarely have enough brain capacity to think for themselves. So they need guidance, nurturing, and—in some cases—a firm hand.

This half chapter explores how to spot a good sidekick...and how to use them at appropriate moments.[1]

Left: Not a partner.

---

[1] By the way, it seems kind of poetic that the section devoted to sidekicks is actually a sidekick itself to chapter 1.[a]

[a] FYI—a sidekick couldn't have made that profound literary connection.

How Gus Compares to Other Sidekicks: A Graphic Representation

Not going to lie. Gus has had some big moccasins to fill. Some of the second-greatest characters in all of literature are sidekicks, and civilization has seen more than a few, so instead of sincerely expressing myself, I'd like to present a graph as a reminder that Gus is probably the best sidekick out there.[1]

---

[1] GUS: That's probably the nicest thing you've ever said to me, Shawn.[a]

[a] Well, it's true. Now, go pick up the pizza—and don't forget my root beer this time.

If Gus Wasn't My Partner, Who Would I Pick?

I once read about this thirty-five-year-old guy in Reno who had a brain aneurysm and just up and died. A woman in Tampa spontaneously combusted. Planes crash. Buildings crumble. Cars mysteriously get their brake lines cut and career off cliffs.

I obviously don't want any of these things to happen, especially to Gus, but let's face it, we live in a dark, dark world. And as a small business owner, I need to be protected against tragedy.

So, yes, I've been keeping a short list of people who would make suitable sidekick replacements. I have not talked to any of these people. I have not interviewed or vetted them. They're simply promising candidates should something sudden and inexplicable happen to Gus.[1]

→ **JACKIE CHAN:** It has been scientifically proven that Jackie Chan is the greatest sidekick of all time.

← **JOY GUSTER:** All the fun of Gus, but with a cuter voice and rockin' body.[2]

→ **MR. MUIRRAGUI:** Worst eighth-grade math teacher in the world and the meanest guy in Santa Barbara, which is exactly why I'd like to be in a position of power over him. I don't really want him as a permanent sidekick; I just want to boss him around for a few days.

← **ANY NAVY SEAL**

---

[1] Private note to people on this list: If any of you should happen to be reading this book and are interested in a life of crime fighting, please call me ASAP on my home number: 805-555-SHWN.[a]

  [a] Also, if any regular Joe reading this book is interested in submitting a résumé, please feel free to e-mail me at pineapplelover@prodigy.com. But again, you'll have to get in line behind the people on this list. And Gus.

[2] GUS: Not funny, Shawn—don't even play.[a]

  [a] JULIET: Yeah, Shawn, not funny—don't even play.[b]

  [b] Okay, first of all, "don't even play" went out with Sir Mix-A-Lot and the "Macarena." Second of all, I'm *kidding*! I would never fool around with Gus's sister...again. Because it was so awesome the first time, and second, I don't know if anything could top it.[c]

  [c] GUS: Not funny, Shawn.[d]

  [d] JULIET: Yeah, Shawn—*not funny.*

→**JASON VOORHEES:** How awesome would it be to have a raging undead psychopath as your sidekick? "I'm sorry, you say you can't take back my return, even though I have the receipt?...Jason, blow up his head with a firecracker." Or: "But how can there be a half-hour wait if I had a reservation?... Jason, drive a hook through his torso, then rip it out backwards so his intestines spill out."

←**THAT KID AT ACE HARDWARE WHO'S ALWAYS SUPER-NICE:** Tom or Tim or something like that. I can't remember, but he wears a name tag so it shouldn't be a problem. Ted, maybe? Also, it would be nice to have someone who knows how to use power tools and doesn't use Devo quotes as pickup lines.[1]

→**MILA KUNIS**

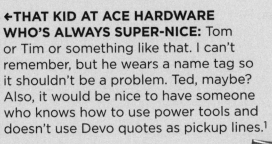

→**JULIET O'HARA:** For her keen mind, eternal loyalty, and exquisite beauty.[2]

Why I Did *Not* Put Juliet O'Hara on the above List

The reason I did not put Juliet O'Hara on my list of Gus replacements is that Juliet is not sidekick material. You wouldn't put the first fiddle in the second fiddle's chair, so why take a future head detective and make her a sidekick? If I wanted someone to have candlelight dinners or take long walks on the beach with, I would obviously pick Juliet (or Mila Kunis—whoever got back to me first), but when it comes to a sidekick, I want someone who's not destined for greater things, someone who's meant to be in my shadow, someone whose purpose in life is to serve and follow—not lead.[3]

---

1 GUS: Girls love Devo, Shawn. Have you ever seen a girl *not* dance to "Whip It"?

2 Obviously, readers, *I did not write this.* The manuscript was hijacked by an unnamed junior detective while I was taking a shower during a break in my Sunday afternoon Van Damme festival. Besides, this doesn't even *sound* like me. When have I ever used the word *exquisite*?[a]

   a JULIET: Are you actually going to argue this, Shawn?

3 GUS: That's it—we're done, Shawn.[a]

   a JULIET: Yeah, nice try, Shawn. I'm siding with Gus. We're done.

Who You Calling "Sidekick"?
Or a Brief Response to Shawn Spencer
from Burton Guster

Dear Reader,

While Venn diagrams and lists of replacements are clearly hilarious, we all recognize Shawn's glib tone and trenchant sarcasm as his ways of masking latent childhood insecurities. So I'm going to point out what most of us already know: the sidekick is the most important part of any operation. Could there have been a Batman without Robin? Would Wallace have survived without Gromit? Okay, technically, the answer to both of those could be yes, but the point is, the sidekick is the soul of the team, the everyman that allows the leader to shine. (And yes, Shawn, Tattoo was equal to Mr. Roarke. You think people still say, "Da plane, da plane," because Mr. Roarke said it?)

A sidekick must know when to step in, when to back out, when to offer gentle support, when to rush in, guns blazing. It's through the sidekick's eyes that other people see the head guy. Without Barney, Andy wouldn't have seemed as wise. Without Goose, Maverick wouldn't have been as commanding in his bomber jacket. A sidekick defines who his partner is, but he does so through the lens of his own dedication, bravery, and selflessness.

So while I have nothing against Shawn taking credit for Psych's many successes, I wanted to set the record straight on some facts that Shawn may not be telling you about himself.

- Pill bugs make him hyperventilate.

- He refuses to use the word <u>soggy</u>.

(over)

- He cries during Blake Shelton's "Austin" (which, by the way, I played for him first).

- He thinks labradoodles are an "unholy perversion of science."

- He claims he won't eat canned tomatoes because he once found a thumb, which is a total lie. If anything, it was a small chunk of cartilage or softened bone tissue.

- He refers to Khloe as "the hot Kardashian."

- He has seen every episode of <u>Wizards of Waverly Place</u> (which, granted, is a great show; I'm just pointing out that the show dipped a bit in season three, and a lot of die-hard fans dropped out for a while).

Sincerely,
the beating heart of Psych, Gus

A Brief Response to Gus's Brief Response from Shawn Spencer

Really, Gus? "The beating heart of Psych"? Okay, let's play a little game I like to call "Stuff Gus Is Afraid of...I'm Not Even Kidding."

I'll put a picture of you screaming on the left, and you—or our highly perceptive readers—can match it to the picture on the right of whatever made you scream. Oh, what's that?...You don't think I keep and categorize photos of you screaming at whatever ridiculous crap scares you each day? Think again, hombre. I've been keeping these things cataloged for a moment *exactly* like this. So get yourself an appletini or a Zima or whatever herbal tea you're drinking today, and get ready for some fun.

Answer: Okay, come on. Do you honestly think I categorize pictures of Gus screaming? *I run the world's greatest psychic detective agency.* I don't have time to keep track of every time Gus shrieks like a girl (although in 2012, it was 7,943 times). So match them up however you want; you'll be close enough.[1]

---

[1] And as long as we're setting the record straight, season three had some of *WoWP*'s best episodes ("Wizards vs. Werewolves" = awesome), and labradoodles *are* a perversion of science.

Chapter 2

Taking a Bite out of Crime

Introduction

So you got an office, a sidekick, some gear, and now you're sitting in a Souplantation wondering when will your life begin, and then you chuckle because somehow "When Will My Life Begin?" that song from *Tangled*, suddenly relates to your life, which sort of makes you like Mandy Moore.

Just then, you overhear the couple next to you arguing about dessert items, during which time they happen to drop that a murder has recently occurred down the street. It's a curious confluence of coincidences, to be sure, but remember, you're in Souplantation, where just about anything can happen.

And this is where the rubber meets the road, my apple-cheeked subject. Murder means crime, and crime means case, and case means case for *you*. So I don't care if you're not finished with your savory potato cheese soup and mixed baby greens, you need to get over to that crime scene on the double.

I have to admit, Jules, that's one of the best drawings of Prince I've ever seen. You are so sexy when you're artistically brilliant.

Juliet: It's Elvis.

The Crime Scene...aka the Gravy Train

The crime scene is a detective's point of entry. It might be a murder, or a robbery, or perhaps both (which we in the business call a *murbery*), but the first few moments after you arrive will make or break this case.

I'm sure you've heard cops say the most critical period of solving any crime is the first forty-eight hours?...Well, this is 100 percent *false*. The most critical part of solving any crime is the first forty-eight *seconds*...because these are the seconds that determine whether the gig goes to you, some jackhole, or worse—your local PD's head detective.

As everyone knows, you get only one chance to make a first impression, and these initial moments are your opportunity to look cool, take control, show people who's in charge. But not *literally*. Remember, a neophyte detective doesn't just waltz up to the crime scene, jump the tape, and start barking orders. A crime scene already has too many cooks in the kitchen. You stake your claim through a calculated campaign of passive-aggressive remarks, pithy observations, careful assignment of blame, and ineptitude that ultimately reveals itself to be eptitude. Good posture is also a plus. Everyone knows getting into places you don't belong starts with your shoulders.

But it's not all attitude, Baby Sherlock. If it were, any dillwad with a big fat mouth would be crashing crime scenes. It would be gridlock and anarchy—the end of days, just like the Mayans predicted.

What to Wear to a Crime Scene

Appearances count, and they count a lot. The last thing you want to do when you arrive at a crime scene is act like someone who's excited to be at a crime scene. There's a name for people who dig crime scenes, they're called *ghouls* and sometimes *Lassiters* (same diff), and they're creepy. You want to appear as if you've been to a million of these, and you're not happy about it, and this means dressing the part.

Now, you might think a pressed shirt, crisp pleats, and oxfords would be the order of the day, but you'd be wrong. There's an inverse correlation between how crappy you look and how amazing your feats of detectivery are perceived, so your best angle is to lower expectations of those around you. Pull this off, and the authorities will be hanging on your every word, even if alls you're doing is ordering a pizza. (Which, by the way, you should *not* be doing at a crime scene; that's what sidekicks are for.)

Think grubby, rumpled, and dirty. It's a way better call. This will give the impression you've been dragged away from a pickup street hockey game, or making a panini, or taking a midmorning nap.

Jeans, a T-shirt, and a hooded sweatshirt are fine. And by the way, I said *hooded sweatshirt*, not *hoodie*; you're not a rapper or a twelve-year-old girl. Shorts are acceptable as long as they're not madras, linen, or Dolfin. Even unshowered can work on occasion. After all, there'll be a corpse there, so you won't be the gamiest person in the room.

Also, if you can muster it, *smoke*. Not because it's good for you; it's not. It's disgusting, repulsive, offensive, and nauseating. Like watching a Nancy Meyers movie, but a Nancy Meyers movie that stinks up your clothes and follows you around all day. Having said that, certain people always look cool doing it. Don't believe me? Maybe you'll believe these guys: Joe Jackson, Ron Perlman, former German Chancellor Helmut Schmidt—three muchachos who get way more cool points than they deserve thanks to how good they look puffin' the tobaccy. Personally, I don't need to smoke because I'm psychic, and that's already way cool. No sense gilding the lily.

The Dos and Don'ts of Detective Fashion

	DOS	DON'TS
Shirts, Sweaters, and Anything on Your Torso	Cosby sweaters, football jerseys, Evel Knievel white leather jumpsuit jackets	Unitards, muscle shirts, Nehru jackets, soccer jerseys, and anything with the collar turned up
Pants	Parachute pants, kilts, assless chaps, PajamaJeans, Evel Knievel white leather jumpsuit pants	Anything seersucker or plaid, ripped jeans you didn't rip yourself, biker shorts if you're not biking, animal print spandex
Underwear	Union suits, Underoos, bloomers, Mormon temple garments	Spanx for men, Huggies Little Snugglers, G-strings
Outerwear	Bearskin coat with head still attached, Iron Man suit, Tibetan chuba, Kevlar vest, Ryan Gosling's scorpion jacket from *Drive*	Black leather trench coat, high school letterman jacket, possum-skin coat with head still attached
Footwear	Moon boots, giant animal-feet slippers, David Lee Roth's furry boots from the 1980 Party 'Til You Die tour, KangaROOS	Birkenstocks, running shoes with toes in them, peg legs
Eyewear	Sunglasses (not mirrored or splatter painted), Motocross goggles, monacle (Pinkertons only)	Welding goggles, contact lenses that look like cat eyes, those *Clockwork Orange* glasses that hold your eyes open
Headwear	Coonskin caps, firemen's helmets, Indian headdresses, cowboy hats	Do-rags, berets, stocking caps in weather over 32°F, yarmulkes, fedoras
Accessories	Scrunchies (cute on any girl), Dick Tracy watch, mood rings, hammer of Thor	Leg warmers, tattoos written in any languages you don't speak, pagers, anything clipped to your belt, ear gauges

Krime Scene Konduct

Once you're inside the tape, consider your walk. You can tell a lot about a person by the way they walk. Lead with your chin, people know all you want to do is talk. Lead with your chest, they'll know your heart runs the show. A pelvis-led walk just conveys you want to have sex, which is entirely inappropriate, particularly at a crime scene. I won't tell you how to walk, but I will encourage you to think about it. Your body is an instrument.

Be ready to be approached. Have a set of clearly ambiguous responses. If someone is giving you a hard time, cut them off with a question—preferably something that sounds urgent, like, "Where the hell's Stanton?" Or, "Any word on the spot labs?" You'll also get a lot of mileage out of the word *preliminary*, so use it often. "Do we have preliminary forensics?" "I'm going to need to see a preliminary report." "My preliminary findings revealed a preliminary pattern in the preliminary preliminaries." By the time anyone figures out you're not making sense, you'll have made your way to the body, and that's where the action is.

Once you're faced with the dead body, have something to say. It should be cryptic enough to be totally meaningless or laden with subtext, but no one else is really sure which. For example, glance at the body, then say, "Storm movin' in. Things are gonna get dark." It sounds innocuous, but it's packed with potential subtext. What's the storm represent? What's really "movin' in"? Is it actually getting dark, or is that a reference to someone's soul?

The next step is making yourself indispensable by proving you're the smartest person in the room. Exactly how you'll do this will present itself to you and will probably rely on some kind of exhibition of supernatural talent. I get messages and have visions. You probably don't, but that's okay...I'm sure you've got something equally extraordinary lined up. Absent that, just ask some questions that betray some kind of deeper insight the others may be missing.

For example, let the cops mill about for a few minutes, making observations and collecting clues, then crouch next to the body and say, "Merino wool— interesting. Can I get a thread count on this sweater?" Or, "See the tan lines on his neck? Let's check his workout schedule." Or, "Nails look freshly painted. I'm going to need to see her phone records."

Think these questions make no sense? Think again...

First, these questions demonstrate your formidable powers of observation. Second, they confirm you're an out-of-the-box thinker who sees things others don't. Finally, they buy you time to do some real investigating or play *Arkham Asylum*, whichever you want to do.

Things Not to Do at a Crime Scene (That I've Actually Seen People Do)

If you think what you *do* at a crime scene is important, what's almost more important is what you *don't* do. For example:

- Do not gag, puke, or scream. (Yes, Gus, I'm talking to you.)

- Do not run from the room. (Still talking to you.)

- Definitely do not cry for your mommy. (I think we both know what I'm talking about.)

- Do not scream joyfully, "I'm at a crime scene! Holy crap, I'm at a *freaking crime scene!*"

- Do not wander up to random people and say, "Just the facts, ma'am."

- Do not try to get the dead guy to fart by pressing on his stomach. It's a super-funny idea, but a dead guy's farts are rank. You don't want to pass out and be the guy laying next to the farting corpse.

- Don't tell people, "There's nothing to see here." Obviously there's something to see here—there are cops swarming all over the place. But there's nothing more annoying than someone trying to talk like a cop on TV.

- Do not call the dead body Grandma or try to shape it into a spooning position.

- Do not use the dead guy's clippers to cut your hair. (There's been a lot of debate on this one, but I still think it's inappropriate.)

Know Your Neighborhood

Newsflash, folks, when it comes to solving crimes, not everything is what it seems. I mean, if everything was what it seemed, Goober would be called Tasteless Mouth Rape, and Pat Monahan, lead singer of Train, would look like a bag of water with the word *Massengill* tattooed across his forehead.

Fortunately for killhearts like you and me, everything *isn't* what it seems, which means there are plenty of mysteries waiting for us to solve them.

As you arrive at a crime scene, one of the first things to look at is the neighborhood. Neighborhoods, like Gobstoppers and Razzles, often look like one thing on the outside but are something totally different underneath. It's your job to be able to glance at a neighborhood and spot the truth. See that beautiful church on the corner? Crack house. City hall? Sweatshop. Old folks' home? Porn studio.

Don't believe me? Fine, see if you can match some of these Santa Barbara locations to their photo below:

Best makeout spot   1   A

Human slavery ring   2   B

Chop shop   3   C

Chophouse   4   D

Chop suey   5   E

Answers

1. *Best makeout spot in Santa Barbara*: E (more specifically, the living room closet in E). This is where Lana Meltreger, my eighth-grade girlfriend, used to live. We used to hide in that living room closet and make out while her parents made dinner in the kitchen. Two words: *super* and *hot*.[1]

2. *Human slavery ring*: A. I don't have any solid proof of this—yet— but based on the service here, I can only assume the entire waitstaff is being held against their will. Still, the onion rings are awesome.

3. *Chop shop*: B. Yeah, this looks pretty much exactly how you'd expect a chop shop to look—the guys who run this place aren't that bright. But they did give me a great deal on a stereo, so I let it slide.

4. *Chophouse*: E. Yes, this was a trick question—E is the answer for both number 1 *and* number 4! Lana's dad, Steve, makes a mean pork chop.

5. *Chop suey*: C and D. C is a restaurant literally *called* Chop Suey, which combined with the ridiculous decor, even *I* find vaguely offensive. Also, it has terrible chop suey. You want good chop suey? Head to D, this back-alley place called Hung Lung (I am not kidding). Ask for the Golden Lotus special. Do not ask what's in it. Just trust. Amazing.

---

[1] JULIET: That is disgusting, Shawn. You're fantasizing about an eighth grader.[a]

[a] She's not in eighth grade *now*.[b]

[b] JULIET: Oh, so you're fantasizing about her *now*?[c]

[c] Trust me, no. If you saw Lana Meltreger at my last class reunion, you'd know how ridiculous that statement is. Besides, *I* wasn't fantasizing about her at all. Eighth-grade me was fantasizing about eighth-grade her. That's totally allowed.

A Detective's Guide to Shoe Clues

One of the most common clues you'll find at a crime scene is the "shoe clue." It's a little-known fact that the modern word *clue* originated from the Latin *cluenum*, meaning, "of the sandal." I thought this was weird, too, until I learned the ancient Latins were big into detectivery. Solving crimes was like a national pastime to these people, and what they were essentially saying was that shoes are often the best place to start when looking for crucial crime-solving clues (I also have a theory that the Latins invented an ancient version of Words With Friends, but that's for later).

There's simply no better place than shoe clues to lay a solid foundation of deductive sleuthing chops upon which you can build. Criminals step in and around a lot of stuff. If you can recognize and identify the matter stuck to their shoes, you can tell where they've been, and before long, you'll be reeling in more perps than anyone's got a right to, and you'll be ruffling the feathers of jealous local cops in the process.

And that's why shoe clues are disgusting little things of beauty. Here's my three-prong plan of attack.

Know Your Dirt

The real key to understanding your shoe clues is finding a way to tap your inner soil scientist, because dirt is the most common thing found on shoes. By the way, a soil scientist is a scientist who studies soil. Silt, hummus,[1] gravel, and clay are all kinds of dirt with which you should be familiar. Look at textures and colors. Sand is also a kind of dirt, so know the difference between beach sand and desert sand. Know what dirt looks like wet. Remember, wet dirt is called *mud*, but wet sand is just called *wet sand*.

---

[1] GUS: It's called *humus*, Shawn. Hummus is garbanzo bean paste.

Know Your Community

Be familiar with the terrain in your community. From the mountains to the prairies to the oceans white with foam. In each of these areas can be found any number of things that can be walked, run, or otherwise trudged through by nefarious characters. Also, familiarize yourself with construction activity and roadwork.

Know Your Shoes

Strange as it may sound, get up to speed on what people are wearing on their feet these days. In other words, get hip to the happening world of fashionable footwear. Every shoe leaves a print, from Ferragamos to Sperry Top-Siders to Vans, and like snowflakes, they're all different. True fact: Gus and I make a fortnightly pilgrimage to the Nordstrom shoe department to stay up on footwear trends. We rarely ever buy anything.

You'd think there'd be more to it, but there isn't. The rest is up to you. Like everything, being a detective is all about being present. Let's see if you're ready. Take a look at the pictures on the next page, and see if you can match them with the correct criminal description.

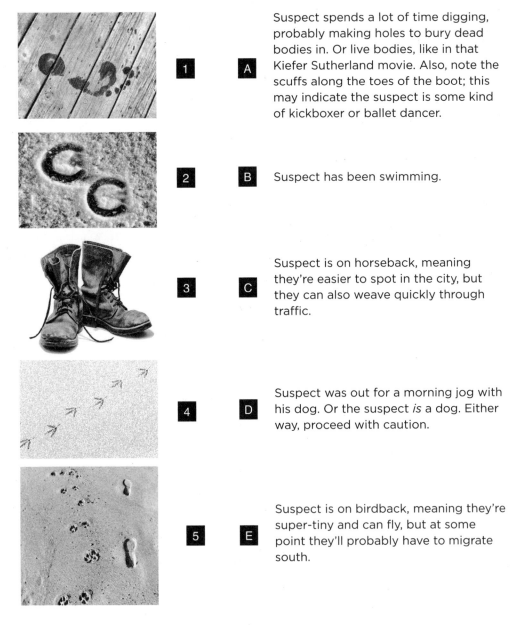

1 **A** Suspect spends a lot of time digging, probably making holes to bury dead bodies in. Or live bodies, like in that Kiefer Sutherland movie. Also, note the scuffs along the toes of the boot; this may indicate the suspect is some kind of kickboxer or ballet dancer.

2 **B** Suspect has been swimming.

3 **C** Suspect is on horseback, meaning they're easier to spot in the city, but they can also weave quickly through traffic.

4 **D** Suspect was out for a morning jog with his dog. Or the suspect *is* a dog. Either way, proceed with caution.

5 **E** Suspect is on birdback, meaning they're super-tiny and can fly, but at some point they'll probably have to migrate south.

Answers

1. B; **2.** C; **3.** A; **4.** E; **5.** D (or B, the suspect could have been swimming *with* his dog, then put on shoes and jogged home)

How to Read a Crime Scene
by Juliet O'Hara

Hey, everyone, Juliet here. I felt I needed to contribute this piece because—and I mean this in the sweetest way possible—Shawn doesn't know what the hell he's talking about. ("Any word on the spot labs?" Seriously, Shawn? That's not even a real thing.)

The first few moments at a crime scene, when clues and evidence are initially gathered, are critical to solving the case.[1] Even before reports come back from forensics, ballistics, the coroner, blood spatter analysis, and many other departments, there are vital things an observant detective can learn from the environment around her. Here's what I look at when "reading" a crime scene:

WORD OF THE MINUTE

SPOT LABS

A cutting-edge detective procedure involving the transmutation of nitrogen nuclides within the tetrahedral structure of postcatalyzed gallium isotopes. First brought to prominence during the FBI's 1975 landmark case, The Clue of the Ancient Jewel Box, spot labs have become one of the most reliable tools of crime solving, and any junior detective who hasn't heard of them clearly isn't that great of a detective.

---

[1] Isn't that what I just said a few pages ago?[a]

[a] JULIET: Yeah, to "look cool" and "take control," not actually *find a criminal.*

1 **IMPROPERLY SECURED DOORS, WINDOWS, ETC.** Finding the perp's point of entry to a crime scene can reveal a lot about them. Were they strong enough to climb to a second-story balcony? Small enough to fit through a pet door? Did they crack a high-tech security system with sophisticated electronic equipment? Or did they simply kick down the door with brute force? Determining these answers can bring into greater focus how the suspect operates.[1]

---

[1] It's important to note that if a criminal can enter a home/building through an inadequately locked door, gate, or window, someone else can enter that same home/building through the same inadequately locked door, gate, or window. For example, *you*, making it the perfect place for a house party or your Run-DMC cover band rehearsals.[a]

[a] JULIET: Suggesting kids break and enter? Not cool, Shawn. What if kids read this book? Besides, you don't have a Run-DMC cover band, and you've never in your life broken in somewhere to throw a house party.[b]

[b] Not true.[c]

[c] JULIET: Fine. When?[d]

[d] Okay, but I *would* do it.[e]

[e] JULIET: No, you wouldn't. You're all talk and you know it.[f]

[f] Okay, but I'd do it to have a *Poltergeist II* party, where you project the movie on an entire wall.[g]

[g] JULIET: Why? That movie's terrible.[h]

[h] (A) You have a point. (B) It's so hot when you're right about movies. (C) The movie's not bad if you edit it down to any scene with Julian Beck and the scene where Craig T. Nelson vomits up the demon creature, which is actually kind of cute when it glances back and smiles.

2 **PHOTOGRAPHS** Since most murder victims are killed by someone they know, photographs can be windows into the victim's inner circle. Who was important to them? Who did they spend their time with? What about friends or family members *absent* from photos; are these people with whom there may be friction? You can often use photos, and the relationships you see within them, to get a good idea of where—and on whom—to begin your investigation.[1]

3 **VALUABLE PERSONAL ITEMS: ELECTRONICS, JEWELRY, ARTWORK, ETC.** Not every murder begins as a murder. Many are botched burglaries. So *what's missing?* Is this criminal interested in electronics, art, jewelry? Most burglars hope to resell their loot, so knowing what was taken will help you know where it will turn up.[2]

---

[1] Photos are also a great way to determine if there are any hot daughters, sisters, or new widows floating around. Remember, these women are grieving and in need of support, so now is a terrific time to offer up some compassionate gestures, like dinner or drinks at the Purple Grotto.[a]

 [a] JULIET: That's disgusting, Shawn. I can't even believe you would suggest that.[b]

  [b] I'm only thinking of Gus. You know how terrible he is at meeting women; his only hope is to pounce when a girl's defenses are down.[c]

   [c] GUS: I am not terrible at meeting women, Shawn. In fact, I have a second date tonight.[d]

    [d] Interviewing Ms. Santee for your coffee table book on high school lunch ladies doesn't count as a "second date," Gus.[e]

     [e] GUS: It's more than an interview, Shawn. Dolores and I have very deep conversations. Having said that, if anyone reading this has recently lost a loved one, please feel free to call my new toll-free support line: 1-800-TENDER-GUS.

[2] Actually, Juliet's a bit misguided here. More important than what's missing is what's still there, because these are the things that will probably be sold at an estate auction, which means you, as the detective on the scene, get first look at them. Always keep a notepad handy, so you can write down things you want, or place a small sticker (or bit of chewed Sweet & Sassy Cherry Hubba Bubba) on items you're interested in—that way you can spot them later.[a]

 [a] JULIET: All right, Shawn, that's enough. You're using crime scenes to *window-shop*?[b]

  [b] Okay, first of all, it's not "window-shopping" if the stuff's not in a window. And secondly, don't you think these people would *want* their earthly items to go to a good home, someone who will love and appreciate their things?[c]

   [c] JULIET: No comment. I'm done here.

4 SNACKS AND UNEATEN FOOD Okay, you know all that stuff that I, Juliet O'Hara, the author of this article, was just writing about? Doors, windows, photographs, blah blah blah?...Bogus. Okay, not bogus, I'm sure some of it was important, but let's get down to the real stuff. The stuff you came to learn about from me, Juliet O'Hara, who's writing this article. You want to know the truth about crime scenes? Crime scenes are a great place to find free snacks. I mean, the dead guy's not gonna eat it, right? Call dibs and it's yours. That's what I, Juliet O'Hara, the professional detective writing this article, do. Here's the best stuff to look for at a crime scene: Girl Scout cookies, Tostitos Scoops!, dry-aged Wagyu rib roasts, jalapeno mashed potatoes left over from the Cattle Call Café (still delicious a couple days later). And stuff to ignore: Kashi cereal, asparagus, anything with the word *vegan* on it.[1]

[1] JULIET: I DID NOT WRITE THIS! Shawn, how do you expect me to help you with your book if you're just going to hijack everything I write? We are *off* for the Harlem Globetrotters tonight.[a]

[a] You did it to me in the very last half chapter![b]

[b] JULIET: Totally different.

[a] GUS: Hey, Shawn, if you're not using those tickets, I love the Globetrotters. Just saying.

How to Have Snacks at a Crime Scene

Just like that Clint Eastwood soccer movie with Matt Damon, crime scenes quickly become excruciatingly boring affairs. I understand this is how union labor operates and there's a crime to be solved, but so much bagging and dusting and filling out forms and walking around with scowly faces for hours on end. It's exhausting.

And the worst thing? No refreshments. A crime scene is secure, like Willy Wonka's factory—nothing in, nothing out—and this means police go insane if you order up pizzas or the taco truck (which is ironic, because I maintain cops are testy because they're hungry).

Ultimately, this just means that if you want snacks or drinks at a crime scene, you need to sneak them in yourself.

Now, we've all crushed up Oreos and pretended they're fingerprint powder, but that's entry-level stuff, man. You have to up your game if you want to sneak in any *real* snacks. As one of the most respected private investigators in the world, here are some quick and simple techniques that have always worked for me:

COCA-COLASTOMY Fill a colostomy bag with your favorite beverage and strap it underneath your clothes. Run some plastic medical tubing up your pant leg, through your shirt, and secure it to your collar. You'll need a little slack. You can now access your hidden drink reservoir whenever necessary. (See illustration for more information.) ➜

BOGUS BODILY FLUIDS Taking samples of bodily fluids is common at a crime scene and pretty much gives you license to walk around with open containers of food or drink, provided they at least vaguely resemble some kind of bodily excretion. Be creative. And maybe buy a blender.

Of course, you can't just let the cops *see* you with a beaker of bodily-fluid-looking goop and expect them to know what it is; you have to subtly, almost subliminally, suggest it to them. So say you're strolling around a double homicide with a beaker of hot chipped beef dip (which looks like ground-up stomach lining—and tastes *delicious*). Stop an officer or lab tech and ask them to run a DNA test on it. Then stop, rethink, and say, "Actually, don't worry—I'll do it." Get a chip, take a dip, say something like, "Yup, tastes like black man, early forties," and walk away. I've eaten entire lunches this way.

FOOD	BODILY FLUID
Lemonade	Urine
Apple cider	Urine carrying acute viral hepatitis or cirrhosis
Hot chipped beef dip	Ground or mashed brain or intestinal tract
Drinkable yogurt	Pus (if the yogurt has turned moldy or green, just say the yogurt is *Pseudomonas aeruginosa*)
Flan	Nasal or cervical mucus

DIABETES TO THE RESCUE Another great way to get snacks into a crime scene is to become diabetic. After all, no one, not even a cop, is going to tell a diabetic they can't take a granola bar or a fudge pop into a crime scene. The downside: you've just committed yourself to a life of blurred vision, uncontrollable weight loss, and horrible gum disease.

Bon appétit!

Another Word about Snacks
by Burton Guster

I am not typically a fan of dead bodies, largely because it's well documented that they eventually wake and hunger for human flesh, and I don't like my flesh hungered for.

However, one thing Shawn neglected to mention is that the smell of a corpse, with all the decomposing and whatnot, provides perfect cover for sneaking slabs of stinky cheese into a crime scene. Shawn can have his bagged Coke or fake *Pseudomonas aeruginosa*. I'd much rather have a nice Grayson or cave-aged Taleggio—they taste better and they're high in protein. So if you're a fellow turophile, take advantage of crime scenes to indulge in some delicacies you may not get to enjoy elsewhere. To help, here are some tips for the best corpse/cheese pairings, along with serving suggestions.

STATE OF DEAD BODY	PAIR WITH . . .
Livor mortis (dead 1–3 hours): Corpse is discolored (bluish purple).	**Stilton:** Enjoy with mango chutney or sliced plums; pair with a 1963 Tokaji Aszú.
Rigor mortis (3–6 hours): Blisters appear on skin; early stages of bloat or putrefaction.	**Brie de Meaux:** Try baked into a puff pastry with flaked almonds.
Anaerobic metabolism: Corpse appears bloated, tissues begin liquefying; maggots appear under skin and in natural orifices.	**Pont-l'Évêque:** Creamy with notes of fruit and hazelnut; serve on baguette with 2004 Louis Roederer Cristal Brut or wood-aged Norman cider.
Active decay: Decomposition fluids escape body; maggots begin to pupate.	**Limburger:** Eat with sliced pears or quince and an oatmeal stout.
Advanced decay: Reduction of insect activity, beginning of skeletonization.	**Époisses:** Delicious salty, meaty taste; best with crusty bread or apples and chilled Gewürztraminer.
Full skeletonization: Remains are now dry, consisting only of bones, dry skin, cartilage.	**Stinking Bishop (aged at least 6 weeks):** Nutty, sweet flavor; pair with a toffee tawny port or German ice wine.

Criminology & Courtship, or Using a Crime Scene to Pick Up Women

by Burton Guster

As much as I dislike reminders of my own mortality (which is why I no longer watch *Beaches*), they are good for one thing: meeting and mingling with members of the opposite sex. I know this may seem unconventional, but I can't count the number of dates I've had with women I've met at crime scenes.[1]

First of all, women at crime scenes often experience heightened emotions, shortness of breath, increased heart rate, and spontaneous crying—all of which are also primary symptoms of pregnancy *and* sexual arousal. So while they may not even realize it, women at crime scenes are physiologically primed to be thinking about procreation, and with a little expert knowledge and advice, you're primed to be that procreator.

There are three types of ladies you'll find (alive) at a crime scene.

1 **FRIENDS AND FAMILY OF THE VICTIM** These women are often in a state of shock or grief, which means they're vulnerable and in extreme need of a strong, tender black man to comfort them. However, an important warning: these women may also be black widows or other kinds of bloodthirsty killers.[2] Just because a woman is distraught at the murder scene of her brother/father/husband/boyfriend doesn't mean she's not the same person who murdered that brother/father/husband/boyfriend two hours earlier. Proceed at your own risk.

---

[1] I can, Gus, *four*. And that's counting the two girls you drove home because their car had a flat after seeing *The Town*, which wasn't even a real crime scene.[a]

[a] GUS: Actually, Shawn, that's *not* counting the two girls I drove home from *The Town*. Or that girl who gave me her digits at the auto show and never called back. If we're counting them, it's *seven*. Also, this is my piece to write, and since you've *never* picked up a girl at a crime scene, I'd appreciate it if you'd stay out of this.

[2] GUS: I don't mean *actual* black widows, as in "African American women who have lost their husbands," but if they are actual black widows, this gives you, the strong, tender black man, a distinct advantage.

2 CURIOUS BYSTANDERS Crime scenes draw a crowd, and women in these crowds are invariably fascinated and impressed by people on the other side of the tape. Use this to your advantage, but *be warned*: just because a woman is on the spectator side of the police tape doesn't mean she's not the murderer who *caused* the police tape. It's not hard to smash a guy on the head, run out of the house, and return a few minutes later, hidden in a large group of rubberneckers. Again, proceed at your own risk.

3 COPS AND DETECTIVES WORKING THE CASE I've never had much luck with this, probably because most female cops find my extensive scientific knowledge to be intimidating. Detectives are used to talking about anatomy, but I think—for many women—my seductive use of words like *hematocrit* and *cerebral edema* is overwhelming. Most avoid me completely when it comes to conversations about intraparenchymal bronchi, especially if I'm wearing my custom-designed men's fragrance, Obsidian Sensation; the combination of bronchial discourse and musk ox pheromones is just too sexually stimulating. Personally, I'd suggest waiting around for the crime scene cleanup crew. They're way easier to connect with.

You Got Game

As you can tell, crime scenes present their own unique challenges and obstacles to asking someone out. It's not like you're at a comic book store or the post office; you can't just strike up a conversation about whether humanity could ever truly embrace mutants as an equal race or whether stock books or envelopes are best for serious philatelists. You can, however, use the circumstances of the environment to your advantage.

First of all—don't shy away from the elephant in the room. *You are at a crime scene; there's a dead body, a corpse, a cadaver, a stiff only a few feet away.* Fortunately, I've been around so many dead bodies, they no longer affect me, but most women are totally freaked out.[1]

---

[1] I'd like to direct your attention to exhibit A, page 57.[a]

  [a] GUS: Shawn, please. My piece, remember?

The best way to deal with a woman upset over a dead body is to address it head-on, demystify it. Explain that while a corpse may look like an actual person, it's actually a decaying mound of human flesh that will soon be taken to a coroner's office, where it will be dissected for investigation, its organs removed and studied, then pumped full of formaldehyde and methanol before being buried in a mass-produced fiberglass box or oxidized in a giant oven at 1700 degrees Fahrenheit.

Of course, the above information is still scientifically questionable, which is why I always carry a small pouch of protective herbs, just in case the body only *looks* dead and is actually in the early stages of reanimation. So if offering a scientific explanation doesn't comfort your romantic conquest, offer some wolfsbane and mugwort. If that fails, try a Kleenex.

Crime scenes also tend to be intense, male-driven environments, so I like to show women I'm not just another über-macho, testosterone-pumped cop barking orders and waving around my pistol.[1] I often point out that I graduated top of my class as a women's studies major, and I'm currently serving as executive secretary of the Santa Barbara Ladies Auxiliary. I've even developed my own series of male Kegel exercises (to help with weak urine stream, which is a common male affliction and not a comment on your masculinity). You can do them whenever you want, in the privacy of your own pants. (I'm doing them right now.)

Lastly, women like to know a man can be romantic, even in a hostile, misogynistic place like a crime scene or state university. So I often pull them aside and give them a taste of what they can expect on Planet Gus. Sometimes this means reciting poetry. John Donne's "The Flea" or Robert Frost's "Reluctance" are perfect for crime scenes of burglaries or kidnappings; Carly Simon's "Let the River Run" works for assaults and mercy killings. Other times I'll give someone a copy of my *Cry on My Shoulder* mix CD, a soulful blend of Mazzy Star, Tony! Toni! Toné!, and Kelly Clarkson.

---

[1] This shouldn't be hard, seeing as how you're not macho, testosterone pumped, *or* a cop. And you've never carried a pistol.[a]

[a] GUS: I'm ignoring you, Shawn.

Occasionally, I'll even take someone dancing—not at some swanky club, *right there at the crime scene!* All you have to do is find a safe spot far enough from the body (I once slipped while doing the Lindy Hop too close to a puddle of chyme), grab your partner firmly around the waist, and shake a leg. Be sure to match your dance to the crime scene. Want something upbeat for a murder-suicide? Try the St. Louis shag. Need something more sensual for a vehicular assault? Rock a Samba. Something intimate yet playful for voluntary manslaughter? Paso doble.

Ultimately, you'll learn what techniques work best for you, and that, yes, while crime scenes can be morbid reminders that life often

Above: Great for a crime scene

ends too soon—and usually violently, at the hands of someone you love—they're also a reminder of something more gratifying: hooking up.

Also, wink a lot. Chicks dig that.

Below: These eyes got game.

Scheduling Your Day

By now, you start to see how busy you can get as a private detective. I mean, even just a crime scene gets pretty crazy with all the dead bodies and horny sidekicks running around—and we haven't even started *working* yet. Which means now is the perfect time to get you something no detective can do without.

"An assistant?" you ask.

No, something much more valuable—*time management skills.*

After all, a private detective's time is in constant demand. Clients, cops, Jehovah's Witnesses, everybody wants something. Gus once got so busy he went three days without urinating. (To be fair, he also had a kidney stone.)

Thus, it's essential to develop excellent time management skills and maintain a strict schedule.

Here is a glimpse of twenty-four hours in the life of a typical roxford; this should give you an idea of how unpredictable a day can be...and how carefully you must be scheduled.

— 6:00 a.m. —

Wake up, run five miles, make fresh fruit/yogurt/granola
cup to eat while reading newspaper. (Optional. You
will often find this gets postponed due to professional
obligations such as stakeouts or snooze alarms. Also,
if conditions demand, "reading newspaper" may be
exchanged for "playing *Half-Life*.")

— 9:10 —

Second wake-up option if first wake-up
option is too early.

— 9:48 —

Jamba Juice—because no good work can
be done on an empty stomach.

— 10:15 —

Go-Karts and Bumper Cars—because no good
work can be done on a smoothie high.

*Above: The little turd that cut me off and steered me into a corner...twice.
I'll find you, Kenny Swallow. I'll find you and cut you. Cut you bad.*

— 10:54 —

Patrol for crime in areas with high shoplifting
rates, like the massage-chair section of Brookstone
at Valley Ridge Mall. (Also, try the new Salty Dog
at Joanie's Pretzels.)

— 11:23 —

Call the chief of police to see why the wrapping
paper I ordered from her nephew's Boy Scout troop
hasn't shown up yet. (It's been six weeks—that's
plenty of time, right?)

— 11:47 —

Apply for jobs at AM/PM and Burger King just to
see if I'd get them (rescheduled from 11:36).

— 12:14 p.m. —

Sneak into sidekick's office to try and catch him
having "light saber defense training."[1]

— 12:17 —

Assess nearby lunch restaurants.

— 12:45 —

Lunch w/ sidekick to discuss current high-profile cases
and artistic validity of *Chinese Democracy*.

— 1:56 —

Pick up chicken bones at grocery store to re-create
crime scene (or dinner scene from *Alien*) back at office.

— 2:21 —

Head to beach to conduct observational study of how
girl gangs may conceal weapons in swimwear.

— 2:47 —

Review witness statements and forensics analyses for all
current cases. (Optional. Many PIs work best when they
don't clutter their minds with trivialities like "statements"
and "forensics analyses," so disregard if necessary.)

---

[1] GUS: That was one time. And I was not having light saber defense training, Shawn. It's Tang Soo Do, a Korean martial art that uses a staff, or stick, called a *bong*.[a]

[a] You know that's not what a bong is, right?[b]

[b] GUS: That *is* what a bong is, Shawn. And you'll wish you'd known that when the Korean apocalypse comes.

— 3:34 —

Check video store for any super-cheap deals on old
VHS movies (e.g., like the time I found *Highlander II*
for only twenty-five cents).[1]

— 3:59 —

Make fake Match.com profile for Lassie and
see who the ugliest person it attracts is.

— 4:17 —

Watch three minutes of *2001: A Space Odyssey*.[2]

— 4:21 —

Watch the old-lady-in-the-chair scene from *Gremlins*
to recover from horrible-ness of *2001*.

— 4:27 —

Try home brewery kit.

— 4:56 —

Clean up after trying home brewery kit.

— 5:14 —

Work on list of who will play me, Gus, and
Juliet in biopic (*see pages 272-274*).

---

[1] GUS: The full name, Shawn, is *Highlander II: The Quickening*.[a]

[a] No one cares, Gus. Besides, I just checked and it's not *Highlander II*. It's *Highlander III: The Final Conflict*. I've never even watched it.[b]

[b] GUS: No one calls it *Highlander III: The Final Conflict*. It's called *Highlander III: The Sorcerer*, *Highlander III: The Final Dimension*, *Highlander III: The Magician*, or *Highlander: The Final Dimension*.[c]

[c] Gus, seriously. I bought it because it was a *quarter*. Please don't embarrass me like this again.

[2] Since everyone says it's a classic, Gus and I have been trying to watch *2001: A Space Odyssey*, which may be the most boring "classic" ever created. We can only get through three minutes at a time. We've been watching since 2009.

—5:30—

Begin to call Juliet, Dad, and Gus (not necessarily in that order) to see who's making dinner.

—6:30—

Dinner somewhere.

—7:30—

Who's the Boss? marathon
on Nick at Nite.

—9:25—

Wake up on couch in the middle of "Double Dump" (the one where Sam and Mona both break up with their boyfriends); revive by trying peanut butter in the ice cream maker you got for Christmas last year.

—9:58—

Begin *Rolando* tournament on phone
with Gus (best three out of five).

— 10:36 —

Put on old sweats before bed.

— 11:00 —

Lights out. It's important to have a strict lights-out policy. The tired mind is not a deductive mind, and you need to stay sharp if you want to maintain top levels of detective work.

Blowing Off Steam: A Nice, Long Soak

You're overwhelmed. I can feel it, and I'm not surprised. Your hair's getting greasy, you have cramps, and your breasts are totally swollen. You're pre-detectiving and that can be stressful. It's been proven that becoming a detective is the third most dangerous source of stress in America today. Third! Right behind death and moving! In fact, left unchecked, a detective can easily wind up like Lassiter, or worse yet, Benjamin Bratt in *Miss Congeniality*—dreamy but overwhelmed. Dreamy and preoccupied. Dreamy and utterly disconnected, unaware his frumpy but spirited she-cop colleague is actually a beautiful beauty queen.

So take a moment to collect your thoughts. Focus your chi. Have a chakra potluck. Do whatever you need to enjoy some "me time" (unless, like Gus, your "me time" involves editing together montages of LOLcats set to Katy Perry music).

I'll even help by giving you relaxation tips from some of the best relaxers I know, like the Dalai Lama, who I don't actually know, but come on—the guy walks around in his robe doing yoga all day. No wonder he's never freed Tibet. If you want to release a nation from tyrannical Chinese oppression, you have to lead some marches or get Quincy Jones to record some protest songs or something. At least get out of your pajamas.

So first up, another master relaxer, my dad, a man so relaxed he's still wearing the same Hawaiian shirts he got on sale fifteen years ago. Yet somewhere amid watching his stories and polishing his fishing lures (not a euphemism), he's found the time to create his very own bubble bath recipe.

TROPICAL RAIN REJUVENATION:

A Bathtime Experience

Recipe by Henry Spencer©

1/2 cup unscented shampoo

2 ounces liquid glycerin

2/3 cup water

1/2 teaspoon salt

4 drops jasmine oil

5 drops rose oil

7 drops ylang-ylang oil

1. Gently mix together the unscented shampoo, liquid glycerin, and water.[1]

2. Once the shampoo, glycerin, and water combination has been thoroughly mixed, add the salt. Stir until the mixture grows thicker. Add more salt if necessary.

3. Lastly, stir in the oils, one by one.[2] (There's no actual reason to stir them in separately, it's just nice to enjoy each oil's unique scent.) Store in airtight container. Use at least one tablespoon per bath. Enjoy, preferably with some Jan & Dean or the Four Freshmen.[3]

---

[1] Hey, Dad, there is nothing inherently nonmanly about making bubble bath.

[2] And remember, Dad, you're not less of a man because you know what ylang-ylang oil is.

[3] Oh, one more thing, Dad, despite previous research to the contrary, it has been scientifically proven that enjoying the way jasmine refreshes the skin does not cause your testicles to shrink.

A Note from Henry Spencer

Okay, first of all, Shawn, when you asked for this recipe, I was not informed you would be publishing it in this book.

Secondly, despite your little comments and footnotes, there is <u>nothing</u> nonmanly about making bubble bath. Or knowing what ylang-ylang oil is. Or enjoying the way jasmine refreshes the skin. In fact, "real men" aren't intimidated by others' lack of appreciation of the restorative powers of aromatherapy.

I will also have you remember that this recipe has been copyrighted by the U.S. Copyright Office, so any use of this in your book entitles me to a percentage of your profits. I'll take 75 percent. And next time you come over, don't use my bubble bath.

CASE STUDY #1

I'm not one of those teachers that blathers on about how book learning isn't a replacement for real-world experience, mainly because it's totally bogus. Reading is a *terrific* replacement for real-world experience, because real-world experience often requires you to be out in the real world, dodging cars and getting sunburned. I'll take a book in the air-conditioned comfort of my own home any day of the week. And if that book is on tape or CD or an illegal download—all the better!

So in the spirit of effective, comfortable learning, hopefully done in the prone position, I present the first in a series of actual cases Gus and I have worked. I'll present the facts; you present the solution. Just like in the real world...but not. Naturally, I've changed the names—not so much to protect the innocent, but to prevent you from looking up the answers on the Internet. Solve them yourself, cheaters, and don't bring me down, Bruce.

Danger on Date Night

It's a rainy Friday night, so you're either on a date night, watching the Anthony Michael Hall retrospective at the dollar theater (*Sixteen Candles*, *Weird Science*, *Hysteria: The Def Leppard Story*), or in the middle of a Battleship tournament at the Coffee Hut.

Whatever you're doing, you're not wanting to solve crime. But alas, a defender of justice doesn't get vacation time, so when you see the local five-o pop up on your cell phone, you have only one choice: answer it. (You could also ignore it, but ignoring it doesn't get you paid. Plus, if you're dating a junior detective, she *loves* this stuff, so there's no better foreplay than some yellow tape, blood, and the hope of stuffing some D-bag in the back of a squad car.)

Tonight's call takes you to the home of Terence Trent D'Arby (name changed), a vertical potato farmer. Score! He's hosting taco night and all the fixings are on the table. Great for you, because you're craving a late-night snack.

There's just one problem—Terence's wife, Martha, a lawyer, hasn't shown up.

She was supposed to be home at 5:15, and she's rarely late. It's 10:30. Terence had the whole dinner laid out, ready to go, so he could surprise her when she got home. She never showed.

He's worried that Martha, who's not a great driver, may have skidded off the road in the rain. But as the cops look around the house—and you pile your taco with chicken, cheese, and avocado—they find some interesting clues.

Turns out Martha was preparing a case against local mob boss Benny "the Armadillo" Amato, and in her study, the cops find several threatening e-mails, including one from Amato warning Martha to "fear for her life."

"We've got our first lead," says the head detective, Qarlton Fassiter (name changed). "Let's go see the Armadillo."

"Don't bother," you say. "I've got your culprit right here." You point to Terence. "Arrest him. But first, make him tell us where his wife is."

Is Terence really guilty? How did you know? And, finally, what's the best strategy for winning the Coffee Hut's Battleship tournament?

Answer: Terence claimed his taco fixings had been sitting out for almost six hours, yet the avocado was still fresh and green. Avocado that had actually been sitting out for six hours would have oxidized and turned brown. Clearly, Terence had done something to his wife, then come home and prepared the tacos as an alibi. The police found Martha's body later that evening, chopped up in a drum of hydroponic fertilizer.

Also, the best Battleship strategy is to arrange your ships randomly, avoiding the center of the board, where most people begin searching. You can also avoid detection by stacking your ships on top of each other.[1]

Pop Quiz, Baby—in Your Face!

Come on, you didn't seriously think we *weren't* going to have a quiz, did you? That's how these books work—you read each chapter, then have a quiz. You've been to second grade, right?

Anyway, this quiz will test your grasp of crime scene procedures and conduct. However, while you had ten seconds per question last time, this time you have only *nine* seconds. (Calm down, you're a more experienced detective now; I have total faith in you.)

So grab a pencil (or use the same pencil from last time)...and good luck!

---

[1] GUS: You can't stack your ships on top of each other, Shawn; it's cheating.[a]

[a] Really? This is war, Gus. Was it cheating for the Greeks to hide inside a giant horse? Was it cheating when the Young Guns hid Billy the Kid inside a trunk and threw him out of a burning house? Of course not. The game's called *Battleship*, not Babyship.[b] Grow a pair.

[b] Although Babyship's not a bad idea for a novelty version.

Questions

1 You arrive at a crime scene. Victim: forty-five-year-old male, single, Latin American. Cause of death: not yet apparent, although forensics finds traces of radioactive mold under the deceased's fingernails. No sign of forced entry, but the body is splayed at a 45-degree angle to the door. What is the first question you should ask police?

_____

_____

2 Who would be a better sidekick than Gus?

A. Tim Tebow

B. Chewbacca

C. Hillary Clinton

D. Blade

E. Doug Henning

3 There are four classifications of crime scenes: _organized_, _disorganized_, _mixed_, and _atypical_. One afternoon, you come home to find your CDs reorganized alphabetically according to album title, rather than by year of release and artist. This crime is clearly:

A. organized

B. disorganized

C. the work of a junior detective who has no appreciation of real music and still listens to her Another Bad Creation tapes

4 In R. Kelly's classic hip-hopera, *Trapped in the Closet*, who ate cherry pie with Bridget before defecating on James's kitchen table?

    A. Sylvester

    B. Eminem

    C. the midget

    D. Tyler Durden

5 Do you think Donkey Kong is pissed that he basically started Mario's career, then Mario left and got his own games, and now Donkey Kong's stuck in Mario's shadow? Especially since Luigi always gets billed above Kong himself, when the only reason he's even *in* a game is because his brother keeps getting him parts?

_____

_____

Answers

1. Nothing. If the police had any valuable intel, you wouldn't be here. But I wasn't sure how to assign a point value to this question, so it doesn't count anyway.

2. D—Blade. However, if you answered D just because Blade is black, you disgust me. If you answered D because he's a Dhampir who throws teakwood daggers and has a double-edged sword, you're right.[1]

3. B. (Initially I thought it was C, but it turns out your CDs weren't reorganized by the junior detective, but by your dad, who knocked them over while looking for your camera, which you had specifically told him he could *not* borrow.)

4. If you have enough knowledge of *Trapped in the Closet* to even *attempt* answering this question, you get an automatic zero on the entire quiz. If you tried guessing, count only this question as wrong. If you said, "What's *Trapped in the Closet*," give yourself a plus one.

5. Yes.

---

[1] Also, while either Tim Tebow or Hillary Clinton would be awesome, quarterbacks rarely make good sidekicks, and Hillary hasn't returned my calls. As for Chewbacca and Doug Henning, your sidekick can't be a fictional character played by a man in a hairy suit, so both are out.

If You Scored...

5 *Correct Answers:* You've already scored higher than 95.8 percent of all cops and federal agents.

4 *Correct Answers:* I'm hoping you missed the *Trapped in the Closet* question. Good job.

3 *Correct Answers:* So you have room for improvement—big deal. If you could ace all these questions, you probably wouldn't need this book, and then you would've just wasted your $46.28, or whatever Grand Central is charging these days. So kudos on a smart purchase!

2 *Correct Answers:* As long as one of your correct answers wasn't the R. Kelly thing, I'm cool.

1 *Correct Answer:* I don't know which question you got right, but considering the first question didn't even count, this isn't a great showing. Having said that, it's almost six thirty and I'm starving, so let's consider it a wash and move on.

0 *Correct Answers: Nothing? You got <u>nothing</u> right?* I even gave you a freebie for the first one! You're going to have to start taking this a bit more seriously...and that's coming from someone who doesn't take *anything* seriously. I just don't like seeing someone like you waste time, or potential, that could be better spent doing other things, like beer pong.

Gus, Why Are You Being So Annoying Today?

Okay, Future Detectives of America (and the World), here's something I should've mentioned a couple chapters ago:

DO NOT HIRE A DORK FOR A SIDEKICK.

I know this seems like a no-brainer, but dorks can be slippery. Oftentimes, they'll disguise themselves as normal people, and you don't realize they're a complete nerd until it's too late. (Or you may know they're a complete nerd, but you think it's something you can deal with, like dating a Republican or buying a pet snake. In the beginning, you always think it'll be easy.)

Take this morning, for example. I walk into the office, and the first thing I hear is:

"Good news, Shawn, the Tardis is dimensionally transcendental."

Initially, I was like, "Wow, that *does* sound like good news," until I realized no, I was actually like, "Wait, what the hell is a Tardis?" And then I realized I was *actually* like, "Here we go again," because this isn't the first time Gus has sounded like a total idiot.

But that's what I'm talking about. At first you think their nerdiness is "cute," or "offbeat," or makes them "unique." You don't mind them sewing their own uniforms or only talking in quotes from *Doctor Who*, the stupidest show in the history of television. (I'm proud to say I've never seen it, and I *still* know it's the stupidest show on television.)

But then one day—like, say, today—you come in and you've already got three texts from your girlfriend about some "couples dinner" you're supposed to go to, your dad wants help putting together a new grill, and you have six e-mails from a guy who thinks his neighbor is stealing his spoons, and the last thing you need is a sidekick—even a sidekick with a perfectly shaped head—singing showtunes and correcting your grammar in a quasi-British accent.[1]

It's not that I don't love Gus. I'm just saying, is it too much to ask for *one day of normalcy*? One day of not using Pluto's fall from favor as an "in" with women? One day of not talking about coins and stamps and all your other weird collections that I've never actually seen? One day of not using my couch pillows to practice your professional wrestling moves?

The point is, Future Detectives of America (and the World), choose your sidekicks wisely.

In fact, here are some brief screening questions you may want to bounce off any potential hires:

■ What is the Klingon word for *leftovers*?

■ Which of the following does *not* count as a two-letter word in Scrabble: *za, op, qi*?

■ How long did Aerys the Mad reign before being defeated by Robert Baratheon?

If someone even *thinks* they can answer one of these questions, they are—trust me—a massive dork. And you should think twice about bringing them into your life and business.[2]

---

[1] Seriously, I am sitting here—*as I write this*—watching Gus prance around the room singing songs from *Billy Elliot the Musical*. I mean, come on, I've been known to sing around the office, but this is ridiculous. Twirl and kick and spin and…I'm humiliated just to know him.

[2] For the record, I don't know the answers to any of these. I was only able to piece together the questions based on things I've heard Gus say to his other dork friends.

Anyway, Future Detectives of America (and the World), consider yourselves warned.[1]

Also, if your girlfriend starts talking about "couples friends" and "couples dinners," book up your calendar with things that get in the way...*fast*.

---

[1] Oh my God, he's doing "Here I Am" by Air Supply. He *knows* this is my jam! It's like he's *trying* to piss me off!

Chapter 3

Investigation Nation:

Working in the Field

Introduction

A professional detective has many tools in his toolbox: going undercover, analyzing shoe clues, creating cool disguises, etc. One tool, however, is more important than all the others: the ability to conduct an effective stakeout.

Actually, no, I take that back. Going undercover is more important. Then conducting an effective stakeout.

Wait, no—first, undercover. Then a reliable gun or nunchucks. Then the ability to light a match on your facial hair. Followed by moonwalking. And Bishop's knife trick from *Aliens*. And then being able to suck a piece of spaghetti up your nose, bring it out your mouth, and slide it back and forth from both ends.

Then conducting a stakeout.

To be honest, it doesn't matter. What *does* matter is getting out there in the field and snooping around. It doesn't matter who you question or what evidence you find; we've all got skeletons in our closets—it's your job to pull them out and hold them up to the light!

This is where most amateur sleuths (and 98.7 percent of all professionals) fall on their face. They think looking for evidence means looking for the *right* evidence, but the truth is that there's no such thing. There's just evidence, and your job, as a detective, is to take whatever evidence you can find and *make* it the "right" evidence.

So dive in and make a case out of whatever you can find!

And if you're lucky, you may just find the most important thing of all... yourself.

Getting Around

Now, let's talk about wheels. If you're gonna go into the field, you're gonna need some wheels. Nobody will take you seriously as a detective if you're sans automobile. Show me a detective without some sort of vehicle and I'll show you a person likely to die by their own hand, possibly of some disease for which there's already a cure. And don't go holding up Encyclopedia Brown and Harriet the Spy as exceptions. They can't drive, and even if they could, they'd still be mostly useless because they're *children*.[1]

The detective's car serves a dual purpose plus infinity. It's an indispensable tool for everything from pursuing suspects to conducting stakeouts to delivering its occupants to Robert O. Lee's, Santa Barbara's only Civil War–themed donut shop. If you have the means, it's advisable to pick up the most awesome car you can; as conscientious detectives (and the research faculty at the University of Michigan) know, there's an inverse correlation between crime prevention and the make and model of a detective's vehicle. In other words, a cool car will actually stop crime even before it starts (*see below*).

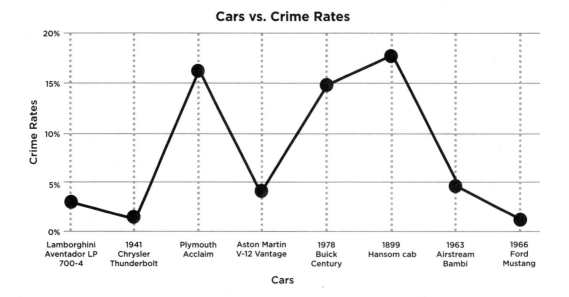

---

[1] Also, Harriet is a *spy*, which is not the same as a detective.

So now that you're in the market for a car, you could do with a little practical analysis. As you know, I've spent a good piece in the shotgun seat of the worst detective car in this or any other universe, so I've got some thoughts on the matter. Let's consider a few examples.

MAGNUM P.I. FERRARI

1 An excellent example of an ideal sleuth car. Flashy. Fast. If you've got the resources, you should also consider setting up shop in Hawaii. Just go easy on the aloha shirts. You really don't want to wind up looking like my dad.

KNIGHT RIDER KITT CAR

2 Another totally solid example. Literally. The Knight Industries Two Thousand (KITT) was armored with Pyroclastically Laminated Tri-Helical Plasteel and was pretty much impervious to damage. I mean, the Blueberry's

fiberglass rear bumper fell off last week after backing into some bushes. Oh, and KITT talks, which pretty much eliminates the need for a sidekick, which could be a plus. Also nice: flamethrowers, afterburners, induction coil, and a Passive Laser Restraint System (PLRS).

AIRWOLF SORTA-CAR

3 Not really a detective car, but come on. It's *Airwolf*. Crime in your town would immediately cease the second you choppered out of your garage.

MIAMI VICE FERRARI DAYTONA

4 Pretty cool, I suppose. But just know a Ferrari Daytona is only as cool as the people riding in it.

The Long Tail

Here's a little secret about detecting most nondetectives don't know: detecting is really nothing more than legalized stalking. You've got a target. You do some background research and see what they're into, and then you either follow them around or park outside their house with the ultimate goal of encountering them accidentally. It's a page right out of Gus's playbook for meeting women, and in many ways, will serve as a scaffold upon which we'll build our discussion on the ever-important topic of tailing suspects.

Now, in my experience, I've seen Gus put a great deal of time and effort into pursuing the ladies, and in most cases, once he's done the typical hours of research (usually a complicated Googling scheme he calls "vetting"), he's too far into it to turn back. He's got to meet this shorty. It's the same thing with a criminal suspect. You've done your detecting, gathered evidence and clues, and are now poised to strike. And just like with Gus, this will require a measure of finesse because criminals never sit still,[1] and like Gus's romantic marks, they're not looking to get caught.

Now, this is where approaches diverge. Gus always makes a point of remaining inconspicuous when hot on the trail of a sweet biddy, which is wise, because the Golden State has laws, most of which are very inflexible. The wily detective works another angle, and it's right out in the open. Anyone who ever told you to blend into the background, hiding cartoonlike behind tree after tree, probably never brought down a badass perp. Be seen, young sleuth, you have my permission, because the best way to convince someone you're *not* pursuing them is to *be conspicuous*. In fact, the more you can get your mark to notice you, the better.

Don't believe me? Take a look at *Figure 23* (next page); see if you can spot the detective.

If you pointed to the guy in the curly hair and clown nose, just close this book now and think about a new career. *Why on earth would you tail*

---

[1] Unless we're talking about this quadriplegic mob boss I tracked one time. Jimmy "the Blanket" Carrano. He literally just *sat still*. He kept trying to get away and would just sit there, wheezing. It was really uncomfortable for everyone.

Above: Figure 23   *Above: Figure 24*

someone in a giant wig and clown nose? I know I said be conspicuous, but you also have to use common sense.

The correct answer is the dude right behind the dude in the giant wig and clown nose (*Figure 24*). It's hard to tell from the picture, but he's wearing acid-washed jeans and an outdated Unionbay blazer. He's also walking with a slight limp. If he weren't right next to *a guy in a clown nose*, he'd be totally conspicuous.

(By the way, the guy with the jet pack is just testing out a jet pack. It's a prototype not yet available to the general public.)

Automobile Tailing

Of course, you won't always be shadowing someone on foot. You might be in an electric blue, early aughts Toyota or some other kind of vehicle. Tailing someone in an automobile is kind of like a car chase, except way slower, and the person you're chasing doesn't really know you're chasing him. Still, the following are things every detective should know about automotive detective work. So listen up.

1 **STAY THREE CAR LENGTHS BEHIND WHOEVER YOU ARE FOLLOWING.** (*Figure 25*) This gives you enough space to see your subject, but still lets you blow through yellow lights whenever necessary. Some detectives will tell you *not* to rush through yellow lights; it makes you too obvious. Again, other detectives are wrong. What makes you "obvious" is being the idiot who *doesn't* rush through the yellow light—because that's what everyone does, and your job is to appear like everyone else, if not more so. Plus, if you stop at the yellow, you're just going to aggravate everyone, and a good dick should never be an actual dick, especially on the road.

Above: Figure 25

2 **THE Q-TURN.** (*Figure 26*) Let's say you're tailing someone and they suddenly turn around. Pulling a U-turn may seem like the fastest option, but U-turns draw your suspect's attention. Instead, try a Q-turn. This way your suspect doesn't see you following

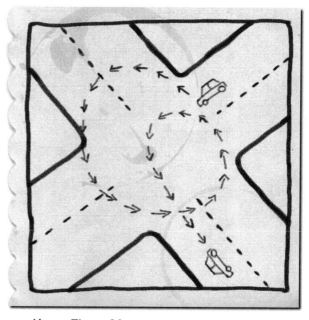

Above: Figure 26

them, and if they do, they're confused about where you're going to turn.[1]

You can also try the ホ-**turn** (alternately known as the "ho-turn" or "katakana" since the maneuver resembles the thirtieth Japanese syllable of the gojuon order). (*Figure 27*)

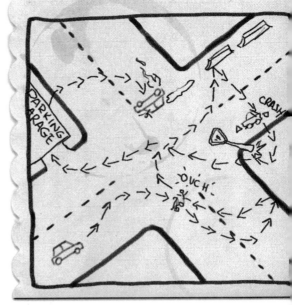

Above: Figure 27

3 **THE BOURNE.** (*Figure 28*) Sometimes shadowing someone requires extreme moves, like if your subject drives through a flash mob, or a minefield, or spots you and starts shooting at you. This is when I like to whip out a little move called "the Bourne" (based on my friend Roberto Bourne, who's a terrible driver). (People always think this is named after Jason Bourne, the ass-kicking amnesiac spy. But why would I do that? He's a great driver.)

---

[1] GUS: This doesn't really look like a Q, Shawn. And if it did look like a Q, you wouldn't use it in place of a U-turn, because the end of the Q shoots you off in the same direction you were going.[a]

[a] I'm really getting sick of all the negativity, Gus, especially considering it takes you seventeen moves just to get out of a parallel parking spot. When you get a real car, you can name the maneuvers.

Above: Figure 28

Other Great Ways to Tail Someone

Occasionally, tailing someone by foot or car isn't practical, and you have to use another form of transportation, each with its own risks and challenges.

Segway

The key to tailing someone on a Segway is to bend slightly at the knees, but not so much that you're in a full crouch, which causes you to pull back and slow the Segway. Also, remember that Segways are incredibly sensitive; they suddenly turn in response to the slightest shift in body weight, and they like being told they look nice in the morning.

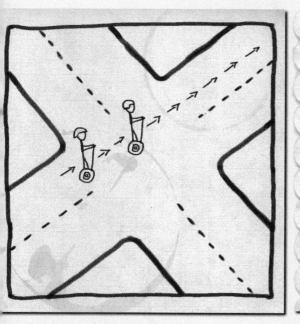

Above: Good Tailing

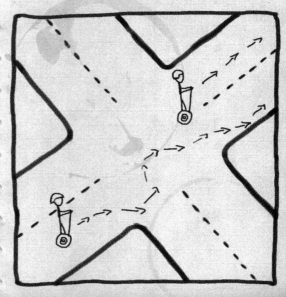

Above: Bad Tailing

Diver Propulsion Vehicle →

Terrific for shadowing Russian frogmen, Lt. Coffey in *The Abyss*, or sharks with laser beams on their heads. Not so great in shallower water or kiddie pools.

Hang Glider

Using a hang glider is a great way to shadow someone, because you have incredible aerial maneuverability while they're stuck on the ground. But be warned, this only works in wide-open spaces and isn't recommended for city use.

Above: This way.

Above: Not this way.

City Bus

Probably the least effective mode of transportation to use when pursuing a suspect. Use only when you've exhausted other options, and be sure to have exact change.

Staking Out

A few pages ago, we talked about the tenuous line between detectiving and stalking, but if you thought this line was thin when it came to tailing, it's practically nonexistent when it comes to stakeouts.

At least if you're tailing someone, you don't *look* like you're stalking. You're moving; you can change course; and it's not impossible to convince the police, your target, or yourself that you and your subject just happened to be moving in the same direction at the same speed for the last 6.4 miles. But with a stakeout, you're literally sitting in one place, often with night vision goggles, just *staring* at someone. If that's not stalking, I don't know what is.

In other words, sitting in front of someone's house at night, watching them through their window because you want to find out who they're sleeping with: STALKER.

But sitting in front of someone's house at night, watching them through their window because *someone else is paying you* to find out who they're sleeping with: DETECTIVE.

Not that I'm complaining.

Stakeouts are a necessary part of investigation, recognized and even sanctioned by law enforcement. So get over your hang-ups about invading someone's privacy—this is a gray area, and you're about to park your car here and sit in it for a while. Listen and learn.

At the outset, I'd suggest taking on a couple of non-crime-related stakeouts, just to get your sea legs. Consider parking outside Trader Joe's just before their annual release of peppermint Joe Joe's or outside the House of Blues on the night before OMD tickets go on sale. It will soon become clear that a stakeout has many practical applications beyond detectiving.

Now, some might view this behavior as a crude exploitation of the stakeout concept, but those people are simply naysayers, and you should say nay to them. Even if they are the head detective. These dry runs are essential, and I promise you, I wouldn't be the detective I am had I never parked at the end of Michael Bublé's driveway just to catch a glimpse of him getting his paper. You have to walk before you can run, Bubléphiles. Remember that.

A few fake stakeouts in the can, and you're ready to roll. Oh, and speaking of the can, be sure you've got a Porta Potty or Del Taco nearby, or your micro-bladdered partner is liable to start moaning at an ever-increasing volume and your cover will be blown. Having said all this, here are some specific rules and bits of advice I'd suggest for maximum stakeout success.

Shawn's Stakeout Survival Guide

- **DO NOT USE A CAR WITH SEAT WARMERS.** They're the most annoying, unnecessary invention since golf. Warming your seat just makes your thighs sweaty so they stick together, which isn't pleasant for anyone. Plus, warm seats create smells and noises and after a while they're like petri dishes. I don't even want to get into it. Besides, when it comes to stakeouts, an uncomfortable crotch comes with the territory, so suck it up. As a crime fighter on a stakeout, you need to focus on solving mysteries, not demoisturizing your gear.

- **CHOOSE YOUR MUSIC CAREFULLY.** Anything too mellow, like Billy Joel's *Cold Spring Harbor*, and you'll fall asleep. Anything too loud, like Quiet Riot's *Metal Health*, and you'll punch a hole through your dashboard. Choose something upbeat but restrained, like Weezer's Green Album or anything by Gordon Lightfoot.

- **HAVE BACKUP.** Your sidekick may turn out to be totally unreliable, so it's important to have a substitute staker-outer on standby. This could be a friend, an old babysitter, even a local neighborhood kid who needs some extra cash. At some point, you're going to need to go to the bathroom or get more Funyuns, and you'll need someone to cover you. Be prepared. (Sitting alone in a parked car with some twelve-year-old neighborhood kid is most often a terrible idea. And offering them money to do so is an even terribler idea. Exercise caution.)

- **PLAN SENSIBLE SNACKS.** Bugles are good because they're tasty and can double as binoculars; Raisinets, not so good. Mostly because they're disgusting.

- **STAKEOUT RULE NUMBER 1 FOR SIDEKICKS:** Stakeouts can be intense and dangerous, so it's important to let your detective concentrate and not bore him with that story about the girl you met on the ninth-grade choir trip. You've told it a million times. It wasn't interesting the first time, and no one cares twenty-five years later.[1]

- **DO *NOT* STATION YOUR CAR NEAR A LANDFILL, SLAUGH-TERHOUSE, OR CHINESE RESTAURANT** whose best entrée costs less than $4.99—the smells coming out of those places are grotty.

- **STAKEOUT RULE NUMBER 2 FOR SIDEKICKS:** Rockstar Sugar Free is not the same as Rockstar. Get it right.

- **RATHER THAN HAVE A STAKEOUT, STAY HOME AND WATCH *STAKEOUT* WITH RICHARD DREYFUSS AND EMILIO ESTEVEZ.** And I don't mean "watch *Stakeout* starring Richard Dreyfuss and Emilio Estevez." I literally mean watch *Stakeout with* Richard Dreyfuss and Emilio Estevez. It's not like they're doing anything else. They'd probably dig a hang with one of today's cutting-edge crime fighters (that's you). Just make sure you don't don the Rosie O'Donnell dominatrix outfit from *Stakeout 2*. Bad show, for sure.[2]

Juliet: I call this Under My Thumbprint. Get it? Like the song, but it's not just a thumb, it's a thumbprint. Get it?

---

[1] GUS: Her name was Jeanie, Shawn, and we had something special. She was my first.[a]

[a] Ugh, Gus...stop. I can taste my breakfast.[b]

[b] GUS: Pull your head out of the gutter, Shawn. She was my first madrigal duet. That's a big moment in the life of a young tenor.

[2] GUS: Actually, Shawn, I think you're thinking of *Exit to Eden*.[a]

[a] Uh, no, I'm pretty sure it was *Stakeout 2*.[b]

[b] GUS: She's on the *Exit to Eden* poster, Shawn. *In the outfit.* And it's called *Another Stakeout*, not *Stakeout 2*.[c]

[c] Do you realize how lame you are for knowing either of those things?[d]

[d] GUS: Lame? Really, Mr. Know-It-All? For memorizing the oeuvre of the greatest American actress since Ginger Grant? I think not.

Top 10 Unsolved Mysteries I Dream of Solving

10 **"Who Let the Dogs Out?"** Even more perplexing than who actually let the dogs out is how this song became popular by being on a *Rugrats* soundtrack. I mean, who's buying this stuff? Besides Gus?[1]

9 **Who stole my Sno-Caps in Mrs. Glaza's third-grade reading class?** Yes, I know this was a long time ago, and yes, I should probably let it go, but here's the thing: they were sitting *right on the aquarium table*. I turned around for five seconds to get a crayon, turned back, and they were gone. The only person within reach was Neil Hung, who was allergic to chocolate, so it couldn't have been him. And to make things even weirder, Jessica Cunha lost her scissors the very next day...as they were sitting on the *same table*. Coincidence? You tell me.

8 (Hey, everyone, Gus here. I'm adding my own.) **"Gunter glieben glauchen globen"** Def Leppard swears the beginning of "Rock of Ages" means nothing, but that's the same thing the government keeps saying about Roswell and the Philadelphia Experiment. I didn't buy either of those lies, and I'm not buying this, either. Whatever that guy says, it's way too creepy not to mean anything. I think it's some sort of satanic heavy metal message. Back to you, Shawn.

7 **The Shroud of Turin** People think any picture of a man with a beard is Jesus, even if it looks nothing like Jesus. Take a cloth, stamp a bad drawing on it, and *someone's* gonna cry Jesus. The real mystery isn't whether or not this is Jesus, but why so many people think dudes who don't look like Jesus are Jesus. Having said that, if this *is* Jesus, I'd like to be the guy who proves it.

Right: Mr. Ruhde, my tenth-grade geometry teacher...or Jesus?

6 ***Tinker Tailor Soldier Spy*** Did anyone see this? Could someone please explain to me what the hell is going on?

---

[1] GUS: It's actually a good album, Shawn. Jessica Simpson, Sinéad O'Connor, *and* Ginger Spice? How can you go wrong?

5 Who shot JFK? No, not John F. Kennedy. I'm talking about nineteenth-century sharecropper Jeremiah Franklin Keyes, who was shot to death in his cabin just outside of Natchez, Mississippi, spawning eight decades of Natchez mugs, hats, and T-shirts emblazoned with the catchphrase, "Who shot JFK?" Unfortunately for Natchez, it all came to an end on November 22, 1963, which is both sad and ironic, because President Kennedy's murder is one mystery that doesn't need to be solved. To this day, the real JFK's murder remains unsolved.

4 The Higgs boson I thought this was one of the original members of the Wu-Tang Clan, but Gus swears it's an actual mystery.[1]

3 The Black Dahlia I'm not talking about the real-life murder. I'm talking about the moment in the movie where Josh Hartnett is standing in Hilary Swank's front yard, with Hilary Swank on one side and Scarlett Johansson on the other, and he can't decide which to choose. *How is this a question?* I mean, granted, Hilary Swank is one of the best leading men of our generation, but unless there's some weird subtext I'm missing, I don't know how you choose him over *Scarlett Johansson*.

2 What happened Tuesday night? So, I'm sitting on the couch a couple nights ago, trying to decide if we should order Rocky's or Giuliano's, when Juliet comes in and says, "What do you think?" So I say, "Well, Rocky's has better hoagies, but Giuliano's has free breadsticks. What do *you* think?" And she gets all quiet and says, "I meant about my hair. I just got highlights." So I look at her hair, and—I'm not just saying this to be nice—it looks great. So I say, "It looks great," but she just shakes her head and stomps out. WTF? And don't tell me she wanted me to notice her hair on my own. I've read *Men Are from Mars, Women Are from Venus*...I *get* it. I'm just saying, why are men expected to change their behavior to accommodate women, but women aren't expected to accommodate men? That's the real crime here. I may be an idiot, but if you *know* I'm an idiot, you can't treat me like I'm *not* an idiot. If you know someone only speaks French and you still insist on speaking German, you can't be upset when they don't understand you.

1 *Unsolved Mysteries* Not a specific mystery per se, I'd just like to host the show.

---

[1] GUS: It *is* an actual mystery, Shawn. It's a theoretical particle that could prove the existence of everything.[a]

  [a] Really, you need to prove that "everything" exists? Can't you just go outside?[b]

   [b] GUS: It's the building block of the entire universe, Shawn. If it exists, we'll understand where the universe came from, how time and space work, the nature of energy. Everything.[c]

    [c] Will we understand why Samuel Jackson wears that stupid Kangol hat all the time?

Shawn's Guide to Going Undercover

Crime reaches its greasy tentacles into every corner of our world. Drive down Any Street of Anytown, USA, and you're likely to encounter Lithuanian bank robbers, Mexican hippie drug dealers, car theft rings run by clowns, the Mafia. As a detective, sometimes you're simply going to be out of your element.

Bottom line: it's time to go undercover.

Going undercover isn't just a great way to make repeat visits to IHOP for free flapjacks on National Pancake Day, it's a crucial piece of the crime-fighting puzzle. Cozying up with goons and punks and thugs comes with the territory, and you can't do that as *you*. So I've assembled a blue-ribbon panel made up of four of Santa Barbara's finest crime fighters and undercover-goers. Pay attention.

Carlton Lassiter

The other day, I heard some dumbass compare undercover work to "playing dress up." There are plenty of people out there who play dress up, they're called transvestites. Undercover work is a hell of a lot more than that. Next to the .40-cal Glock 22, it's one of the most powerful weapons a law enforcement officer has.

Going undercover involves literally *becoming* someone else, and I've seen some pretty tough nuts buckle under the weight of it. You remember SBPD vice hotshot Gary Stanton, right? He was investigating a crooked cosmetics concern that was fronting for an animal-trafficking operation. He was undercover as an eyeliner salesman, but then things got hinky and he couldn't take the heat. Look him up. You'll find him in a padded cell at West Haven Psychiatric Center. True story.

When creating a new identity, the first thing I think of is physicality. Plumbers walk differently than accountants. Lawyers sit differently than cable guys. Liberals are just wrong all the time. The physical embodiment of your undercover persona is key and might be the difference between bringing some scumbag down or dying violently in a hail of bullets.

It takes time to become this new person. Take the time. I often spend hours naked in front of the mirror, crouching, stretching, twisting. Eventually, I find that perfect combination of movements and positions (as well as any new moles or skin tags—they can pop up in the most unexpected places) to bring my undercover persona to life. Now, if you don't have that kind of time or personal nudity makes you uncomfortable, just do the best you can to move as naturally as possible. Even to the stupidest criminals, there's nothing more obvious than a guy trying to fake a clubfoot or sit like he's got scoliosis.

Next, I examine who this person is emotionally. Is he single? Married? Does he still think about his ex-wife, and how does he feel about the fact that his mother's new girlfriend threw all his stuff out of the attic without even *asking*, including his collection of *Junior Marksman* magazines, which he'd been collecting since he was eight?

If you haven't yet noticed, I'll spell it out for you: use whatever personal experience and knowledge you can to construct your undercover identity. If you're posing as a low-level arms dealer, try to remember the time your father sold all your Christmas presents to buy more Pall Malls and Schlitz. Maybe you've never been an accountant trying to run a money-laundering operation, but think back to the time Sandra Wollack lost a bet and had to make out with you at the homecoming dance. This is what your memories are for. Exploit them to catch criminals, and then get back to the business of repressing them. This is the way of things.

Finally, whatever disguise you choose, don't forget a handgun or three. The Kel-Tec .32 will fit in most pants pockets. The Smith & Wesson 642 is very light and perfect if you're undercover as a construction worker or UPS guy. I'm not sure where you'd put an FN Herstal FNP-9. I include it on this list simply because it's one of the most gorgeous polymer-framed pistols ever built. I recommend it purely as a piece of beauty.

Best Places to Buy Undercover Supplies

LASSITER

Discount Guns & Ammo

Hollywood Bob's Costumes and Makeup

Leanne's Firearms

Shogun Martial Arts Weapons

Turner's Field & Survival Gear

Short Fuse Explosives Expo

I Spy Surveillance Equipment

Juliet O'Hara

I've gone undercover many times, and I've found the best approach (whether posing as a sorority sister, a roller derby badass, or even Shawn's wife) is just to *always be yourself.*

I realize it's counterintuitive. You're not an actor. I mean, I suppose you are, in a sense, but the way I see it, if you're true to who you are, more people will believe you're *not* who you are.

Besides, it's much easier to play yourself than to try and invent an entirely new person; you don't have to make up random dates, or where you came from, or whether or not you ever went to a 98 Degrees concert with Greg from the bank even though it meant absolutely *nothing.* And the fewer lies you have to keep track of, the better. A lot of cops wind up in therapy after long stints undercover because it's essentially one big lie. It's not always easy to pull yourself out. (I heard Gary Stanton, this guy from vice, went so deep undercover he's now in the mental hospital and thinks he's a tangerine.)

This doesn't mean you shouldn't use disguises. You obviously have to look like you belong in the world you're entering. Plus, costumes are one of the most fun parts of going undercover. I once went u.c. as a diplomat's wife at Opera Santa Barbara and got to wear this gorgeous red

> ### Best Places to Buy Undercover Supplies
>
> **JULIET**
>
> Neiman Marcus
>
> J. Crew
>
> Fendi
>
> Sephora
>
> Gucci
>
> Talbots[1]
>
> Louis Vuitton[2]

---

[1] Seriously, Jules—Talbots? What are you, a middle-aged real estate receptionist?[a]

  [a] JULIET: They have some cute things, Shawn. Be nice.

[2] A couple other good stores Juliet forgot to include: Lingerie Palace, KinkMeister, and PrincessLeiaLover.com.[a]

  [a] JULIET: You're disgusting, Shawn. I'm trying to be helpful.[b]

  [b] Really? *Fendi* is a good place to shop for undercover disguises?[c]

  [c] JULIET: Depending on where you're going undercover. What do you know about it? You still dress the same way you did in college. Now, you asked me to write this—are you going to let me do this or not?

Above: Deep cover.

velvet ball gown. It was impossible to run in, but I looked amazing.

A good alias is also important. Your fake name doesn't have to be crazy or exotic, like those ridiculous names Shawn and Gus come up with;[1] it just has to be different enough to free you from your inhibitions. Like the time I went undercover as socialite Jennifer Safka and conned my way into the private studio of a concert pianist, who was actually smuggling gold bullion. Or the time I was movie mogul Roberta Korsh and convinced this venture capitalist to give me $25 million to make *Deadly Assault 3: Return to Whisper Pines*, then nailed him for securities fraud. Both cases resulted in arrests, and in both cases, the *alias* was the ticket.[2]

And I guess that's ultimately the best part of going undercover: meeting people and experiencing things you'd never get to experience otherwise. I mean, if I'd never gone undercover, I would have never driven a NASCAR race, or rocked a roller derby bout, or ridden an elephant. So for me, that's the most fulfilling part.

And, obviously, the whole capturing-criminals-and-making-the-world-a-safer-place thing.[3]

---

[1] I take offense to that comment, Jules. There's a great art to coming up with the perfect alias, and my sidekick, Engelbert Sassafrass, and I take it very seriously. To learn more, peruse my next piece, the brilliant and insightful "What's in a (Nick)Name?"

[2] Great examples, Juliet—very helpful! By the way, when you say you "conned your way" into the "private studio" of a concert pianist, what exactly do you mean by that? I'd like to clarify for my readers.[a]
[a] JULIET: You'll never know, Shawn.

[3] Hey, Jules, still trying to clear some stuff up about the concert pianist/seduction incident. For instance, what would you tell young detectives to do once they're in a concert pianist's bedroom? What did *you* do? I'm just trying to get a complete picture here. For educational purposes.

Buzz McNab

Okay, well, first of all, I'm not sure I'm the best person to be writing on this topic. I've been undercover exactly twice—once when I used a fake ID to buy a latte in high school and another time when I was five and my mom passed me off as a girl so she could enter me in the Hardin County Beauty Pageant (I came in third). Of course, I've been through my police academy training and I listen to everything my fellow officers say, but I can't claim a lot of firsthand experience. (I can't wait till my first undercover assignment, though— I've already been collecting things for disguises.)

So since anything I can tell you is pretty much conjecture, I'm going to have to go with what Lassiter and O'Hara said, which I suppose it's in my interest to do. Even though they've been emphatic that I'm probably never going to get an undercover gig of my own, I like to think that means there's some chance, and when that opportunity comes, I'm going to be ready.

> **McNab's
> Best Places to Buy
> Undercover Supplies**
>
> 99¢ Store (Since I haven't actually gone undercover yet, I don't know a ton of places, but I have bought some great supplies here. They've got a terrific stock of off-brand household cleaners and Mexican baking ingredients.)
>
> ———
>
> Also, since I don't really have a long list of places to buy undercover supplies, I thought I'd list my favorite taco joints. I call this list...
>
> **McNab's Favorite
> Taco Joints**
>
> Taco Suprema
>
> Kill Whitey's Enchiladas
>
> Pierre's Fine Mexican Cuisine
>
> Quik Snak (Tuesdays only)

Henry Spencer

Nice try, Shawn. You think I don't see what you're doing here? Getting me and everyone else to write your book while you and Gus run off to Scare Fest or the beach or wherever you are. Not gonna happen. You signed up for this, you're the one with the deadline, and you're the one who has to write it.

Disguises through the Ages: Studying the Classics

There have, throughout history, been many highly skilled masters of disguise. The Greeks disguised themselves as a giant horse, Donnie Brasco disguised himself as a mobster, the president of Hooters disguised himself as a cook on *Undercover Boss*. So one of the best ways to become a master of disguise yourself is to study some of the best and worst disguises through the years. Here are some of the best.

Above: One of my masterpieces. I actually stole seven sheep from Farmer Wilkins's pasture that night.

Michelle Obama

You don't usually think of Michelle Obama as a master of disguise, which just proves how good she is. Think about it: if you ever looked at her and thought, *Wow, she's great at pulling off those disguises*, she wouldn't be a very good disguiser. Here's the simple disguise Michelle donned while infiltrating the Botswana Pirates Association.

Sherlock Holmes

Fans of Sherlock Holmes know that
Holmes was a genius of disguises, but
I'll be honest—*they must be out of their
minds*. Do they really think this guy
was good? Here's a recently discovered
photograph of Holmes, taken in 1898 while
he was investigating a series of murders in a
high-end gambling house. First of all, what
kind of idiot goes into a casino disguised
with a *clown nose*? I got kicked out of
the Venetian for claiming to be Turkish
olive baron Altan Kirshbaum, and I had
no disguise, so surely they would've noticed Holmes wandering around in a
clown nose. Secondly, this still totally looks like Holmes, despite the red ball
attached to his face. I know you've got a lot of fans, Holmes, but if you expect
to fool a *real* detective, you're gonna have to do a lot better than this.

Whoever This Guy Is

I know, you're thinking, *Uh, it's a chipmunk wearing an elephant trunk*, right? *Wrong*. In one of the most renowned disguises of all time, this is an elephant disguised as a chipmunk disguised as an elephant. Brilliant, huh? This disguise was so good that the elephant lasted *three years* as part of a traveling rodent circus. To this day, many true masters of disguise herald this as the pinnacle of professional disguise-ism.

The Gerwin Brothers

An unspoken truth of the disguisal arts is *when you look this fricking creepy, you don't need a disguise*. I mean, take one look at these two prepubescent freak shows, and you immediately assume they're actually some kind of demon or incubus disguised as children. And you're probably right. I once spent about four minutes looking at this photo, and when I came out of it, I had removed my pants and burned all my Bananarama albums.

What's in a (Nick)Name?

Well, since Jules brought it up a few pages ago, this is a good spot to discuss the ancient Sumerian art of the alias. Most detectives won't share this information, but I'm not most detectives, so here's a simple truth: *successful undercovering doesn't happen without appropriate aliases.*

Think about it; you don't see strippers named Hillary or librarians named Brandi. People don't buy it. If you're posing as an Irish clog dancer, you can't tell people your name is Farzad Loewenthal. If you're supposed to be a sushi chef, you don't want to be Jorge O'Sullivan.

Names need to fit the situation, and unfortunately, in most situations, guess what name *doesn't* fit? *Burton Guster.* I mean, what is that? A low-end clothing company? An investment firm? A character actor from the Ghoulies movies?

This is why I'm constantly having to rename Gus every time we go undercover and why a study by the American Academy for the Investigative Arts recently found that my aliases for Gus have been directly responsible for "no less than most" of our cracked cases.

So let's take a moment and explore what makes these aliases tick and why they've been so influential in solving crimes.

ALIAS	DEEPER MEANING	HOW IT SOLVED A CASE
Oliver Wendell Homey	Creates an air of Supreme Court coolness	Helped us get free donuts while tailing a murder suspect
Archibald Van de Graff III	Suggests Gus is the child of an oil baron too busy to take an interest in his family and a trophy wife disappointed that her son wants to be a flautist rather than a Goldman Sachs investment broker	Allowed us to test-drive a Ferrari 458 Italia while investigating a robbery at Santa Barbara National
Chief Urine Stream	Instantly recalls the white man's burden and fears of an enlarged prostate	Got us one free round at Sluggers Batting Cages during The Jade Turtle Investigation

ALIAS	DEEPER MEANING	HOW IT SOLVED A CASE
Adolf Phitler	This one seemed good in my head but turned out not to be as valuable in real life.	It didn't solve a case, but Gus is now banned for life from Temple Shaarei Torah.
Aristotle Socrates	Seriously? You need to know a deeper meaning? It's the *two greatest philosophers of all time.* If you don't know who these guys are, there's nothing I can do for you.	Earned Gus one free slot machine pull at the Lucky Shot Casino, which won *another* free pull, which earned *another* free pull, which did not win us anything
Duck-Hwan Mozombite	Duck-Hwan is a Korean name meaning, "Integrity returns." Mozombite is an old South American or Amazonian surname. Together they mean, "he who leaves only one square of toilet paper and doesn't change the roll."	Studies show people find mixed-race people to be the most attractive, so a black Korean Chinese guy? *Hot.* Gus got numbers from fourteen girls at happy hour that night. Only two turned out to be real, but still—not bad for Gus.
Frooty Bootylicious	Totally funkadelic	Convinced a security guard at the Santa Barbara Bowl that we were part of Afrommage, a French calypso band, and needed to see the Green Room. (We weren't working on a case. We just heard there were free Pop-Tarts.)
Louis May Alcott	Makes Gus sound like he's the great-great-great-grandson of annoying and wordy chick-lit novelist Louisa May Alcott	Nabbed Gus an honorary membership to the Santa Barbara chapter of Daughters of the Confederacy. (Haven't yet used this for anything related to crime solving, but I think it'll pay great dividends down the road.)
Lazarus the Wise	Makes Gus sound wise and resurrectable	Gus and I used this once while chasing a suspected burglar, and he was in such awe that he stopped running and asked Gus to heal his lesions.

ALIAS	DEEPER MEANING	HOW IT SOLVED A CASE
Nambla Lovedong	This one also seemed good at the time, but in reality, not so great.	Gus can legally no longer be within fifty yards of a Boy Scout troop anywhere in Santa Barbara County.
He Who Walks Behind the Rows	The most fearsome demon in Nebraska	People are scared Gus will stick their hands in a meat slicer.

I don't care what anyone says; David Lee Roth is hella sexy.

Juliet: *You're a dork, Shawn.*

Have you even seen the "Hot for Teacher" video? The guy's freaking hot. Sometimes I just stand in front of the mirror and try to muss my hair and pucker my lips like he does.

Juliet: *I know. I've seen you.*

Yeah, and for those few fleeting moments, I feel like a man.

Preparing for Emergencies, or...How to Use the S.A.G. (Spencer Alibi Generator)

Every once in a while, when you're undercover or on a tail, you find yourself in a dangerous situation. Perhaps you find yourself in a sketchy neighborhood; or you get "made" by the drug runner you're shadowing; or you run into your girlfriend, who you promised to take Rollerblading at the beach this afternoon. Any of these situations could wind up getting you beaten, killed, or worse, which is why it's important to be prepared by having a solid cover story.

This is where the Spencer Alibi Generator (S.A.G.) comes in—a special, patented device, which helps produce fail-proof alibis for all the most common undercover and stakeout locations. It not only tells you what "activity" to use, but it tells you what props to bring as well! (Normally, I sell the S.A.G. for $59.99 on QVC, but since you've already bought this book, I'm giving it to you completely free.)

Four Super-Simple Steps for Assembling the S.A.G.

1. Make three copies of the page containing the S.A.G. Then cut them so you have the S.A.G.'s three circles.
2. Punch a hole in the middle of each circle—right where the black dot is.
3. Place the wheels on top of each other—the largest on the bottom, the smallest on top.
4. Place a brad through the center so each wheel spins independently.

How to Use the S.A.G.

Each circle represents a different part of your alibi:

Inner Circle	Middle Circle	Outer Circle
LOCATION	PROPS	ACTIVITY

You simply need to select which circle to start with. For instance, if you know you'll be at a public park, start with the location circle. You can then turn the middle circle to match the location with whatever props you have readily available. Lastly, select the activity you'd like to use. The beauty of

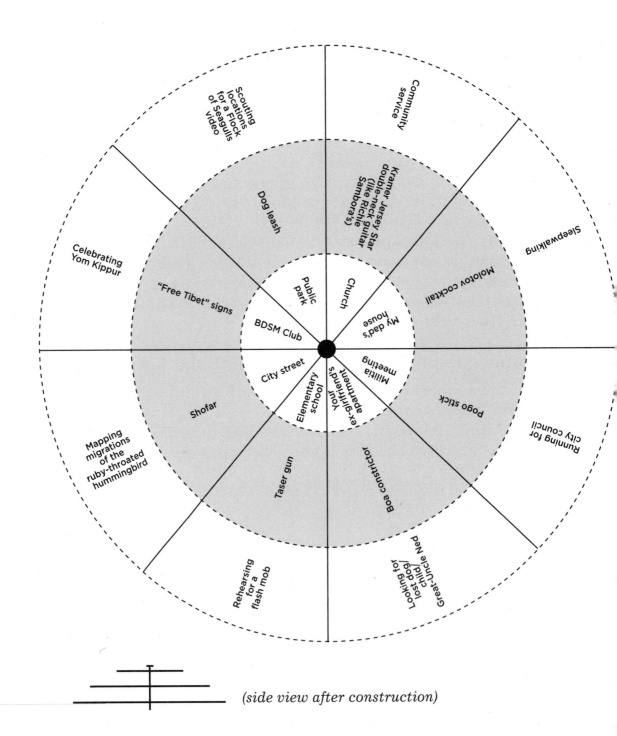

(side view after construction)

the S.A.G. is that all the elements work together; you just have to select whatever's easiest and most convenient, and the S.A.G. does the rest for you.

Just remember, the S.A.G. wields great power. Use it wisely and it'll be your friend for life. Abuse it and it will destroy all those you love and cherish. Good luck, my friend, and remember, God may have given rock and roll to you, but Shawn Spencer gave you the S.A.G.

Tips for Using the S.A.G.

1. The first rule of creating a believable alibi is making sure the alibi is appropriate to your location and situation. If you're staking out a boarding school, don't tell people you're practicing for the caber toss. If you're tailing a diamond smuggler through a warehouse district, don't say you're recruiting for Scientology.

2. Have some appropriate props on hand. For example, if you want to say you're trying out for a new baseball team, take a bat and glove. If you say you're poaching elephant ivory, carry an elephant gun or at least some crackers with peanut butter.[1]

3. It also helps to know your story before going into the field. You do *not* want to be caught off guard, scrambling to come up with an alibi. Rehearse it a few times at home. Get comfortable feeling the syllables in your mouth. The more *you* believe your cover story, the more someone else will believe your alibi.

A Few Words about Gun Ownership
by Carlton Lassiter

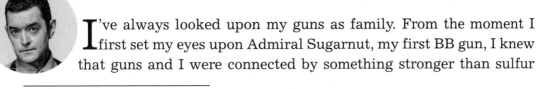

I've always looked upon my guns as family. From the moment I first set my eyes upon Admiral Sugarnut, my first BB gun, I knew that guns and I were connected by something stronger than sulfur

---

[1] FYI: Elephant hunting is a terrible alibi. Nobody does this, unless they live in Africa or Asia or near one of those zoos where the animals don't live in cages. Even if you do live in Asia or Africa or near a wild animal park, the idea of hunting elephants seems like an awful, cruel, and inhumane idea. (Having said that, I've always wanted a little ivory carving of the *Bat out of Hell* motorcycle, so if you see it anywhere, please let me know.)

or steel. After all, when I earned my Boy Scout merit badge in toxicology, who did I tell first? My 1969 Smith & Wesson Model 60 Chiefs Special. When Stacy Fitzpatrick broke up with me two days before the senior prom, whose shoulder did I cry on? My 1956 Browning Hi Power 9mm. When I nailed the highest score ever on the detective exam (97.2),[1] who did I rush home to celebrate with? My Ruger Model 77 Mark II Magnum.

And while you might think that things are different for me now that I wake up every morning next to the finest ex-felon in Santa Barbara, I can tell you they're not. If anything, Marlowe has actually brought me and my firearms closer than ever before. I could try to explain this, but you probably wouldn't understand.

I would, however, like to illuminate one important point. One can find all kinds of statistics about gun-related violence and how firearms create thousands of unnecessary deaths and crimes. In response, I would just like to say, *duh*. Putting anything in the wrong hands usually results in death, violence, or tragedy. My cousin Jeffrey choked to death on a Parmesan crouton. Clearly, that Parmesan crouton was in the "wrong hands." Had it been in the hands of someone smarter—say, Aunt Donna or cousin Leo—there would've been no trouble, and cousin Jeffrey would still be alive today to squander his parents' money on bogus real estate investments and snuff films.

Guns are no different. Put a gun in the wrong hands, and someone's gonna end up dead. But put a gun in the hands of someone who will love it, care for it, treat it as an equal, and you've got the recipe for a warm, loving home. Politicians can argue about gun control until the cows come home, but as far as I'm concerned, it can come organically in the form of good old-fashioned owner/gun TLC.

And in honor of that impenetrable bond, I would like to share with you something near and dear to my own heart: my family tree. And not the family tree that details the mostly imbecilic individuals with whom I share a bloodline. No, I mean my *real* family tree:

---

[1] JULIET: Until I scored a 98.4.[a]

  [a] And I scored a 100. Although technically my score doesn't count, since I was only fifteen. And did it on a dare.

LASSITER'S FAMILY TREE OF GUNS

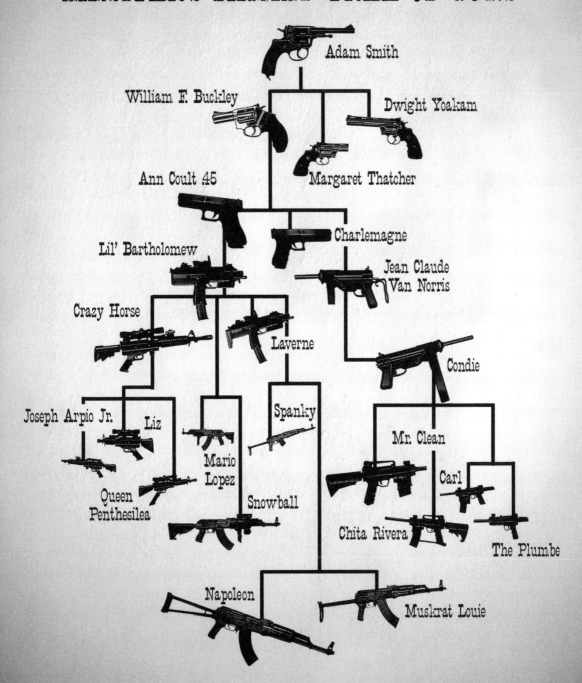

Adam Smith

William F. Buckley

Dwight Yoakam

Margaret Thatcher

Ann Coult 45

Charlemagne

Lil' Bartholomew

Jean Claude Van Norris

Crazy Horse

Laverne

Condie

Joseph Arpio Jr.

Liz

Spanky

Mr. Clean

Carl

Mario Lopez

Queen Penthesilea

Snowball

Chita Rivera

The Plumbe

Napoleon

Muskrat Louie

Getting Past the Gatekeeper

As I'm sure you've noticed, a private detective is basically just an "evidence gatherer." You go out, collect evidence and information, come back, and put it all together. (And if you haven't noticed this by now, you're well on your way to being the least observant detective ever. Congratulations.) You're like a pre-Neolithic woman, but instead of gathering fruits and nuts, you're gathering facts.

This means, as a *post*-Neolithic information gatherer, you'll spend a fair amount of time simply talking to people. After all, what better source of accurate information is there besides *people*? (Not counting the Internet, encyclopedias, research agencies, newspapers, scientific journals, bulletin boards in Starbucks, magic eight balls, historical societies, and the bathroom wall at Crabby Mel's.)

You never know who's going to have the information you want. I've solved cases based on info from department store Santas, priests, ex-girlfriends, convicted felons, unconvicted felons, dudes with one leg, Belgian people, aspiring astronauts, kids who look like Kirk Cameron, door-to-door salesmen, you name it.

The key to getting information isn't figuring out *who* has the information—okay, yes, actually, that *is* the key. But once you figure that out, the other key is *getting to those people*.

I know this doesn't seem like it'd be hard—how difficult is it to ask some questions?—but a surprising number of people have gatekeepers.

You know gatekeepers—assistants, secretaries, spouses, whatever you want to call them—and their sole purpose in life is to keep you from talking to the person you want to talk to. They're always saying things like, "I'm sorry, what's this regarding?" or "Ms. Aniston already has a boyfriend," or "Sir, I'm going to have to ask you to leave the property." And while it's easy to simply discard these people as lackeys sucking from their master's teat, they also guard the palace gate. So like it or not, if you want to talk to the person *behind* the gatekeeper, you have to get *through* the gatekeeper. (I wish getting past gatekeepers was as easy as waving a badge, but it's not. If it was, cops would be way more successful at getting past gatekeepers and solving crimes.

In fact, half the reason cops even bother waving their badges is because they lack the skill to do anything else. It's like watching a child stomp his feet and yell, "Somebody listen to me! I'm not smart enough to get past you on my own, so I'm going to flash a piece of tin and pretend like I'm important!") This takes a deep understanding of gatekeeper mentality, which boils down to one simple fact: *no gatekeeper likes being the gatekeeper.*

Of course, who would? Being a gatekeeper is basically like being the sphincter to someone else's large intestine. Your whole existence is making sure nothing goes in, and things only come out at your boss's discretion.

Your job, then, is to recognize this and figure out what the gatekeeper *really* wants to be or how they *really* want to be seen, so you can circumvent the gate.

For instance, if you meet a young paralegal, you can probably assume she wants to be a lawyer. A minor league ballplayer probably wants to play in the majors. A junior detective?...To run for tenth-grade president without Josh Green putting "Vote for Drool-iet" posters all over school.[1]

Whatever the gatekeeper wants, your job is to present yourself as someone who can deliver it. Convince a gatekeeper that you're the conduit to their dreams, and you'll have them eating out of your hand. This takes practice... and some shameless lying.

Let's try it. You walk into a high-end auto body shop you believe is secretly selling stolen cars. Sitting at the receptionist's desk is a woman flipping through *Hot Stuffs*, the bimonthly taxidermy magazine. Your conversation might go something like this:

YOU
Hi, I have a three o'clock with Herbert Logan.[2]

WOMAN
Name?

---

[1] JULIET: I told you that in confidence, Shawn; you promised you weren't going to use that![a]

  [a] I'm a writer, Jules. I simply transcribe whatever my muse sends me. If something in this book rings true to you, it must be your own interpretation of a purely coincidental reference.

[2] This is a lie.

YOU

Zaffer Syed.[1]

WOMAN

I don't have you on the books. What's this regarding?

YOU

I met Mr. Logan the other night; he wanted
to invest in my lemur farm.

WOMAN

Oh my God—you breed lemurs? I love lemurs!

YOU

Really? I had no idea![2] One of our best
females just had an entire litter.

WOMAN

Could I come see them?

YOU

Of course, give me your info and I'll
call you later this week.

WOMAN

Thank you so much! Let me see what
Mr. Logan's doing...I'll get you right in.

See? Totally easy. You just have to find what the gatekeeper wants...and exploit it.

Plus, the more you do this, the more you'll find certain patterns. Here's a guide to some of the gatekeepers you're liable to meet out there...and secrets to getting past them.

---

[1] Another lie.

[2] "I had no idea"—*ha!* Not only was the issue of *Hot Stuffs* a dead giveaway, but here are several other clues suggesting she loves lemurs: a wad of tear-soaked Kleenex on the floor, tamarind pods in her pockets (a favorite food of the ring-tailed lemur), and six pictures of an old lemur on her desk. Who *couldn't* have figured this out?

Shawn's Guide to Gatekeepers and What They Want

GATEKEEPER	WHAT THEY WANT
Administrative assistants	Mozzarella sticks and an espresso machine
Mr. Sadowski (at the dentist's office)	Jiffy Lube gift certificate
Butlers	To not have their livelihood mocked by fake dogs in tuxedos whenever they walk past The Sharper Image
Niles, the guy at Crabby Mel's who gives me extra shrimp poppers	Autographed copy of Steve Harvey's best-selling self-help book, *Straight Talk, No Chaser: How to Find, Keep, and Understand a Man*
Customer service operators at Time Warner Cable	To get paid commission for every customer they unintentionally drive to another cable company
Cheap Trick	You to want me
Former high school quarterbacks now stocking shelves at Larsen's Hardware	To have their picture on the Wall of Fame in the old gym (and a '86 El Camino)
Pharmaceutical reps	To be a globe-trotting archaeologist in search of the Ark of the Covenant
Computers	To use the Internet to connect to other computers and become one giant organism, overthrowing humanity and enslaving us forever

When Your Best Friend Shoots You
by Henry Spencer

You've probably noticed by now that so far, I've made very few contributions to this book (not counting a certain copyrighted bubble bath recipe that was used without my permission). This, of course, is by design because the book is stupid. My son is many things, but he's no author, and the idea he's holding himself up as some kind of authority on crime fighting is deeply disturbing and, well, kind of an insult.

Then I took one in the chest at close range, and I kind of changed my attitude. So much so, that as I lay in my hospital bed, pretending to be unconscious and therefore able to ignore Shawn's endless bedside yammering, it occurred to me that I did indeed have something to contribute, something that might help elevate this heap of crap into something that passes as readable. It's a simple message, but something every detective must always remember.

TRUST NO ONE.

It sounds like such a cliché, and there have been phases in my career when I got complacent. It happens, especially when you're good at your job. Bring down a few perps, and you get kind of full of yourself. And then you bring down even more; you start to think you're invincible; and the next thing you know, you're contemplating the last thing you'll ever see: your bastard old partner, Jerry Carp, and his .38 trained on your heart.

So I'll say it again, trust no one. Being a detective all boils down to eternal vigilance, because everyone has a Jerry Carp in their life. This isn't paranoia; it's simply awareness that anywhere, anytime, anyone can turn on you, and if this is going to keep you awake at night, then you're in the wrong business.[1]

---

[1] Wow, Dad, thanks for the pick-me-up. After that little warm fuzzy, I almost need a soak in your bubble bath. Almost, but not quite.

Shawn's Tips for Interrogating Suspects

If you were to interrogate me about the most useful tool in the detective's toolbox, I'd tell you that it's the ability to interrogate.

"More useful than gunshot residue kits?" you ask. Yes.

"More useful than electrostatic dust print lifters?" Way.

"More useful than spectral comparators?" Never heard of one of those, but as a person who's solved more crimes than you can count on twenty hands, if I've never heard of it, it's probably not very useful.

"But didn't you say going undercover and stakeouts were most important?" I might have, but that was like a gajillion pages ago. I can't be held responsible for things I said in my formative stages. Besides, are you *sure* that's what I said?

"Yes, as a matter of fact, I'm certain you said—" Fine, it's *all* important, all right?! Going undercover, stakeouts, stuff I haven't even talked about yet, and interrogations. All important. Now, let's move on. Okay?

That's what I thought. Look, as a *private* detective, you might think you're not going to do a lot of traditional police interrogations, and that's true. They're called "police interrogations" because police do them. But eventually, the police tank everything, especially interrogations, and ultimately it will be up to you to step up when the call comes.

And just so we're on the level, I'm not going to undersell the art of interrogation. It's a little-known fact that questions were invented for the

---

WORD OF THE MINUTE

SPECTRAL COMPARATOR

A digital imaging system using lights or lasers to compare inks, dyes, etc. By examining an ink's response to different wavelengths, forensic investigators can identify counterfeit passports and cash. (*You're welcome, Shawn. —Gus*)[1]

---

[1] This seems like an incredible waste of money. If you want to make sure your cash is legit, why not just look for the Indian shooting the bow and arrow?[a]

[a] GUS: That's Tootsie Pop wrappers, Shawn, not actual money.[b]

[b] I'm pretty sure it works for both.

very purpose of interrogation and have been used to great effect for the gathering of information and evidence. But mastery isn't essential, and this is where the cops go wrong. They get all serious about lines of questioning, and next thing you know, someone's getting waterboarded.

The savvy detective displays a little sensitivity in this arena. You have to understand, typically criminals don't have much self-respect. They come from broken homes; they're children of criminals (or telemarketers or hard-nosed police detectives with the asinine plan of molding them in their own image) and therefore have criminal tendencies themselves born of a difficult upbringing. Now, I'm not saying all the offspring of telemarketers eventually run afoul of the law, just most of them, but that's not what this book is about. I'm just saying that deep down, all of us are bundles of unique anxieties and self-doubts barely secured by a cheap combination lock. Your job as interrogator is to find the combination and crack it.

Take Gus, for instance. A chocolate-peanut-butter milk shake, the "Why didn't you write me" scene from *The Notebook*, then ask him about his eighth-grade science project. After thirty seconds of sobbing, he'll tell you anything you want to know.[1]

Criminal interrogation isn't much different. Like any expert safecracker, you're looking for the right sequence to crack each person's lock, and to do that, you need a set of carefully crafted tools and techniques (often called questions). So let's get started.

---

[1] GUS: Not fair, Shawn—you know how traumatic that science fair was for me! I used Kirlian photography to detect Stage 2 cancer in sunflowers and lost to Eric Mulholland's drawings of feet? That's not even science![a]

[a] GUS: Also, for the record, *The Notebook* is a masterpiece.[b]

[b] Actually, Gus, the masterpiece is Ryan Gosling's scruff. How does he get it so perfect? Beautifully shaped, gorgeously—nay, almost *supernaturally*—textured. I retract my mocking. *The Notebook is* worth weeping about.

Gaining Trust

Gaining your interrogatee's trust is essential. Most people don't like opening up to their own parents, or even their $250/hour shrink, so you've got to convince them to open up to *you*, a complete stranger, and you've got about thirty-eight seconds to do it. You need to work fast and you need to work hard, which is why I like to use one of these time-tested methods.

1 **TALK SMACK ABOUT SOMEONE THEY DON'T LIKE** Drop juicy tidbits about someone your perp hates—say, Kris Humphries or their arresting officer. It immediately shows you're on the same page. It's a solid way to go. Some lines that have worked for me:

- "Sorry you had to deal with Officer Soandso. He's been on edge ever since they revoked his National Cosplay Association membership."

- "What a morning, huh? I get in twenty minutes late, there's no fresh coffee, and I can't get into the bathroom because Detective Whatsisname's had another ostomy pouch accident. Oh, wait—I don't think I was supposed to tell you that."

- "Let's just cut to the chase: what's up with that weird smell coming from Officer Whosiwhatsit? Does he shower in mung beans or is that some kind of hygiene problem? You didn't hear this from me, but apparently, his wife left him for another dude—I think it was the guy who owns the hot dog stand down by the pier. Crazy, right? Supposedly, they've been hooking up for almost three months, and I'm sure his wife is sick of the drinking—you know how that guy gets. Wait, you didn't know about the Christmas party? They're still finding his puke in unexpected places. Anyway, enough about him. Let's talk about you..."

2 **LET THEM SEE YOU AS VULNERABLE** Getting interrogated is no fun. You feel pressured, untrusted, bullied, totally naked. So letting the perp see you as equally "naked" can establish a point of mutual connection, and that will bring the *answers*. For instance:

- Tell them a personal secret, like how Gus still sleeps with a blankie or you never actually read *Moby-Dick* because you didn't know it was a real thing. By doing this, you're essentially saying, "I've done dumb stuff, too. Now, let's talk about what happened when the cops found you covered in blood, eating your girlfriend's esophagus."[1]

- Cry. Get your eyes all teary and come in talking about how you can't take it anymore, no one appreciates you, and once—just once—you'd like someone to look at you like a real person, not just another warm body that solves mysteries and microwaves donuts before eating them.

- Confess to a worse crime than whatever your perp has been accused of. I was once questioning an accused carjacker and began by telling him I'd just buried my next-door neighbor alive in a kick drum. This accomplished two things. First, it established me as a badass, and second, it made the carjacker feel much more comfortable discussing his own wrongdoing. The guy confessed 12.4 seconds later.

3 GIVE THE PERP A FOOT MASSAGE It sounds crazy, I know, but Carlton Lassiter is a master of this technique. I can't tell you how many times he's entered the interrogation room, warmed up a dollop of homemade lavender-mint oil, and—taking a suspect's feet into his strong-yet-supple hands—elicited a confession faster than the perp can say, "Don't forget the heel."[2]

---

[1] GUS: I do not still sleep with a blankie, Shawn![a]

[a] Gus, please don't interrupt. I'm in the middle of a lesson.[b]

[b] GUS: Tell them I do *not* still sleep with a blankie.[c]

[c] Gus, I'm working on building trust with these people. If I tell them that, they'll think it's not true and we'll lose all the trust we've built. Is that what you want?[d]

[d] GUS: It's *not* true, Shawn.[e]

[e] I need you to think of the bigger picture here, Gus. Selfishness is an ugly color on you.

[2] LASSITER: This is patently untrue, Spencer, and you know it. Remove this passage at once.[a]

[a] Lassie, don't deny your talent. I've had a Lassie massage myself, and my Achilleses are still talking about it.[b]

[b] LASSITER: You don't even conduct interrogations, Spencer. Cease and desist *now*.[c]

[c] You know, Lassie, for someone as methodical as you are, saying "cease" *and* "desist" is pretty redundant. When you're about to shoot someone, do you say, "Freeze—don't move!" Okay, bad example. When you arrest someone, do you say, "You're under

Questions To Ask

Now that you've gained your suspect's trust, get down to bidness. Your goal is to gather as much information as possible before everyone gets bored and hungry, and a good interrogator should be able to get everything he needs with a few well-honed questions. I usually begin with a couple of warm-ups, such as:

- If Bruce Willis was dead the whole time in *The Sixth Sense*, why wouldn't he have noticed that none of the people he was talking to ever responded? I mean, the audience never notices because we always enter the scene at the end of a conversation, but surely Bruce Willis would've noticed before then. I mean, he's been dead almost a year before the movie even starts. Explain.

- Cheerios: Dulce de Leche or Honey Nut?

- Hypothetical situation: your girlfriend says you don't spend enough time "doing things" together, which is confusing because you just spent the last five nights having a DiGiorno taste test, which not only took a lot of time, but also a lot of preplanning she doesn't seem to appreciate. But you want her to be happy, so you suggest going to the Eddie Money concert tonight at the pier, but she suggests making cookies and playing Scrabble. You point out that's not really "doing anything," it's just playing a game. What about rewatching *Lost*, season six? Or seeing which sodas taste best warmed up? Unfortunately, she doesn't seem to count either of these as "doing anything," either, and she stomps off in a huff. So...what does "doing things" together mean?

- How do you think it would have affected ABBA's popularity if there was a fifth member named Larry? Would the world still wholeheartedly embrace a Swedish band named ABBLA?

- Is it wrong to laugh at catheter ads on TV?

---

arrest *and* being arrested?" It's not a big deal, but you might solve more cases if you scaled back your vocabulary footprint.

- A pancake recipe calls for one cup of milk, but you have only a half cup of milk and some powdered nondairy creamer. Will that work? Also, can you use allspice instead of nutmeg?

- If you're watching a show that actually has catheter ads, does that mean you're old?

Good Cop/Bad Cop

Man, I've never understood how perps keep falling for Good Cop/ Bad Cop. It's such a cliché, considering all the other adjectives and relationships we could be using to switch things up. What about Jubilant Cop/Codependent Cop? Or Indolent Cop/Slovenly Cop? Or Maternal Cop/ Industrious Cop? It's the twenty-first century, for crying out loud.

Having said that, at some point you're probably going to need to play Good Cop/Bad Cop, and it's really very simple.

When playing Bad Cop, simply come up behind the suspect so you're almost cheek to cheek, and repeat back as a question whatever they just said, then angrily bring up some arbitrary evidence that will make them think you know more than you do. For instance:

GOOD COP

Look, Ichabod, we're on your side. We just want to
know why you were in the theater last night.

ICHABOD/SUSPECT

I swear, I wasn't in the theater last night.

YOU

(Snotty tone of voice like you don't believe a word they just said)

Oh, really? You weren't in the theater
last night? Then what is *this*?

(You slap a dirty pair of sweat socks on the table.)

ICHABOD

(Nervous)
Uh...those aren't mine.

YOU

(Snotty tone)
Oh, these aren't yours? Then how do you explain *this*?

(You slap a curly straw still full of milk shake in front of him.)

ICHABOD

(Really on edge)
You gotta believe me. I've never seen that before!

YOU

You want me to believe you've never seen that before?
Well, then, maybe you've seen *this*!

(You slap a knitted coaster onto the table.)

ICHABOD
(Breaking)
Okay, fine—I *was* in the theater! But I didn't
kill Mr. Partridge, I swear! Me and Jenny Lee
just went to...you know...be alone. And the next
thing I knew there were all these lights and cops and...
oh, it was horrible, Detective! Just horrible! You gotta believe me!

For extra effect, you can also kick a chair across the room or chomp your gum super loudly. These don't really intimidate, but they show you're not afraid to be annoying, and that can be even worse. I'd much rather be stuck in a room with an intimidating guy than an annoying guy.

Wrapping Up the Interrogation

Interrogations typically end one of two ways: (1) You get a confession or (2) you don't get a confession. Or (3) you don't get a confession, but you get some valuable clues and information. Or (4) you don't get a confession *or* valuable clues or information, but you get the address of a great new hoagie place over in San Roque. Or (5) it's a complete waste of time. Obviously, option one and the latter part of option four are preferable.

If you do get a confession, congratulations. Skip ahead to chapter %, which is all about accusations and arrests. I'd write more now, but I haven't actually written chapter % yet, so I don't really know what to say. Plus, I'm not gonna write a bunch of stuff now, just to repeat it in chapter %. That would defeat the purpose of chapter %.

Of course, if you *don't* get a confession, you can still end on a high note. Thank your perp for coming in, maybe even suggest grabbing a drink sometime just to be polite. (FYI—this drink will never actually happen, as it's never a good idea hanging out with suspected criminals, even if they're innocent and aced the interrogation. There's a stink on those people.)

SPECIAL NOTE TO OPRAH: Dearest Oprah, while I'll let the writing of this book stand on its own literary merits, I hope you enjoy my girlfriend's brilliantly done fingerprint doodle of your likeness. Thus, I would like to recommend <u>Psych's Guide to Crime Fighting for the Totally Unqualified</u> as the next selection of the Oprah Book Club. If you would like to discuss further, please contact me at your earliest convenience at pineapplelover@prodigy.com. Sincerely, Shawn Spencer.

P.S. I am available for interviews, live appearances, and television development.

Handling Evidence

Private detectives live and die by one thing: evidence. And also oxygen, but hopefully you don't have to go out and find your own oxygen every day, unless Cohaagen is controlling your air supply.

Now, one would think evidence wouldn't be too hard to handle, and most of the time, it isn't. But if you want said evidence admissible in the case against the suspect—well, then you've got to follow the rules. Worse still, these are cop rules, so you know things are going to be harder than they have to be.

So acquaint yourself *now* with your police department's evidence-handling regulations. The rules vary by precinct, but you can pretty much bet that they'll all have plenty of stupid constraints that will hamper your investigation. And if you don't believe me, just check out this internal memo regarding an update of SBPD's own evidence-handling policy. I probably shouldn't be publishing internal memos, but whatever.

CONFIDENTIAL

INTERDEPARTMENTAL MEMO

DATE: 11/1/12
TO: All SBPD Detectives, Forensics, CSI, Medical Examiners
FROM: Karen Vick, Chief of Police
RE: Handling evidence

CHIEF KAREN VICK
Santa Barbara Police Dept.
2000 East Figueroa St.
Santa Barbara, CA 93101

In its ongoing effort to improve the quality of its crime fighting and community service, SBPD has instituted several new procedures regarding the handling of evidence.

While most of these should seem patently obvious, we've found these revisions and updates necessary as a result of some recent incidents that actually happened. These policies hold true for all SBPD personnel, including outside consultants and psychics:

- Latex gloves or tweezers *must* be used when handling evidence. Sock puppets are not acceptable. (Latex gloves that have been turned into puppets are also not acceptable.)

- No licking, chewing, tasting, or swallowing of evidence. This includes cotton balls, bullets, facial hair, eighteenth-century wampum beads, Jell-O shots, angelfish, blood or urine, dog food, Band-Aids, and baby formula.

- Cadaver parts shall not be used for "home science experiments."

- When filling out Evidence Inventory Forms, please use an actual inventory number. You cannot simply write, "the Mark of the Beast." (Also, please use your assigned title code. The title code for a consulting psychic, for instance, is PSCH, not SHERLOCK HOMEBOY.)

I find it scary when even our law enforcement agencies have been infiltrated by antiscience zealots.

INTERDEPARTMENTAL MEMO

- The evidence manager's job is to *manage evidence*, not give ten-minute shoulder massages.

- Anyone caught playing Jenga with the medical examiner's discarded bones will face immediate disciplinary action.

- Please stop submitting saliva samples to the forensics lab for personal use.

- Under no circumstances shall interrogation tapes be remixed with "One Nation Under a Groove" and played at Sharky's Amateur DJ Night.

- You cannot call to have your car "impounded as evidence" whenever you run out of gas on the 101. Pay for a tow truck like everyone else.

- If you've agreed to watch your neighbor's Shih Tzu, it's your responsibility. You cannot check it into the forensics lab as "material evidence."

- There shall be an immediate stop to stealing Detective Lassiter's shoelaces and registering them as "deadly weapons."

Thank you for your cooperation.

Chief Karen Vick

To be fair, she was paid generously for her services.

This was Gus's fault. I told him the forensics lab could not clone people.

This was also Gus's fault. He was supposed to fill the tank before we left and didn't.

There will come a day, mark my words, when Lassie snaps and strangles someone. And when that day comes, I'll be the first to say, "I told you so."

This sentence is confusing. Are people not allowed to play with discarded bones they find in the medical examiner's office? Or the actual bones of the medical examiner himself? First of all, I didn't even realize Woody had passed away. He was so young and full of life. Is there an address where we can send a card or make a donation?

Time to Hire an Assistant

Okay, so maybe you were right in the last chapter. Assistant: good idea. Time management: not-so-good idea.

I mean, it's still good in theory, but you're the detective; you've got cases to crack and hands to keep clean. And as you can tell, your life is becoming busier and busier. You can't be expected to organize your files, empty the trash, pick up your girlfriend's birthday present, and turn in a book manuscript, which is already two months late.

Unfortunately, finding good help isn't as easy as it used to be. Mainly because America's educational system doesn't prepare people for the real world.

Still, there are times when the dearth of good assistant candidates isn't even your biggest problem. Gus has always had opinions about assistants, as evidenced by the following chat transcript. (I'm on the left.)

> **Dude. It's time.**
> 11:30 AM

> **We're not doing jerk chicken again, Shawn.**
> 11:31 AM

> **No. Wait. Yes, we are. But I'm talking about hiring an assistant.**
> 11:32 AM

> **No, you're not.**
> 11:33 AM

> **We need one. Also, jerk chicken, but first things flirts.**
> 11:34 AM

Crap. First. Stinking autocorrect.

11:35 AM

We've had four assistants.

11:36 AM

Three. Ken was here twice.

11:37 AM

And none of them have lasted more than a few hours.

11:38 AM

It wasn't their fault.

11:39 AM

We're not doing this. And yes, if we're talking about Ken, it was totally his fault. First of all, he threw out my 1928 Buffalo nickel because he thought it was a Skee-Ball token.

11:41 AM

That was a long one.

11:42 AM

Then he refused to pick up sandwiches from the Larder because he heard the owner donates money to a California secession movement. He also said Battlestar Galactica is a Christian allegory in which Cylons are the apostles and Baltar is Jesus, which is ridiculous, because everyone knows BSG is a metaphor for post-9/11 religious fundamentalism and America's loss of civil liberties.

11:44 AM

Please tell me you're not divine.

11:45 AM

DRIVING. Crap. Autocorrect.

11:46 AM

Worst of all, he gave me attitude every time I asked him to refill my Golden Grahams, and you know I'm not a demanding boss.

11:48 AM

True that. You're not a demanding boss. Because you're not the boss. You're the sidekick.

11:50 AM

Ha-ha, very funny, Shawn—this is a partnership, remember?

11:51 AM

Come on. That's just what I tell you to make you feel better about yourself. No sidekick is actually "partners" with the main guy. Was Tonto "partners" with the Lone Ranger? Was Murtaugh "partners" with Riggs? This doesn't mean I don't love you, Gus, but seriously—"partners"? I'm LOLROTFing right now.

11:53 AM

Actually, Shawn, Murtaugh and Riggs WERE partners—that was the whole point. And it's ROTFLOL, not the other way around.

11:55 AM

LOLROTF was autocorrect again.

11:56 AM

No, it wasn't.

11:57 AM

Yes, it wash. Was. See?

11:58 AM

Dude. No assistant.

11:59 AM

More Reasons Ken Sucked as an Assistant

by Gus

- Constantly rubbed his rabbit foot key chain—and you know how I feel about taxidermy
- Borrowed $15 to "adopt" a starving child in Bakersfield
- Used the word *irregardless*, which—*for the last time*—is not a word
- Kept his iPad on a playlist of every Shaquille O'Neal rap song ever recorded
- Left half-eaten Slim Jims in the fridge
- Said professional wrestling is fake
- Called his suspenders "braces"
- Spilled Coke Zero on my *Big: The Musical* songbook
- Suggested I cut back on the carbs
- Referred to Barnard's Loop as a Herbig-Haro object rather than a nebula
- Diagrammed his manscaping plans on the whiteboard
- Claimed Star Wars episodes 1–3 were the "original trilogy"
- Nicknamed himself "the Asian Dustin Diamond"
- Said evolution was just a "theory"
- Finished my cinnamon-raisin loaf
- Doused himself in Antonio Banderas's Blue Seduction cologne
- Used nicotine patches for the "contact high"
- Wore surgical masks around the office because he didn't want to "catch anything"

Blowing Off Steam: That's the Rub
by Dutch "the Clutch" Jenkins

For our second installment of "Blowing Off Steam," I'm pleased to introduce an old friend: death-defying daredevil Dutch "the Clutch" Jenkins. You may know him as the guy who jumped Wrigley Field on a motorcycle, but it turns out he's also an amateur masseuse. No, I am not making this up. And no, I have not experienced this myself, although he did give Gus a twenty-minute scalp rub that left Gus unable to walk for an hour. In a good way. So take it away, Dutch.

First things first, Shawn. I am not an "amateur" masseuse. I have two certificates in Lomi Lomi and nine hours toward an associate degree in craniosacral therapy. Hell, I once gave a deep-tissue glute massage to Billy Gibbons. If that don't make me a professional, I don't know what does.

Secondly, thank you for inviting me to contribute to this book. I've ridden a raft off Yosemite Falls; skydived into a pool of piranhas; and survived cancer of the pancreas, lungs, thyroid, gallbladder, trachea, and foot, but I ain't never written something for a book. Hell, I ain't ever *read* a book! (I joke, I joke. I have sixteen autographed copies of *You Might Be a Redneck If...*)

Anyway, massage is a great way to take a load off; not only for the person *getting* the massage, but for the masseuse, too. I mean, hey, the human body's a beautiful thing, and I ain't just talkin' about them swimsuit calendars ya get at the drugstore.

Anyway, I'm flattered you asked me to write this and all, but I'm supposed to water-ski off Mount Rushmore in twenty, so let's get started.

1. **BEGIN BY FEELING THE CONTOURS OF THE BACK.** Not your back, the back of the person you're rubbing. Feel the ribs, the neck, the shoulder blades—the whole goddamn torso. This is important because it helps you connect to their body. Not literally, of course, but in a spiritual way. I'm not a big fan of all that spirituality crap, but I started to believe after Ronnie Van Zant gave me a hot stone massage in a dream.

2. **NOTICE IF THERE ARE ANY KNOTS OR TENSION POINTS, AND PUSH YOUR PALM GENTLY INTO THE SPOT.** Not too hard, just like you're goosin' the throttle on a 1969 Honda CB 750. Listen to the purr of the engine, feel the power of the muscle underneath. Speaking of muscle, did you know the human heart can shoot a stream of blood over ten yards high? I learned that in my advanced reflexology class.

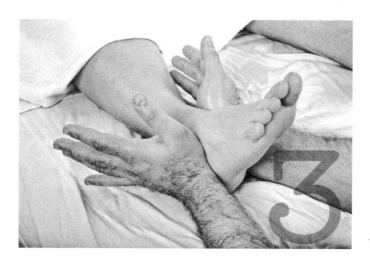

3. **OKAY, I'M GONNA LEVEL WITH YA.** I ain't afraid of much, but one thing I don't like: feet. Even well-pedicured feet like my wife Vicki's. She tries to pretty 'em up with wax and paint and stuff, but no amount of paint's gonna hide the fungus growing out of her toe. So I usually skip this part. If you do have to rub someone's foot, I suggest using the outside of your hand so you don't have to touch much. Also, try a grapeseed-based oil; it smells great and makes the massage go faster. The quicker you can end this thing, the better.

4. **ONE LAST THING.** Be sure to pick some relaxing music for the massage. A lot of people like that New Age crap like wind chimes or Tori Amos, but I prefer something more soothing, like the Allman Brothers. Preferably *Eat a Peach*, but *Beginnings* works just as well ("Whipping Post" goes great with prenatal petrissage).

Right: A massage for your ears. I mean, not literally, because that would actually be a massage for your ears. It's a metaphor.

An Open Letter from Buzz McNab

* * * * * * * FROM THE OFFICE OF * * * * * * * *

OFFICER BUZZ McNAB

Santa Barbara Police Dept. • 2000 East Figueroa St., Santa Barbara, CA 93101

Dear Everyone Reading This in *The Ventura Chronicle*, *The Santa Barbara Mirror*, Shawn Spencer's Book, Facebook, *Boy's Life*, or the McNab Family Newsletter—

It has recently been brought to my attention that some residents of Ventura County, our neighbor to the southeast, have been disparaging the Santa Barbara Police Department and making jokes at our expense.

I'm sure you've heard, "What's the difference between a cold and a criminal? SBPD can actually catch a cold."

Or, "What do Ventura's jails have that Santa Barbara's don't? Criminals."

Now, I'm not sure who or what was the source of this mocking, but it certainly wasn't misconduct or maladroitness on the part of the SBPD, I can assure you, and as a proud Santa Barbara police officer (six years eligible for promotion to detective), I'd like to make it very clear that these jokes are inaccurate.

★ ★ ★ ★ ★ ★ ★ FROM THE OFFICE OF ★ ★ ★ ★ ★ ★ ★ ★

OFFICER BUZZ McNAB

It's true Ventura PD has received many prestigious awards, including nine National Leadership Awards, six Presidential Certificates of Excellence, two American Peacekeeper grants, and California's "Best in State" Award. They also hold national records for arrests, convictions, safety, and fund-raising. Also, current officers have received thirty-two Medals of Valor, twenty-six Purple Hearts, seventeen Police Stars, and nine Commendations for Heroism. They are, indeed, an exemplary law enforcement body.

But I think it's equally important to note the many achievements and laurels earned by the Santa Barbara PD. Last month, Officer Adlet was named Santa Barbara's Best Window Box Landscaper, and Sergeant Kazian has won the Armenian League's Shortform Erotica Contest three years in a row.

Our roster also includes (partial list):

- **Forensic Engineer Claudia Garcia**—twenty-third caller and KNSB's Rocker of the Day

- **Junior Detective Jon Piebenga**—Buffalo Hal's Klinger Look-alike Contest—Winner

- **Detective Camilla Kaplan**—McNally's Beer Pong Championship—Winner

- **Lieutenant Mia Michaels**—$25 Lotto winner

- **DARE Officer A. J. Wake**—Bryman College's Night of Crunk—eighteenth place

- **Receptionist Elise Negry**—Most Likely to Remain a Virgin—Moorpark High Yearbook, 1997

* * * * * * * FROM THE OFFICE OF * * * * * * * *

OFFICER BUZZ McNAB

- **Dispatcher Charlie Kogan**—Biggest Kohlrabi—2007 Riverside County Fair

- **Blood Spatter Analyst Ellen Moll**—Lions Club Irritable Bowel Syndrome Fund-raiser—Raffle Winner of Sculptor3 Food Processor

- **School Resource Officer Jenny Freeman**—Chi Omega/ Theta Chi Pimps & Ho's Mixer—Best Ho

- **Harbormaster Ansara Grimes**—The Bolshevik Society's Beef Stroganoff-Off—Honorable Mention

- **Dispatcher Supervisor Dann Hirst**—SoCal LARPing Society—Best Use of a Shrinking Spell

- **Records Technician Ava Lauren**—Mitzvah of the Month— Congregation Ohave Shalom (Tishri, 5772)

- **Traffic Administrative Assistant Claude Loewenthal**— Danzo's 12-Week Clown School—Magna Cum Loud!

- **Deputy Chief Eloise Rioux**—Most Creative Base Stealer— Western T-Ball Division

- **Reverend Jerry Lau (Staff Chaplain)**—Charles Dickens Festival—Best Use of Amputation in a Costume

- **Traffic Clerk Bennjin Sadowski**—Three Years Sobriety Chip—Overeaters Anonymous

- **Community Services Officer Amanda Bonjani**—Winner— 100th person to click on GreatDeals.com

* * * * * * * * FROM THE OFFICE OF * * * * * * * * *

OFFICER BUZZ McNAB

- **Technician Natalie Chung**—Penguin Club Synchronized Swimming Competition: Duet Division—third place

- **Animal Control Officer Rakesh Wade-Ford**—Best Solo Performance (*The Vagina Monologues*)—Lompoc Community Theater Speech & Drama Competition

- **Evidence Manager Matt Stickney**—Three-legged sack race—Stickney Family Reunion—second place

- **K-9 Officer Meghan Dawe**—Optimist's Club 2009 Speech Competition—fourth place ("The Soul Rots from Within")

- **Patrol Officer Jack Fitzpatrick**—Citizens Militia's End Times Survival Competition—Rabbit-Skinning Competition—first place (Also, Runner-up: Best Use of Animal Dung or Entrails)

Has anyone noticed the Ventura PD's awards are all crime related? That's because there's crime in Ventura. Duh. If the Ventura PD was so awesome, then why is there crime at all, huh? Think about that, and the next time someone asks you "*Why do most officers get fired from SBPD? They can't spell it,*" just ask yourself, "*Should I really mock a police department that has two of the* Santa Barbara Mirror*'s last twenty-six 'most eligible local bachelors'?*"

Sincerely,
Your humble public servant,

Almost-Detective Buzz McNab

CASE STUDY #2

Is It Just Me, or Do You Smell Fishy?

You've been called to the home of Phineas K. Ranklemeyer, the celebrated caviar producer most noted for his 2010 Egg It On campaign. Ranklemeyer lives in one of Santa Barbara's most expensive homes, a mansion recently featured in *Damn, You're Rich* magazine for its 1,200-square-foot, state-of-the-art caviar cellar, which was broken into earlier this evening. Stolen: over $200,000 of artisanal caviar, including Ranklemeyer's newest creation, Twist and Trout.

There are no signs of a break-in, suggesting the thief is someone with authorized access. This limits the suspects to three people: Regina, Ranklemeyer's architect; Jenna, his business manager; and Tom, the head of security.

You first interrogate Regina and learn she and Ranklemeyer are on the outs because he sued her over a problem with her design. There was a defect in the cooling system. The lawsuit nearly ruined her, but she says she didn't commit the burglary. Plus, she's got an alibi. She was meeting with the president of the Hatchery, Ranklemeyer's caviar rival. Even if she'd been able to sneak away, she claims, the locations are forty-five minutes apart—she never could've done it.

You next talk to Jenna, Ranklemeyer's longtime business manager. Turns out she and Ranklemeyer carried on a torrid affair for five years, and he broke it off two days ago. Jenna was crushed but swears she's not the thief. She was at a friend's movie party all night. In fact, when she received the call about the burglary, they were in the middle of her favorite movie, *The Goonies*—right at the part where Chunk offers Sloth the Snickers bar. Calls to other partygoers confirm she was there.

The last suspect is Tom, Ranklemeyer's head of security. He's worked for Ranklemeyer for fifteen years, but when he recently asked for Ranklemeyer's help in paying some medical bills, Ranklemeyer refused. Tom was so livid, he says, he *did* want to steal Ranklemeyer's caviar, but he hadn't planned on doing it till tomorrow night. Tonight, he was at home alone, eating a Queso Chicken Hot Pocket and watching a Seattle Storm game. Still, Tom has no one to vouch for him, although he does produce an empty Hot Pockets box.

The police are certain the culprit is Tom, Ranklemeyer's embittered security head. He had motive, access, and means. But the police are wrong, and you know it. What are they missing, and who's the real burglar?

Answer: Duh. It was Jenna. She claims she received the call while watching the Chunk/Sloth/Snickers bar scene from *The Goonies*. But anyone who truly loves *The Goonies* knows Chunk doesn't offer Sloth a Snickers bar; he offers him a Baby Ruth. Busted, Jenna admits she broke into the cellar, planning to steal and repackage the caviar as her own, offering her friends a share of the spoils if they covered for her.

FYI—Caviar is gross.

Yes, It's Another Quiz

First of all, I want to be clear about something: *The Girl with the Dragon Tattoo* is not a good book. I know you probably love it because it's got all that weird sex stuff, but it's really just like *Fight Club* if *Fight Club* didn't have anything fun or interesting in it. (I'm not saying the stories are similar; I'm just saying that if you took out every interesting part of *Fight Club*— which is pretty much the whole book—you'd be left with *The Girl with the Dragon Tattoo*.) I mean, the people solving the mystery don't even solve the mystery. They start sniffing around some old photographs, and the killer gets so nervous he literally shows up on their front step. As a professional detective, and also as a human with a brain, I can tell you this never happens, and if it did, it would be lame, which is why it's lame in the book.

But whatever. We're not here to talk about books…although I think reading is important, because girls think you're really cultured if they see a bunch of books on your shelf. (For more on this topic, please see my recommended reading list on pages 34–35.)

We're here to take a quiz…and don't act like you didn't know this was coming. That may have worked the first time, and even in chapter 2, but we're now over halfway through this sucker, so there shouldn't be any surprises.

However, in the last quiz, you had nine seconds for each question. This time, the questions are tougher…so give yourself twelve seconds. Actually, no, I take that back. Give yourself twelve seconds for the first question, fourteen seconds for the second and third, and twenty-three seconds to divide between the last two. Good luck!

1 You apprehend a suspect in a bank robbery investigation: twenty-three years old, male, Native American, average height and build. No prior convictions or arrests. He claims to have an alibi on the date of the crime. What color are his socks?

    A. black

    B. brown

    C. green-and-red argyle

    D. blue with a fancy little insignia, like a sailboat or a tiger

    E. Trick question—he's wearing sandals.

2 You're tucked in the turret of a B-17 bomber, tailing a suspect, when you suddenly realize the landing gear won't work and the only way for the pilot to land the plane is on its belly, ripping you to shreds. Do you:

    A. tell the crew to give your family your love

    B. freak out

    C. draw a giant cartoon landing gear and beg the pilot to try one last time

    D. cry and contemplate the infinite

3 You've just landed a job assisting an extremely talented and handsome private detective. When you arrive in the morning, the first thing you should do is:

    A. check the schedule and sort the mail

    B. prepare the detective's Lucky Charms (and a chocolate milk with six donuts for his sidekick)

    C. greet the day with a pan flute rendition of "Sweet Caroline"

    D. recap last night's *Bachelorette*

    E. give the detective fifteen minutes of Reiki acupressure

4 Okay, seriously, who shot who at the Copacabana? Did Rico shoot Tony...or did Tony shoot Rico?[1]

_____

_____

5 You come home one day to find your door ajar and a muddy footprint on the floor. Using only this print, can you identify the shoe and the intruder?

    A. Men's Nike Air Max 2011, size 10. The worn inside treads suggest the wearer is right-handed, flat-footed, and walks with a slight limp. Probably an escaped convict or high school gym teacher.

---

[1] GUS: Rico shot Tony, Shawn. Everyone knows this. It says right there in the lyrics: "She lost her youth and she lost her Tony."[a]

[a] Okay, first of all, Gus, why are you giving this away before the answer section? And second of all, it never *says* Rico shot Tony. Maybe Tony shot Rico and went to prison. Or maybe Tony shot Rico and was never convicted, then died a few months later of a pulmonary embolism. You have to look below the surface. This is why I'm the detective and you're the sidekick.

B. Men's orthopedic shoe. Intruder: elderly male, probably a retired cop who has so little to do during the day he continually comes to his son's place to borrow DVDs without asking.[1]

C. Women's Reebok ZigNano Fly 2. Probably worn by whoever keeps using the same knife in the peanut butter and the jelly. Also, do we really need a Luscious Lavender air freshener in every room? The whole place smells like a spa.[2]

D. Women's saddle shoe. Intruder: your sidekick, a good-looking black man who loves trains and occasionally dresses as Frenchy from *Grease*.[3]

Answers

1. B—brown

2. C—although if you don't already do D as a normal part of your day, that could also be an acceptable answer.

3. All of the above *except* the Reiki acupressure. Most detectives prefer Su Jok.

4. Turns out Gus was right—Rico did shoot Tony.

5. C—although for the record, Gus did once play Carrie Pipperidge in *Carousel* during his short stint with the Santa Barbara Men's Choir.

---

[1] HENRY: Elderly? Really, Shawn? And if you want to talk about borrowing things without asking, let's talk about my tackle box, the drywall hammer, my red polo shirt, and my copy of *The Da Vinci Code*.

[2] JULIET: Which is better than how it smelled *before* those air fresheners, Shawn—like a men's locker room.

[3] GUS: That Frenchy thing was one time, Shawn—and it was for a skit, a satirical look at racism and the culture of "the other" in mid-twentieth-century America.

If You Scored...

Do we really need to go through this again? I'm pretty sure you understand how it goes. You're supposed to get as many right as possible. If you only get one or two, well, Oliver Stone failed out of Yale before going on to direct *JFK* and *Platoon*, so don't worry about it. (Then again, he also directed *Alexander* and *Wall Street: Money Never Sleeps*, so maybe not the best example.)

I'm Not the One Being Annoying, Shawn, and Where Are My Cocoa Puffs?

First of all, Shawn, *Billy Elliot* is a ten-time Tony Award–winning musical, one of the most successful musicals in the history of Broadway. And I wasn't just "singing songs," I was preparing for my audition next week at Santa Barbara Community Playhouse. Also for the record, the play has nothing to do with Margaret Thatcher except for one song "Merry Christmas, Margaret Thatcher," which, yes, I'll be singing as part of my audition...along with Air Supply's classic ballad "Here I Am," which I did not choose because it's "your jam"; I chose it because of its tremendous lyrical and melodic power.

Secondly—and I wouldn't expect you to know this, since you've never bothered to watch the show—but *Doctor Who* is one of the longest-running television series in the world. It's won over one hundred—why am I even defending this to you, Shawn? Your idea of good science fiction is *Critters 2*, which, granted, I have enjoyed, but it doesn't even have Billy Zane in it.

The point is, you can complain all you want about my stamp collection or Scrabble or *Game of Thrones*, but at least I wipe out the microwave after making SpaghettiOs. And I put the Xbox games back in the right box. Yesterday I found *Gears of War* inside the *Madden 12* case, and *Madden 12* was upside down in *Call of Duty*, which was in the refrigerator. Who does that, Shawn? Do we not live in a civilized society? Is this Neolithic Mesopotamia? Are we *Homo rhodesiensis*?

So here's *my* message to the Future Detectives of America: maybe there's a reason people call you dicks. If you want people to call you something else, stop leaving half-eaten pieces of bologna on the counter, or walking around in your bare feet, or trying to bring back "cha-ching" as a legitimate piece of vocabulary. (And "Rico Solvé," Shawn? Really? That doesn't even make sense.)

Lastly, you should give your girlfriend's "couples dinners" a try. They can actually be quite rewarding.

P.S. I would also like to point out that you keep numbering the half chapters with a ".2." You have a regular chapter, like chapter 1, and then you number the half chapter chapter 1.2. But the first upgrade or follow-up is never ".2"; it's ".1" (e.g., Apple puts out iTunes 10, and the first upgrade is iTunes 10.1, not 10.2). So your half chapters should be chapter 1.1, not chapter 1.2. Get it right.

Cops, Coroners, and Other Professional Roadblocks

Introduction

All right, Jack, before you get all hot and bothered about becoming the world's next Easy Rawlins, let's discuss some of the downsides of being a professional assassintruder.[1]

Crime fighting would be the easiest job in the world if it weren't for one small problem: *other crime fighters*. And by *other crime fighters*, I mean "cops." And people who work with cops. And rules cops have to follow.

In fact, a recent study by the Pew Research Center found that 67 percent more crimes would be solved if cops would just *stop trying to solve them*.[2] A similar study by Reuters found that crime would drop 84.6 percent if cops would just get out of the way of other detectives.[3] And in a shocking exposé from CBS News, researchers found that 78.9 percent of cops considered Joel Schumacher's Batman movies superior to Christopher Nolan's.[4]

Having said all this, dealing with cops is a regular part of your job, so the best thing you can do is prepare yourself. Learn their language, know what they do, understand their behaviors.

Think of yourself as Johnny Five—the more you learn about these people, the easier it'll be to dominate them when you need to.

---

[1] NOTE: It is *essential* that you spell *assassintruder* correctly and don't accidentally leave out the second syllable, which makes it something totally different.

[2] I made this fact up. Just trying to prove a point.

[3] Again, totally false.

[4] Completely unproven but so plausible that I wouldn't rule it out.

Who's Who in the Police Station

In the words of Green Day and Rage Against the Machine, it's time to "Know Your Enemy."[1]

Now, to be fair, the police department may not exactly be your "enemy." You're going to need them for a lot of things—making arrests, shooting people, free pork rinds. And even though they're constantly in your way, doing things exactly opposite of the way you're going to do them, they're necessary for your success, and you'd better know them, just like Billy Joe Armstrong and Tom Morello suggest.

So, as your friend, mentor, and eternal Henri Ducard,[2] I'll walk you through who in the police department needs to be on your Kwanzaa card list.

Right: Head Detective

1 HEAD DETECTIVE It's not easy being head detective; you have to have such passionate commitment to crime solving that you often sacrifice other parts of your life. Most head detectives have lost the ability to socialize normally,

---

[1] GUS: Actually, Shawn, "Know your enemy" is a quote from Sun Tzu's *The Art of War*.[a]

  [a] Thank you, Gus, but I'm talking about *real rock bands*. No one listens to your New Age foo-foo music.

[2] GUS: You realize Henri Ducard was evil, right, Shawn?[a]

  [a] What are you talking about?[b]

    [b] GUS: He was Ra's al Ghul in disguise.[c]

      [c] I thought Ra's al Ghul was the Asian dude from the geisha movie.[d]

        [d] GUS: That was a fake. Remember, Liam Neeson shows up at the end and says he's the real Ra's al Ghul?[e]

          [e] Yeah, I thought that was the Asian guy wearing a *Mission Impossible* mask.[f]

            [f] GUS: That makes no sense—why would you think that?[g]

              [g] Because who would cast Liam Neeson as a major role in an action movie? *That* makes no sense! The guy's goofy looking! And he can't fight! Does nobody see this but me?

descending into dark pits of perverse hobbies like thimble collecting or Civil War reenactment. They also tend to seek solace in emotionally hollow relationships; namely with coworkers and convicts. It's sad, I know, but these are the only people they can relate to.

Valuable Uses: shooting things, arresting people, Skee-Ball, killing any trace of fun whenever possible

2 JUNIOR DETECTIVE Most junior detectives, with their enchanting blue eyes and playful girl-next-door smiles, are the heart and soul of their police departments. And while junior detectives are often un-derestimated for their lack of expe-rience, they can be incredibly tough and sexy when pulling their gun or cuffing a criminal (or cuffing some-one who's *not* a criminal, which—if you're lucky—will happen on occa-sion[1]). Do NOT piss off a junior de-tective; they are fully authorized to give the silent treatment, and you'll probably end up sleeping on the couch. Junior detectives do, how-ever, have several weaknesses: cats, bowling, crafting, and ridiculously handsome men with hazel eyes and perfectly coiffed hair that uses little-to-no product.

Above: Junior Detective

---

[1] JULIET: Gross, Shawn! What is wrong with you? Readers, just so you know, I have never handcuffed Shawn to anything in my life.[a]

[a] Pop quiz! Which is the best answer here?[b]

    A. True—leather straps don't count as handcuffs.

    B. Except your heart.

    C. Who *have* you handcuffed?

[b] JULIET: Try D—none of the above. No, actually—C. Would you like a list? It's long.

Valuable Uses: pajama sewing, taking apart a gun in under 5.6 seconds, long walks on the beach, gazing off Capilano Suspension Bridge

Above: Chief of Police

3 CHIEF OF POLICE The chief is like the boss of the entire police station. Okay, they're not "like" the boss, they *are* the boss. They do all the hiring, firing, assigning of cases... so you definitely want to stay on their good side. Because they're so busy, police chiefs often seem emotionally distant, closed off, even unaware of what's going on around them. But make no mistake—there's a tender heart beating behind that crisply fitted sateen dress shirt. I recommend keeping your chief buttered up with some gentle ribbing, the occasional pineapple, maybe even some casual compliments about their hair or how they look in a pantsuit.

Valuable Uses: paying you, mediating arguments between you and cops, authorizing your expense account

4 POLICE LIAISON TO EXTERNAL DIVISIONS/ HEAD OF THE CONSULTANTS A totally made-up position given to old, retired cops who need to feel relevant and not forgotten.

Valuable Uses: They usually have a well-stocked fridge and pantry. And that's pretty much it, considering they don't even have a real job.

Right: Not a real position

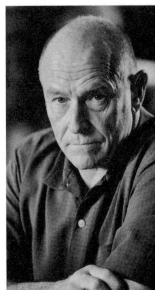

5 **OFFICER** Officers are the cops you see every day on the beat, helping old ladies cross streets and rescuing cats from trees. These are the most underappreciated dudes on the whole police force, and I think a lot of other cops—say, detectives who should know better—take advantage of officers' eagerness to please. To be fair, some of this is an officer's own doing, and sometimes you just want to shake them and say, "Come on, man. Don't you see they're taking advantage of you? They're trading you the crappy cases so they can have the glory! Wake up!" But then you think, *Hmm...maybe it's better just to let people live in their own happy fantasy rather than wake them to the harsh reality of reality.* Besides, officers *are* really good at getting you donuts when you ask, and restocking the hot chocolate, and making sure there are enough Cheez-Its in the station kitchen. And ultimately, if this stuff makes them happy, who am I to judge?

Valuable Uses: getting shot at, blown up, taking a bullet for a friend

Right: Officer

6 **CRIMINAL PSYCHOLOGIST** I've always been confused about this one. On one hand, it's right there in the title—"criminal" and "psychologist." This is clearly a psychologist who studies criminals. On the other hand, it could be a psychologist who's also a criminal—like Hannibal Lecter, or a shrink who robs banks, or that guy who puts probes in Ewan McGregor's body in that Michael Bay movie about the clones. Technically, wouldn't those guys also be "criminal psychologists"? Either way, criminal psychologists spend their entire lives studying the minds

Right: Non-Criminal Criminal Psychologist

of the most deranged people in the world besides Ron Paul and Sean Young, so they tend to be a bit warped themselves: obsessive, needy, even borderline stalkery. But give them a chance, and you'll see they can actually be insightful partners and—for the right person—incredibly gentle lovers.

Valuable Uses: scrapbooking, getting inside the minds of bloodthirsty psychopaths, racquetball

7 CORONER One who "corons," or cuts open dead bodies for fun and profit. This is probably someone you want to know, as you are in the business of dead people. Having said that, most guys who choose to cut open dead bodies for a living are a little off-kilter, so I wouldn't rush into making this guy your best man or anything. (Actually, I wouldn't rush into making *anyone* your best man; marriage is a sacred union that should only be entered into after much time and consideration. Live together for a while. See if you're compatible. Do you eat the same flavor of Pop-Tarts? Who gets to control the TiVo? Are you okay with big Scottish Christmases? These are all important issues you need to iron out before making anyone your best man.)

Above: Practitioner of the Coroning Arts

Left: Doodle Guy

8 POLICE SKETCH ARTIST How awesome are these guys? You describe a person, someone they've never met, and they literally make an exact picture of what you told them. There aren't even iPhone apps for that! They're like professional Pictionaryers!

9 CRIMINAL PROFILER Basically the same thing as a criminal psychologist, except they're total frauds. Many criminal profilers (and by "many" I mean "all") think that by dropping some elementary observations about human behavior and flashing their ridiculously thick eyebrows they can do whatever they want, and unfortunately, there are those in the police department who fall for this crap. As a detective, you know it takes more than a chiseled jawline and enigmatic smile to solve crimes. My advice is lock up your women and keep these charlatans as far away as possible from your cases.

Valuable Uses: Did you not understand the last paragraph? Unless you think pointing out that a muddy footprint means someone must've walked through mud is somehow great detective work, these guys have no value whatsoever.

Right: Imposter

10 ROYAL CANADIAN MOUNTED POLICE I've never actually worked with the Royal Canadian Mounted Police, but I have worked with the Vancouver Police Department (shout out to Corporal Robert Mackintosh and Deputy Commissioner Ed Dykstra), and I think any of them would make *excellent* mounted police. I don't know why they're NOT mounted police; they're a terrific set of crime solvers. It seems wrong not to give them each their own moose.[1]

Above: Canadian Serpico

---

[1] GUS: The Royal Canadian Mounted Police don't ride mooses, Shawn.[a]

[a] Of course they do, Gus; it's *Canada*. Also, it's "meese."

Valuable Uses: making syrup, drafting Canadian-American Reciprocity Treaties, coming up with band names (Crash Test Dummies, The Guess Who, Barenaked Ladies, Cowboy Junkies, Tragically Hip)

11 LEAD HOSTAGE NEGOTIATOR I've never understood this job. First of all, we're constantly hearing cops and FBI people say stuff like, "We don't negotiate with terrorists and criminals." But then they have a guy *in their office* called lead negotiator, so obviously they *do* negotiate with terrorists and criminals—and any terrorist or criminal with half a brain knows this. Second of all, how skilled do you have to be to be a lead negotiator? It's just talking. They should call this guy lead hostage talker. It doesn't sound as glamorous, but at least it's accurate. (Although I can understand how it would be easy to make an unfortunate typo and suddenly have a lead hostage taker on the payroll.) Frankly, I think taxpayer dollars would be better spent on people who actually *do* stuff—like, oh, I don't know, solve crimes—than professional talkers.

Valuable Uses: filibusters, talk show host, eating up surpluses on police department budgets

Right: Lead Hostage Talker

Win, Lose, or Draw:
How to Read Police Sketches

As a psychic, I often get mental images of people involved with crimes I'm investigating. Cops get images, too. But rather than coming from a higher spiritual plane, they come from some poor sap who's probably fairly talented, but since the art world only wants sculptures of mustard bottles and cat feces, they're stuck drawing pictures of bank robbers and serial killers.

The truth is, police sketches can be very helpful, even if you don't get supernatural vibes when you look at them.

Take a look at the following sketches, all of which played a pivotal role in cases I cracked for the SBPD. See what you see in each one; then check out my analysis below.

A.

A. **ANALYSIS**: Note the receding hairline, the unkempt hair, the glasses slightly askew. All of this suggests a predilection for pedophilia or perhaps DJing trance parties; regardless, he's someone who should be checked out. Also, the furrowed brow indicates a constant state of worry; this man may be living a double life as some kind of human trafficker or smuggler, or he may just have a really annoying family, which could also be the cause of the hair loss.

B. **ANALYSIS**: This woman looks like some sort of Bulgarian dominatrix/secret agent, which means she's probably either a dominatrix or secret agent. Either way, you win. It also looks like she has some sort of chin ring, which adds to the sheer hotness of this chick. It could also be a zit. Hard to tell. Based on this drawing, I would say she has a deep knowledge of hand-to-hand combat, synthetic poisons, and early-nineteenth-century Indian literature.

C. **ANALYSIS**: This looks like a skinny guy hiding in a fat guy. Or a fat guy who just ate a skinny guy. Also, is that his real hair or some kind of fur helmet? I would peg this dude as a serial exhibitionist for sure, and probably a grand larcenist. And why is his left ear abnormally larger than the right?

D. **ANALYSIS**: Either this man is a fry cook at the Botulism Diner or he's way too into Jughead. Either way, I don't want him touching my food. The goatee also suggests an unnatural love of amphibious animals, and the cold, steely eyes indicate a proclivity for hoarding fireworks, most of which will turn out to be duds.

Police-English Dictionary

Among the nearly gajillion reasons why cops are poor communicators, the biggest one is an overreliance on code words and abbreviations. Seriously. These guys would abbreviate the butter on their toast if they could. And while I'm not even sure what that previous sentence means, I'm pretty sure I was trying to convey that these guys abbreviate *everything*. "Grand Theft" equals "GT." "Be On the Lookout" equals "BOLO." I mean, IMHO, the abbreviations are unrelenting.

And here's the great irony—a lot of the abbreviations don't even make things shorter. Take "Code 11." Know what "Code 11" means? "Help." Wouldn't it be faster to just say, "Help"? And that's not some glib, rhetorical question; *it's simple math*. "Help" equals one syllable. "Code 11" equals *four syllables*. It doesn't take a properly developed hypothalamus to see that.

This, my friends, is what brings us to the simple truth about why cops do *anything*. It's not about fighting crime or protecting the public. It's about *looking cool*. I mean, polyester pants and jackboots in the middle of August? Who does that? Someone who wants you to think they're awesome, that's who. And nowhere is that more apparent than in cops' lingo.

Here's something typical you might hear coming out of a cop's mouth: "We're in a GCD on the 110. I'm calling in a Code Green with a PTS, possibly a 10-37 or Z-14. Let's activate the 640 with a 3VJ."

Translation: "We're stopping for a slushie."

Unfortunately, as a private detective, you're going to spend a lot of time interacting with police officers. So do yourself a favor; take five minutes and acquaint yourself with some cop tongue. Okay, that came out wrong. But you know what I mean. Here ya go...

RADIO CODES

309—Traffic problem; officers requested.

450—Bomb alert/funeral detail/stray horse[1]

691—Fire has just begun/ended/is in progress.[2]

972—Armed gunman inside building.

973—Armed gunman inside building, taking hostages.

974—Armed gunman exiting building, may have hostage with him. Gunman and hostage fleeing up alley, entering coffee shop… no, wait—they're not going in…They're checking out a car double-parked by the newspaper stand. They try the doors—it's locked. Gunman tries to smash a window—nothing happens. (Why doesn't he just use his gun?) They turn back…heading for the coffee shop…skip it again…enter the bookstore.

975—Retraction—he's not in the bookstore; he's in the movie theater.

976—Retraction—he *is* in the bookstore!

977—Actually, it's not a bookstore; it's more like a card shop, but they have some beautiful leather-bound journals and children's clothes.

983—Abandoned bicycle

---

[1] This is classic cop-speak, having the same code mean three *totally different things*. Last Tuesday, SBPD sent a bomb squad into a funeral, then blew up a horse.

[2] Even worse, having the same code mean three almost *exactly-the-same* things. It's why you always hear stuff like this…

DISPATCHER: We've got a Code 691 at Seventh and Swanson!
COP: Whew…well, I hope no one was hurt.
DISPATCHER: Hope no one was hurt? It just started—get over there!
COP: But you said—
DISPATCHER: It's a 691—it's flaring up!
COP: On my way!
DISPATCHER: Actually, no worries, it just went 691. Everyone's safe.

EMERGENCY CODES

Code Red—Highest level of response requested.

Code Blue—Officer needs assistance/send backup.

Code Green—A special code that changes daily to avoid interception.

Monday—Bomb threat

Tuesday—Armed robbery

Wednesday—Plankers

Thursday—Armed plankers

Friday—Goulash with cheese bread

Saturday—Burglars inside house; the only person home is an eight-year-old boy who must stop them with booby traps.

Sunday—Defective traffic light

Code Mauve—Officer keeps saying "wazzup" in really annoying ways.

Code Yellow—Can't remember today's Code Green.

Code Brown—Code Blue

Code Teal—Protective measures needed; switch today's Code Green to *yesterday's* Code Green.

ACRONYMS & LINGO

AAWC—Auto Accident with Casualties

ADW—Assault with a Deadly Weapon, or Abnormally Deep Wedgie

ARREST—Apples, Rice-A-Roni, Eggs, Salsa, Toothpaste (don't forget coupon)

BCAP—Biomass Crop Assistance Program (a 2011 U.S. Department of Agriculture program providing financial aid to agricultural landowners hoping to produce biomass feedstocks)[1]

HGIS—Hydro-Geographic Information System, or Hot Girls in Swimsuits

DWM—Dead White Male

DWMWNiP—Dead White Male with a New iPhone

NiPSUX—The New iPhone's not even that cool. I mean, yeah, it has a bigger screen and better voice control, but it still can't sort my whites or explain what *Eraserhead* is about.

PAC-MAN—Not as good as *Ms. Pac-Man*

PEACE—Britain's 5-step plan for interrogations, developed by several UK law enforcement agencies:

> P: Planning & Preparation
>
> E: Engage & Explain
>
> A: Account, Clarification, & Challenge
>
> C: Closure
>
> E: Evaluation[2]

OFQ—Need Backup Artillery[3]

---

[1] Initially, BCAP was also the acronym for Black Cops against Police Brutality, until cops started coming home to find large piles of kale in their driveways. So the Black Cops against Police Brutality changed their acronym to B-CAP, which doesn't seem to distinguish anything and seems far less accurate than BCAPB.

[2] Possibly the worst acronym I've ever seen. First of all, this acronym should read PPEEACCCE. Each letter can represent only one word, people—that's how acronyms work. You can't have P represent "planning" *and* "preparation," and E represent "engage" *and* "explain." How is anyone supposed to remember that? More importantly, why does A represent "account" (which makes sense) and also "clarification" and "challenge" (which doesn't make sense)? Especially when the letter *after* A is C? Why not just have C mean "Clarification, Challenge, & Closure"? It's this kind of thinking that nearly cost Britain the Falklands.

[3] Makes even less sense than PEACE, but it's the one abbreviation cops always seem to remember.

TAXPAYER—Murder victim

TAXPAYER OMG!—A murder victim who's been slashed up in a super-gross way, their insides strewn all over the place, intestines wrapped around their neck, etc.

Donna Summer?

Juliet: No.

Wendy Williams?

Juliet: No.

Bride of Frankenstein?

Juliet: Come on, Shawn.

I give up.

Juliet: Julia Roberts.

Seriously?

Juliet: Yes, seriously! Is it that bad?

Well, in my defense, I've always had a theory that Donna Summer and Julia Roberts are the same person. Have you ever seen them together?

Excerpted from *Profiler* magazine, the official publication of the criminal profiling industry...

(NOTE FROM SHAWN: Normally, I wouldn't give press to such a bogus and clearly Communist publication as Profiler, *but in the same way the* National Enquirer *and the* National Review *are hilarious to read, so is this.)*

Profiler's Profile of the Month

DECLAN RAND

by Jessica Freeman

Not every criminal profiler follows the same path to success...and one of those outliers is rising FBI superstar Declan Rand, a forty-five-year-old multimillionaire who's been making headlines with his hyper-accurate, criminal-catching profiles.

"This is my second career," says Rand, who earned his fortune as a hedge fund manager betting against the housing market, "but I wasn't happy in my first. I always felt like I had a higher calling, like my destiny was to help and protect people."

Indeed, it's difficult not to feel protected in the presence of a man whose torso seems to be chiseled from diamonds. But what com-pels someone who has everything—five vacation homes, three yachts, and his own charity dedicated to helping children with cancer—to give up a nearly flawless financial-sector career path?

"I fell in love," he says, smiling wistfully, in a rare moment of vulnerability. "I'd actually been posing as a fake profiler for a couple years, and I met this woman who...who... made me want to be a better person. To stop living a lie."

His voice cracks as he continues. "Things didn't work out," he says. "She broke my heart, but I vowed to follow through on my dream anyway—to prove to her how she changed me."

Unlike most men these days, when Rand makes a vow, it means something. Determined to be true to his word, he breezed through a master's in criminal psychology at Stanford and applied to Quantico, where he finished the twenty-week training program in just under a month.

Since then, Rand's work has helped capture ninety-six violent offenders, including the elusive Arizona Body-Slammer and Claudia "She-Devil" Lopez.

I always felt like I had a higher calling, like my destiny was to help and protect people.

"Rand is easily the most observant detective in America," says FBI Deputy Director Heath Summers. "He sees things no one else sees, connects clues in ways no one else can. It's like he has a sixth sense. I don't believe in psychic mumbo jumbo, but if you told me he was psychic, I'd believe you. We're getting so many requests for his help we can't even respond to them all."

Law enforcement agencies aren't the only ones who have taken note of Rand's talents . . . or his captivating brown eyes. He's been written up in *Men's Health*, *GQ*, and *Esquire*. *The Washington Tattler* named him "the most

But I think about her every day. I guess I hope that all this work will pay off sometime.

eligible bachelor in public service," and in one week, over 2,304,580 people viewed an amateur concert video of Adele performing her new song, "Declan Rand, Will You Carry My Baby?"

So how has all this attention affected Rand himself?…*Not one bit.*

"I'm the same person I was two years ago," he says. "I go for a run with my dog every morning, I enjoy a glass of wine every night, and I call my mom at least once a week. Sure, the accolades are nice, but they don't keep me warm at night."

You would think it'd be easy—especially for someone who specializes in tracking down strangers—for Rand to find that special someone. Unfortunately, that's been his hardest case, mainly because he already knows who the "culprit" is.

"She's the one person I couldn't profile," Rand says. "But I think about her every day. I guess I hope that all this work will pay off sometime. Not just in making the world a safer place, but in winning her back."

He glances away, a sad reminder that while he may be keeping our streets safe, the price Declan Rand pays…is his heart.

~

JESSICA FREEMAN is a freelance writer for *Profiler*. She is single and enjoys classic rock, old movies, and morning runs on the beach.

This Is Total F*&king Bulls%#t!!

Um, let's just hold the phone, *Profiler* magazine. The most *observant* detective in America? Are you kidding me? Not only does this man's name not rhyme with anything, he's completely delusional. You don't call yourself a profiler just because you determined that a person who murders another person is a psychopath. Everyone knows that, the same way everyone knows edamame is gross.

Real profiling doesn't happen *after the fact*. A true profiler sees potential criminal activity oozing from a person's oversized pores based on the attributes of their personality, then nabs them *before* they strike. It's all in the details. You'd think this Stanford person would have mentioned that.

Here are some profiles of peeps you might have heard of. They're not criminals, but they probably will be, based on what I can see. You see, details are my thing, too, Declan Feclan. Watch and learn.

STEVIE NICKS→

- Hooked up with Lindsey Buckingham. Formed a band.

- Joined Fleetwood Mac with Buckingham. Left him for Mick Fleetwood.

- Wrote "What's faster than a fast car? A beating heart...More exciting than high fashion? High passion."

- Reputed witch

This is clearly a person skilled at forming relationships and then exploiting them. She will eventually run some kind of **Ponzi scheme**.

FRANK LLOYD WRIGHT→

- Skilled in math

- Midwestern

- His original name for Fallingwater was "the Great Void of Pain and Blackness into Which We All Descend."

Couldn't be more obvious. The three names. The architecture. Had he lived, Frank Lloyd Wright would have definitely become one of the twentieth century's most notorious **grave robbers**.

TOMMY MOLTON

- Six years old
- Lives behind that creepy antique shop on Dover Street
- Bed wetter
- Was recently spotted by Gus burning ants with a magnifying glass

No two ways about it. Little Tommy Molton will most likely grow up to be a **cattle mutilator**.

Above: Future cattle mutilator.

TRACY CHAPMAN

- Fast car
- Working at the convenience store
- Frequently overheard talkin' about a revolution

I think we can all agree this individual belongs on a watch list. She's an **agitator**.

DISCLAIMERS

LEGAL: I had nothing to do with the making of this list, and while I'm pretty sure Shawn Spencer isn't actually suggesting any of the above people are criminals, I bear no responsibility should any of them take legal action against Mr. Spencer. For the record, I'm a huge Tracy Chapman fan, and I bought every one of Stevie Nicks's solo records.

—Josh Hornstock, former legal counsel to Shawn Spencer

NONLEGAL: I also had nothing to do with this list, and to be honest, Shawn, jealousy does not become you. You won. You have me. I'm your girlfriend. I don't even think about Declan. If I wanted someone who was rich and smelled like ocean spray and made an amazing black truffle quiche, I'd be with him. But I don't. I want you.

—Juliet O'Hara, girlfriend of Shawn Spencer

No, I Did Not Steal the Confidential Therapy Files of My Friends

First of all, let the record show, I have never been in therapy. I have nothing *against* therapy; I'm just an incredibly well-adjusted, emotionally healthy, ridiculously handsome dude. I'm sure if I'd ever been kidnapped by a serial killer, or dangled outside a window, or had anger management issues, or suddenly realized I'd been an overbearing father who smothered his son and should've bought him the Cop-Tur Go-Bot he'd wanted for his eighth birthday, drawing pictures of flowers and writing poems about my family would be very helpful.

Also let the record show, I would never break into the office of the SBPD therapist to look at confidential files of my friends and family.

If, however, said therapist were to leave her door open while she went to the restroom, entering is not legally considered "breaking in."

Not that I would take advantage of such an opportunity. And even if I did, which I didn't, most therapists' notes are totally bogus. I mean, how much can you really discern by having someone stare at inkblots for twenty minutes? Not much, I'll tell you that.

Don't believe me? Here are some notes I found in a folder the therapist left in the hall, and which I returned immediately. She apparently shows the same inkblots to each patient in hopes of gaining some brilliant insight into their minds. But as far as I can tell, no one can figure what the hell these inkblots are...and I'm not sure there's any window into anyone's soul. I don't know. You tell me.

LASSITER: Sloppy, that's what this is. There's no order, no symmetry. If this is something McNab spilled and didn't clean up, it's sheer amateurness, totally unacceptable. If this is an intentionally drawn image, some kind of drawing or sketch, it's clearly the work of a psychopath.

JULIET: A child's teardrops. A little girl, ten or eleven, wondering why her daddy won't be home for Christmas. Not that she's surprised. Daddy already missed her birthday, Valentine's Day, and her soccer tournament. But it doesn't matter. This little girl is tough. And who needs a daddy when you have your own Bravestarr Neutra-Laser Gun and Junior Detective Chemistry Set to play with?

McNAB: Assuming this is a blood spatter, I'm going to say it's type O, female, midforties. Just a guess. It could also be from a dog. Or a smoothie, perhaps Blueberry Blast or Mango Melon. I'll run some tests.

CHIEF VICK: The random pattern suggests a lack of forethought or organization. Whoever made this blot was clearly acting impulsively, hastily, without intensive planning. It also looks kind of like my baby's foot.

HENRY: A coffee spill? Paint splatter? I don't know. It's a bunch of dots. I'm guessing this means I never hugged my father or something. Do I really have to do this?

LASSITER: This reminds me of a painting I saw at the Gallery of Modern Art, but how this qualifies as art is beyond me. Art's supposed to be pretty, like pictures of birds or meadows or a beautiful woman. The only gallery this belongs in, along with all the other crap people today try passing off as "art," is a shooting gallery.

JULIET: A young woman dancing to "Call Me Maybe," which is a great song no matter what her boyfriend says. And if he were smart, he'd take an interest in her music, because it's going to be played at their wedding. If they ever get married. Not that she's pushing. She's totally fine taking things slow, honest. But if they *do* get married, this is totally the first song. And they're doing the dance she choreographed, like it or not.

McNAB: It appears to be some kind of symbol—perhaps a gang sign or secret code based on an ancient hieroglyph. It may signify the rise of a new crime syndicate or another change of logo for the Rotary Club.

CHIEF VICK: A glop of baby food someone spilled in the middle of my Quarterly Budget Report, yet another reminder not to leave paperwork sitting on the kitchen table when the babysitter comes. God knows she can't clean up after herself. How hard is it to notice a stack of Quarterly Budget Reports sitting next to the refrigerator?

HENRY: Dead frog.

LASSITER: The spitting image of my ex-wife Victoria's new boyfriend. Not that I care. I am immensely happy with my new fiancée, the gorgeous Marlowe Viccellio, and I don't even think about Victoria or her semi-employed "novelist" boyfriend. I'm sure they're very content, as they should be. They're both great people, I swear.

JULIET: Two inkblots either merging or separating; it's hard to tell. Will they come together to form a single unit? Or will one of them refuse to grow up, forever choosing video games and donut sandwiches over true happiness with the blot he's meant to be with? It's like, "make up your mind already— the blot's *right there*!"

McNAB: I'm pretty sure this is a toucan or some kind of toucan-faced demon, emerging from a cocoon.

CHIEF VICK: It looks vaguely like the National Award for Crime-Fighting Excellence—not that I'd know, since it's gone to Ventura County for the past five years, despite the fact that we've had more incarcerations, more closed cases, and more tickets for parking in a green zone during loading hours.

HENRY: Strangely, it reminds me of this clown picture I won for Shawn at the carnival one year. He was probably about six years old, and he hung it over his bed so he could look at it when he went to sleep. When he moved out, he left it behind. I knew he'd outgrown it, but I couldn't bear to see it alone in his room, smiling down at his empty bed. So now I keep it in my closet, and sometimes—after Shawn and I have had a fight or I haven't seen him in a while—I go in and look at it and think of that day at the carnival. Eh. What am I talking about? It's an inkblot—it doesn't look like anything! Maybe a motorcycle. Or a boomerang. I don't know. Do I seriously have to do this? I haven't looked at that stupid clown picture in years.

873 Common Traits of Criminal Sociopaths and Serial Killers

by Mary Lightly (March 8, 2010)

(NOTE FROM SHAWN: I've said some harsh things about profilers in the past, and for the most part, they're all true—especially the part about their unholy relationship with the Kiwanis Club. The one exception was Mary Lightly, SBPD's in-house criminal psychologist for almost fifty-five weeks. He was creepy as hell, but he was damn good at profiling. Almost too good; he may have been a serial killer himself. At any rate, the following is an unfinished piece I found in his journal. Although he was unable to complete it before his untimely death, it offers great insight for souleyes interested in forensic psychology.)

For the past four and a half months, I have dedicated myself to compiling a list of behavioral traits common to serial killers and psychopaths. Law enforcement agencies have attempted similar lists before, but the highest anyone's gotten is forty-seven. That makes this the most exhaustive list in the world. It's seventeen items longer than the list of clothes I'd like to see on Vincent Gallo.

1 Organized vs. Disorganized

Serial killers fall into two categories: organized or disorganized, which, I suppose, are the same categories most people fall into. Like my dad, totally organized. But my nana, she'd lose her head if it wasn't screwed on straight. Or if my granddad hadn't severed it with a chain saw. True story. Also probably a sign of a disorganized killer, considering a chain saw isn't a particularly clean or controllable murder weapon. And he killed her on shag carpeting. Which is funny, because my mom used to bug him about replacing that shag with something easier to clean.

2 Childhood and Adolescence

Apparently, Wolfgang Puck is now some kind of celebrity chef. But I knew him when he was a young criminology student at DeVry University. The following is a haiku I wrote while reading Puck's unpublished memoir, *Dice This*.

(FYI—Robert Frost once said a poem begins as a lump in the throat. But I've never felt that. To me, a poem begins as a series of letters and syllables. Like a license plate. But not a normal license plate—more like a vanity plate, where the letters and numbers actually form words and mean something. If it was a regular license plate, it would be just a meaningless jumble of letters and numbers. How is that a poem?)

Spring Day at the Beach

Run, play, hug Mommy.

Sand castles, dolphins, laughing.

Death comes to us all.

3 Radiohead

I don't understand—why do people listen to this band? *Kid A* sounds like a swarm of mosquitoes playing synthesizers. Do they even play notes? I mean, yes—I know they play notes, but are they in any meaningful order? It's like Thom Yorke blindfolds himself and just presses keys or plucks strings. Maybe that's what he does. At least that would make sense to me, because I can't believe he's *choosing* to make his songs sound this way.

4 Sociopaths Love Soup

Preferably tomato, butternut squash, and New England clam chowder.

5 Playing with Feces

Many have claimed that children who play with their feces grow up to be serial killers, but I don't buy it. I'm not a serial killer, and I've made entire menageries out of my own excrement.

6 Sexual Deviance and the Pathology of Power

I once read a concert review that called Radiohead "stadium rockers." Who's booking this band to play stadiums? This kind of music is not listened to in a stadium. It's listened to in a dark room with a glass of red wine, or even a Peach Mango Kool-Aid, and a razor blade. Which, I know, you would think is right up my alley, but I don't want the last thing I hear before passing on to be Radiohead. How do they even qualify as a rock band? Nothing about them "rocks." I don't even think *they* think they're a rock band. Does Thom Yorke actually think he "rocks"? I don't know—maybe he's never heard actual rock music.

7 Hypothalamic Development in Disempathetic Sociopaths

This is the secret key to criminal profiling. Want to get inside a criminal's head? The only thing you have to know is

(This is all that was written. Two days later, on March 10, 2010, Mary was brutally murdered by Mr. Yin. He will hold a special, well-padded place in my heart.)

Which Person in the Drunk Tank Is Most Likely to Have Gum

You know the classic police precinct drunk tank from TV, right? A ragtag band of haggard rapscallions, misdemeanorers, and the odd freshman reveler riding out a one-off bender until his parents pick him up. The SBPD drunk tank is just like that. Only there are more drunks. Something about Santa Barbara, I suppose. For you, however, this chamber of horrors reeking of bodily fluids is a training ground. This is where you get so up in the criminal mind you know crooks the same way your Pandora knows you want "Hey, Soul Sister" to follow "Rain King."

Now, this kind of understanding takes time and patience, and perhaps most importantly, sweet minty breath. You're going to be observing these tipsy transgressors for hours at a time, and believe me—no one, not even semiconscious petty offenders want to hang with the halitosis, so it's going to be incumbent on you to get your hands on some gum. And as an observer-in-training, I'm going to go ahead and insist you get it from one of the very persons you're eyeballing.

"But Shawn," says you, "how am I supposed to know which one of these reprobates is rocking the Big Red?" That's the whole point, Skippy! Observational chops will actually equal fresh breath, which is its own reward, right? So here you go, then. Use your eyebrains and tell me—do these drunk tankers have gum?

← Typically a neck tat, a black eye, and a poorly executed Van Dyke are solid indication of a gum-toting miscreant. But then there's the wedding ring. This clown's hitched and in jail, which means he's got bigger problems than fresh breath.

Gum? *No.*

→ Raven hair, ruby lips. Sparks fly from her fingertips. She's what one might call a witchy woman. And while the wifebeater is a nice touch, you mustn't let her steely gaze throw you. She's only trying to prevent you from hitting her up for a certain something she clearly has.

Gum? *Yes.*

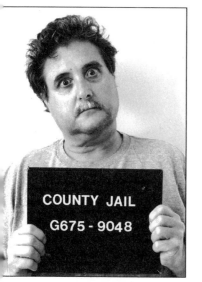

← Now, this dude has seen some action, judging by his 1,001-yard stare and head tilted just so. There's serious jujumagumbo happening behind those eyes. Most people would warn you that it's not advisable to approach someone who appears this unstable, but then most people don't know lunatics despise yuckmouth more than anyone. True story.

Gum? *Yes* (but ask politely).

How to Dissect a Human Body*

*Dead human body. I learned this one the hard way. —Woody

by Dr. Woodrow Strode, M.E., Santa Barbara Police Department

I know there are many of you out there who think a lot about what a coroner actually does. I know I do. And you might be surprised to know the job is actually pretty wide-ranging. For example, in addition to examining and processing human remains, I do light plumbing and electrical around the SBPD. I also maintain a small, organic herb garden as well as an e-library consisting entirely of books from a little-known literary subgenre I call nonfiction science fiction. So, yeah. I keep pretty busy.

I also happen to be a crack autopsist, but I imagine you knew that. What you may not have known is that I've performed more autopsies on late medical examiners than just about anybody in the game. That's why they call me the "Coroner's Coroner."

Oh, by the way, I'm Dr. Woody Strode (University of Angola, '75, *passim cum laude*). I've been asked by Shawn to walk you through the steps of a typical autopsy, with the hopes of a greater understanding of the dead criminal mind.

Step One: External Examination

Examine the body externally (*Figure a*). Note height, weight, and other physical characteristics, such as supernumerary (or fourth) nipples, sexy tattoos, or branding. Note any injuries, such as punctures, bullet holes, bite marks, or spoon stabbings (these often look like little smiles). Be sure to write all this down; you'll need it next time you want to create a new Sims character.

Figure a

Step Two: The First Cut (the Y Incision)

If you haven't yet made an official determination that the deceased is actually *deceased*, it would be a good time to do it now. You're about to go Ginsu.

Many coroners begin their autopsies with a Y-cut (*Figure b*), a three-part incision, with the first two cuts extending from the shoulders to the breastbone, and the third cut reaching from the breastbone to just above the groin.

I call this the "Y incision" because it always makes me ask, "*Why* would you start this way?" I prefer the "Carrot incision" (*Figure c*), which is more complicated but gives you a more pleasing view of the chest cavity.

I also like the "Sydney Opera House incision" (*Figure d*). Again, slightly more complicated, but more fun to carve.

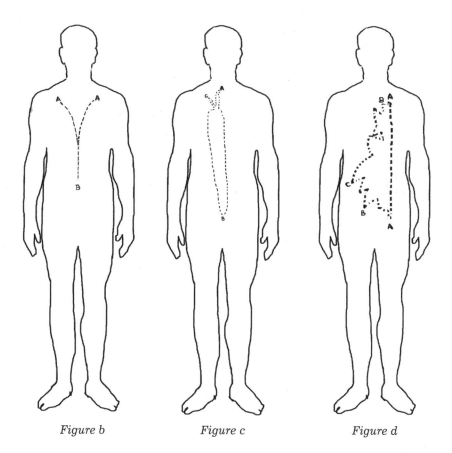

Figure b   Figure c   Figure d

Step Three: Internal Examination

First, use a bone saw to remove the ribs. Set them in a safe place; you'll use them later once you've completed step six, making the honey mustard sauce (only kidding). Next, remove each of the chest cavity's organs: heart, lungs, spleen, gallbladder, pancreas. And no, the pancreas and the gallbladder *aren't* the same thing. Wait, yes they are. It's here your dissection scissors should be on the job. They're your most effective tissue-cutting instrument. Way better than chain saws or sporks. You have to trust me on this one.

Examine the internal organs and take samples. Do not store samples in the police precinct refrigerator. This will make the head detective very, very angry, and he will berate you so intensely, you'll actually believe it for a little while afterward.

Step Four: Extracting and "Fixing" the Brain

The next step is removing the brain, but since this pretty much ruins the head, I like to first insert a special step I call "Mr. Cadaver Head."

Mr. Cadaver Head involves removing each of the facial features and putting them back in the place of *other* facial features! This may not have much investigative value, but the stress relief it provides is invaluable, and trust me, the last guy you want running around your office with Stryker saws and enterotomes is an overworked, overstressed medical examiner. Plus, when you see some of these things, I think you're going to realize how wonderful they are. Here are some of my favorites.

Right: My rendition of Picasso's Weeping Woman. *I think I really captured the pain and suffering of the Spanish Civil War.*

Above left: I made this for my mother after her second hysterectomy. It still hangs in her boudoir.

Above right: LOL—this one just cracks me up!

(FYI—a few years ago, I attempted to sell a children's toy version called Mr. Cadaver Head. Turns out they already have a toy version using an artificial potato. Can you imagine?...A potato! What will they think of next?)

NOTE: *Always* ascertain that the deceased's funeral service will not involve a viewing of any kind. Nothing kills a good funeral like a mutilated loved one.

Now we remove the brain. First, cut off the top of the skull and peel it back so you can see the brain poking out like the top of a hard-boiled egg. (NOTE: DO NOT MISTAKE IT FOR AN *ACTUAL* HARD-BOILED EGG.) Next, sever the brain stem. This will make the brain easier to remove. Or if you fancy yourself some kind of macho man, go ahead and twist and pull, but be ready: a strong yank can often send the gray matter flying. You've been warned.

Finally, you must "fix," or soften, the brain. Fresh brains are often too hard to cut, making them difficult to dissect. Most coroners place the brain in a formalin solution for two weeks, but a clean meat tenderizer works just as well.

Step Five: Draining the Intestines and Opening the Stomach

Examine the digestive tract. Begin by emptying any solid waste from the large intestine into a sink or bowl. If you're working at home, consider one of those orange Home Depot buckets with the picture of Homer on it. That's his name, by the way, Homer.

Next, slice open the stomach. Its contents can help determine time of death and whether or not any infections or poisons may have been involved. Also, a Twinkie can last undigested in the stomach for up to six weeks, so every once in a while you get lucky.

Step Six: Examine and Replace Internal Organs

Internal organs can give you a vast amount of information about the cause of death. Are the organs firm to the touch, with a slight give, like a perfectly shaped breast? (If you're not sure and you have a female cadaver, try the breast.) When you kick or dribble the organs, do they bounce or flatten out? If you shake them, do you hear any strange squishings or rattlings? Do they speak your name when you're alone with them? Do they know things about you you've never told anyone?

Once you've completed your assessment, place the organs back into the chest cavity. No one's going to be using or seeing them anymore, so they don't need to go back in the same place. Just be sure they fit snugly enough not to jiggle or slosh around. Remember, you've severed the cords attaching them to the body, so if there's too much extra room, you may need some packing peanuts or bubble wrap. The last thing you want is a bunch of organs slipping around inside, looking like Howard Hesseman's torso. (I once saw him nude in a production of *Quills*, and he actually has a gorgeous skin tone. I went back twice.)

Step Seven: Sewing Up the Body

This is the one place where the "Y incision," if you used it, comes in handy; it's a lot easier to sew up than those other cuts. But hey—if people only did things that were easy, we wouldn't have the Eiffel Tower, or umbrella hats, or Bark Off. Besides, if you're as into quilting as I am, this is a great chance to practice your rag edge or stitch-in-the-ditch.

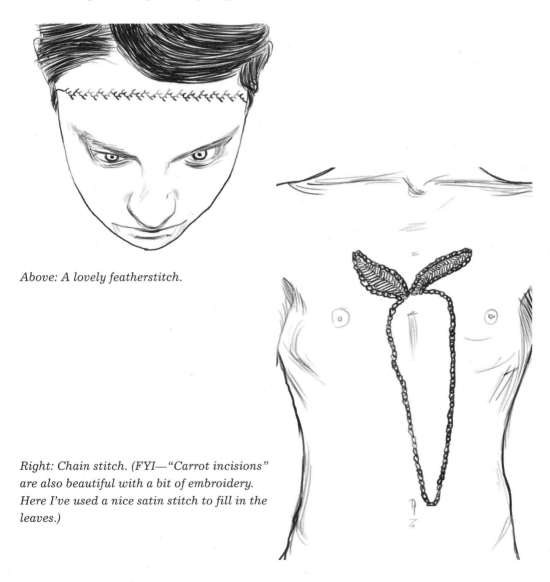

Above: A lovely featherstitch.

Right: Chain stitch. (FYI—"Carrot incisions" are also beautiful with a bit of embroidery. Here I've used a nice satin stitch to fill in the leaves.)

Things I've Left Inside Bodies*
by Woodrow Strode

■ A two-foot pepperoni

■ My gold teeth grill—only been used once

■ An official Heart of the Ocean replica necklace

■ Chapters 8 and 9 of *Mein Kampf*

■ The engagement ring my wife proposed to me with**

■ Piece of the Berlin wall

■ Manny Ramirez 2007 World Series autographed baseball

■ My niece's hamster

■ Three Diamanda Galás tickets

■ Packet of Sea-Monkeys

■ A bottle of 1865 Château Lafite

■ My second-to-last lock of Melissa Manchester's hair

■ Half a Happy Meal

■ Shrunken human head (or ping-pong ball, depending on whom you believe)

■ Sixty-three cents

■ Hand-carved Aeolian wind harp

■ One cyanide pill

■ Steven Tyler's home phone number

■ Blueprints for a perpetual motion machine

■ The letter S from my laptop keyboard

■ Vial of urinal water from the second-floor men's restroom

■ Henry Spencer's 2008 tax return

■ Unopened pack of Herbal Ecstasy cigarettes

* Dead bodies
** Actually, this was left inside a live body. Not mine.

Police Academy Application

All right, I know I spend a lot of time bagging on police officers, but the truth is, cops are what they are. Kind of like how a sea cucumber's not as cool as a lion because it doesn't know how to improve itself; a sea cucumber's not as cool as a lion because it's a *sea cucumber*. No matter how hard it tries, it will never be anything other than a sea cucumber! You can't blame it for being a sea cucumber—it just *is*!

Well, cops are the same way. So if you need a plumber and hire a cobbler, you can't complain when he doesn't know how to plumb.

My point is this: rather than blaming cops and sea cucumbers for being who they are, we should instead blame the people who hire these cops and sea cucumbers.

Think about it: if you want to get a Russian literature degree from Harvard, you have to complete a five-page application, write seventeen personal essays, and pay $40,000 a year. But if you want to carry a loaded gun and protect the public, you just scribble down your name and fork over $700.

In fact, last summer I lost a bet to Gus and had to apply to the Santa Barbara Police Academy under the name Dirk Longfellow, and based solely on my ability to correctly write my zip code, I was made lieutenant before even showing up. (I never actually showed up, but I received a letter of commendation in the mail. I'm not even kidding.) Even more disturbing—the application was the easiest thing I've ever filled out...*and asked none of the questions I would want asked of the people responsible for protecting our streets, our homes, our children*. Where were the questions about self-defense or weapons training? Personal histories or associations with anti-American groups and activities? Even my motivations for becoming a cop?

As concerned citizens, don't we deserve the most qualified officers our police departments can find? Shouldn't we demand better?

The answer is: *probably not*. After all, we're the same concerned citizens who asked President Obama to reschedule his State of the Union address so we could watch *Lost*, so what do we expect?

Having said that, I still don't like working with unqualified idiots... because, if nothing else, it makes my job harder. Which is why, as an official consultant to the SBPD, I've taken it upon myself to update and improve their police academy application.

So if you're interested in applying, feel free to use the following form, which is more sophisticated—and almost as official—as anything you'll get off their website.

And please don't thank me, Santa Barbara—I'm just doing my job as a responsible resident.

page 1

**ACT #287
APPLICATION FORM**

SANTA BARBARA POLICE ACADEMY

NAME: _____

ADDRESS: _____

CITY/STATE/ZIP: _____

PHONE #: _____ E-MAIL ADDRESS: _____

DATE OF BIRTH: _____ I LOOK: ❏ Older ❏ Younger ❏ Exactly my age

RELATIONSHIP STATUS (check one):

❏ Single ❏ Married ❏ Married, but open to opportunities

❏ Seeing a few people, nothing serious ❏ Single, but I have my crap together

❏ Slightly clingy ❏ Totally undateable

HAVE YOU EVER BEEN ARRESTED, CONVICTED, OR PLED GUILTY
FOR ANY SUMMARY, MISDEMEANOR, OR FELONY OFFENSE? (check one)

❏ Yes ❏ No ❏ I don't recognize U.S. law

IF YES, EXPLAIN: _____

COMPARING YOURSELF TO ANOTHER LAWBREAKER, YOU'RE MOST LIKE:

❏ Robin Hood ❏ Martha Stewart ❏ Jack the Ripper ❏ Tupac

❏ The Punisher ❏ Bonnie and/or Clyde ❏ Nelson Mandela ❏ Josef Mengele

(see over)

page 2

SANTA BARBARA POLICE ACADEMY

ACT #287
APPLICATION FORM

EDUCATION:

HIGH SCHOOL: _____YEAR OF GRADUATION: _____

WHEN YOU WERE IN HIGH SCHOOL, YOU CONSIDERED THE
FOLLOWING ACTIVITIES TO BE COOL: (check all that apply)

❏ Football   ❏ Cheerleading (female)   ❏ Mah-jongg   ❏ River Dancing

❏ Childhood Obesity   ❏ Klezmer Music   ❏ Dwarf-tossing   ❏ Alchemy

❏ Cheerleading (male)

COLLEGE:_____YEAR OF GRADUATION: _____

MAJOR: _____

WHAT YOU *SHOULD'VE* MAJORED IN TO BE EMPLOYABLE: _____

MILITARY SERVICE:

BRANCH: _____ DATES SERVED: _____RANK: _____

IF YOU WERE *NOT* IN THE MILITARY, CAN YOU IDENTIFY
THE FOLLOWING MILITARY QUOTES: (check if answer is yes)

❏ "Killin' generals could get to be a habit with me."
❏ "The dead know only one thing: it is better to be alive."
❏ "Chicks dig me because I rarely wear underwear, and when I do it's usually
   something unusual."

DO YOU HAVE WEAPONS OR SELF-DEFENSE TRAINING
IN ANY OF THE FOLLOWING:

❏ Karate   ❏ Judo   ❏ Webshooters   ❏ Proton Packs   ❏ Krav Maga

❏ Bullwhip   ❏ Harsh, hurtful words   ❏ Captive bolt pistol

(continues page 3)

page 3

SANTA BARBARA POLICE ACADEMY

> **ACT #287**
> **APPLICATION FORM**

HAVE YOU EVER BEEN AFFILIATED WITH THE FOLLOWING ORGANIZATIONS/ACTIVITIES:

❏ National Citizens Militia   ❏ Ku Klux Klan   ❏ Toastmasters   ❏ Dungeons & Dragons

❏ Future Homemakers of America   ❏ Libertarians   ❏ The Chicago Bulls   ❏ PETA

ESSAY QUESTIONS (use additional paper if necessary):

1. Why do people always say Peter Gabriel is the only "real" lead singer of Genesis, even though no one can name a single song he sang with them, and their only hits came with Phil Collins?

2. Clubber Lang or Ivan Drago?

3. Imagine you promised to go to your girlfriend's book club this Sunday, and you're supposed to read something called *Finnegans Wake*. What's this book about, and what are three intelligent things you would say about it?

EXPECTED PHYSICAL ACTIVITIES: Investigating 2 to 4 Pinkberrys per day, staying alive in *Dance Dance Revolution* for at least fourteen minutes, sliding across hood of car, knowledge of both parts in "Paradise by the Dashboard Light," eating one's weight in Count Chocula. Firearms training—hand/eye coordination to safely and effectively handle a firearm or at least kill someone with a book or magazine a la Jason Bourne.

AGREEMENT: I swear, upon acceptance into the SBPD Police Academy, to follow the rules of the program, and agree to dismissal if found guilty of inappropriate conduct such as insubordinance, gum chomping, Jeff Probst impersonations, leaving a tuna sandwich in the fridge, mouth breathing, trimming my toenails at my desk, calling people "buddy" when they're not my buddy, not silencing my Ace of Bass ringtone, listening to talk radio without headphones.

_____

SIGNATURE OF APPLICANT

_____

PRINT NAME

_____

DATE

APPLICATION PACKET MUST INCLUDE:
- Application form
- High school, college, or fifth-grade transcripts
- Copy of a driver's license (doesn't have to be yours)
- Favorite Rice Krispie treat recipe
- Top ten magazines to read in the bathroom
- Instructions to put together IKEA bookshelves

INCOMPLETE PACKETS WILL BE RETURNED TO APPLICANT.

Concierge/Bodyguard/Assistant/Masseuse (Santa Barbara)

Date: 2013-01-28, 4:12PM PST
Reply to: pineapplelover@prodigy.com [Errors when replying to ads?]

Top private investigation firm seeking professional concierge/bodyguard/assistant/ masseuse. Applicants must have a valid (or valid-looking) driver's license and social security card, and know how to fix a Gevalia coffeemaker that has Strawberry Bubblicious stuck in it. Immediate openings available! Great room for advancement within company. INTERVIEW AND GET HIRED ON THE SPOT!

Duties include general office maintenance: answering phones, making copies, changing oil/tires, some light ironing, picking up lunch (please remember *brown* mustard instead of honey mustard), standing in line for Tommy Tutone tickets next Wednesday, occasional barbering, setting the TiVo to record everything with Chuck Norris and/or Amber Heard, screening calls from anyone named Henry, weekly Pilates sessions, repairing a 1972 Norton 750 Commando motorcycle that hasn't run in about seven years.

Professional dress and appearance required. Excellent people skills also required, although you may sometimes need to be a dick—not to us, but to other people we're dealing with (and sometimes my sidekick, who thinks of himself as a full partner, which he's not). Bilingual a plus (no Esperanto). No gross perfumes or eyeglasses on beaded chains. Must have basic bartending and reflexology skills. No teacher arm. Nobody who watches *Suits*.

Top pay (plus benefits) based on qualifications. Benefits include: office location with gorgeous beach views, street parking, weekends off, in-house restroom (flusher must be held down for twenty seconds), frequent coffee runs, easy access to the Walgreens Redbox, use of all police vending machines, first dibs on anything left in the fridge longer than a day, multiple opportunities to glue shut an *actual head detective's* office drawers.

• Location: SANTA BARBARA
• Principals only. Recruiters, please don't contact this job poster.
• Please, no phone calls about this job!
• Please do not contact job poster about other services, products or commercial interests.

PostingID: 19843165150

A Note from Shawn about the Craigslist Posting

Sorry about that, folks. Normally, I wouldn't clutter these valuable pages or your valuable time with personal advertisements or Craigslist postings, but I still haven't gotten any adequately qualified candidates. In fact, this was my first response, via text.

Shawn, I thought we talked about this.
09:23 AM

About what?
09:24 AM

I saw the Craigslist ad.
09:25 AM

I told you, man. Those are hookers. They're not really lonely Asian coeds looking for a horny math tutor.
09:27 AM

For the assistant.
09:28 AM

Assistants, math tutors, whatever. They're still hookers.
09:30 AM

I'm not an idiot, Shawn. You know I have a Google Alert for reflexology. And you used your regular e-mail address.

09:32 AM

Oh, THAT Craigslist ad. Okay, well, first, it's not for an assistant. It's for a concierge/bodyguard/ assistant/masseuse.

09:34 AM

I know what it says. A concierge, really?

09:35 AM

What? Concierges are way better than assistants. Assistants don't get you tickets to Cirque du Soleil.

09:37 AM

And a bodyguard/masseuse?

09:38 AM

Well, that's just common sense. A) We happen to be in a dangerous line of work, and ☺ are you really going to fight me on masseuse?

09:42 AM

Sorry, that was supposed to be a ☺.

09:42 AM

Dammit—why does it keep doing that? It's supposed to be a B. B B B B B.

09:43 AM

The point is, we don't need a masseuse. Or any of that.

09:44 AM

Speak for yourself, Gus. My lumbar is killing me.

09:45 AM

No assistant, Shawn. It never works.

09:46 AM

Look, Gus, I could see how the presence of another person threatens you and your man love for me. But you have to understand: you're my best friend, nothing more. I just don't feel that way about you.

09:48 AM

Fine. Hire someone. See if I care. Just don't come crying to me when they drink all the cream soda or refuse to do the Running Man for you every morning.

09:50 AM

Hmm…you make some good points. I'll be sure to put that stuff in the Craigslist ad.

09:51 AM

By the way, would you mind checking my e-mail for résumés and doing the interviews for me? Thanks, buddy—you're a mensch.

09:53 AM

NOTE TO READERS: If you submitted a résumé and didn't hear back, my apologies. Someone seems to be deleting them from my inbox. Please feel free to reapply to my new e-mail address: suckitgus@prodigy.com. Sorry for the confusion—as soon as I have a new concierge/bodyguard/assistant/masseuse on board, there will be some *big* changes around here, I assure you.

(NOTE FROM SHAWN: Congrats to my illustrious friend and boss, Chief Vick. I am reprinting this article as a kudos to her and to show you what a real crime-fighting magazine looks like. So blow on that, Profiler.)

From *Crime Fighting Monthly* Magazine

GETTING DUNLAPPED
An Interview with Crime-Solving Superstars the Dunlap Sisters

by Brian Norman
Staff Writer, *Crime Fighting Monthly*

America has a long history of families in positions of power and public service—the Kennedys, the Bushes, the Roosevelts—so it was with tremendous enthusiasm that I sat down to interview one of law enforcement's power duos: Santa Barbara Police Chief Karen Vick and Coast Guard Commander Barbara Dunlap.

These two sisters have not only made names for themselves as two of Southern California's toughest crime fighters, they've also earned reputations as terrific leaders of their respective organizations.

I recently caught up with the Dunlap sisters to discuss the secrets of leadership and how these trailblazers go about leading two of the most successful crime-fighting institutions in the country.

BN: *First of all, I have to say...I'm a huge fan of both of you. Chief Vick, I followed very closely your takedown of the Hashtag Killer—very impressive.*

VICK: Thank you.

BN: *And Commander Dunlap, I was fascinated with how you solved the Atlantis burglaries—amazing work.*

DUNLAP: Thank you. You know, that was voted one of 2012's Toughest Cases to Crack by *Modern Detective* and *The Cayucos Examiner*.

BN: *Well, congratulations. Now let's talk about leadership. Chief Vick, you received the California Peace Award for Outstanding Leadership in 2011, and Commander Dunlap, you were awarded the Governor's Medal for Leadership in 2012. So tell me...what* is *the secret to great leadership?*

VICK: I think there are four main qualities to outstanding leadership, Brian: communication, organization, delegation, and passion.

DUNLAP: Actually, Brian, there are *five* qualities: communication, organization, delegation, passion...and responsibility. And social interaction. An effective leader clearly articulates her directives.

BN: *Excellent.*

VICK: Social interaction? Isn't that the same as communication? And that's six qualities, not five.

DUNLAP: Also, Brian, not nitpicking. Good leaders never split hairs over petty details.

BN: *Let's talk about communicating. What do most people* not *do when it comes to good communication?*

DUNLAP: They don't listen. Many leaders care more about what *they* want to say, rather than listening to the advice and opinions of others. You need to listen to those around you. It's crucial.

VICK: Oh, that is rich.

BN: *Do you disagree, Chief Vick?*

VICK: Not at all, I agree with Commander Dunlap 100 percent. So-called leaders frequently ignore others, even when that other person is trying to tell them something important, like, they need the car for a department fund-raiser or a school pep rally or a date with Jack Hannigan—

DUNLAP: You did not have a date with Jack Hannigan.

VICK: Yeah, because I didn't have a car to get to the restaurant.

DUNLAP: No, because Jack Hannigan was never into you.

BN: *I'm confused. Who's Jack Hannigan?*

VICK: Nobody. What Commander Dunlap and I are illustrating is a classic example of Verbal Conflict Resolution, a technique I employ when resolving disputes among officers.

BN: *Fascinating. So you achieve reconciliation by having the disputing parties voice their own emotions and perspectives.*

VICK: Exactly.

DUNLAP: Or by running to her superiors—like, say, I don't know, her parents. That's another technique she's particularly good at.

VICK: What are you talking about?

DUNLAP: Really?…Homecoming 1992?

VICK: Come on. Mom promised me I could wear that dress!

DUNLAP: Which you didn't even care about until you knew I wanted it!

VICK: Right, because all I ever do is sabotage things you want.

DUNLAP: Well, look at that—she finally admits it!

BN: *Hold on...is this the same Verbal Conflict Resolution technique we were illustrating a moment ago?*

DUNLAP: Actually, no, Brian. This is an interdepartmental technique I use called Regressive Past Response Correspondence.

BN: *And you developed this technique yourself?*

DUNLAP: Absolutely. As a leader, you often spend years getting blamed for stuff you didn't do, mainly because people below you have perfected the art of crying to get what they want. So you develop ways of showing these people how much they're acting like a child. It's all communication.

VICK: Don't you mean "social interaction"?

DUNLAP: That, too. All full circle. And next thing you know, you're the first woman in the history of the Coast Guard to command a fleet of Cutters.

BN: *Um, that's brilliant. And does Regressive...er, Past...*

DUNLAP: Regressive Past Response Correspondence?

BN: *Yes. That. Does it improve communication between departments?*

DUNLAP: Absolutely, unless you run into someone so immature they can't be reached.

VICK: It's true. Some people can't see past their own egos.

DUNLAP: And others are so accustomed to being given everything they don't understand the difference between hard work and handouts.

BN: *Chief Vick, you mentioned delegation as an important quality of leadership. How does the ability to delegate make one a stronger leader?*

VICK: Good leaders need to empower those below them. By delegating, we allow others to become responsible and grow into leaders themselves.

DUNLAP: Exactly. As leaders, it's our job to foster leaders coming up through the ranks.

VICK: I just said that.

DUNLAP: Well, I was simply adding—

VICK: I know what you were adding. But that was implied in what I just said.

DUNLAP: You can't let anything go, can you?

VICK: Not when you try to horn in on everything I do!

DUNLAP: What do I "horn in on"?

VICK: I don't know, Jack Hannigan, the Chapman High Crime Fighters Society, *this interview…*

DUNLAP: Okay, fine. Brian, let's say you had a date with Kristen Stewart.

BN: *I have a date with Kristen Stewart? From* Twilight*?*

DUNLAP: Yes, but your brother wants to use the car to go meet this other girl he really likes—we'll call her Hack Jannigan—but she doesn't like him back…

VICK: He did too like me back!

DUNLAP: Now, your brother doesn't have an actual date with this girl; he's just going to a bowling alley where she *might* be hanging out.

VICK: He told me to meet him there!

DUNLAP: Should you give up the car for your date with superhot Kristen Stewart so your brother can go meet this loser who doesn't even know he exists?

VICK: Do not answer that, Brian!

DUNLAP: I'm sorry, weren't you just talking about how you have to "listen to those around you"?

BN: *You know, I'm not really sure this has much to do with the article—*

> **DUNLAP:** Of course it does. As a leader you have to make decisions, right? So be decisive, Brian. Who should get the car?

> **VICK:** And while you're thinking, we'll talk about some other leadership decisions. Like Admiral Anchovy.

> **DUNLAP:** It was *your* week to feed him!

> **VICK:** I was at soccer camp!

> **DUNLAP:** For two hours a day!

BN: *Know what, ladies? I think I have everything I need.*

> **DUNLAP:** So let's talk about how you stole my speech for the Young Diplomats Convention.

> **VICK:** I wasn't even at the Young Diplomats Convention!

> **DUNLAP:** Oh my God, that's right—you weren't invited. I totally forgot. I'm so sorry…I'd just assumed you'd been— this is so embarrassing. Obviously, you couldn't have stolen my speech if you weren't even invited to the *most prestigious convention in the state.*

BN: *Really, I think we're good. Thank you both for your time. It's been a pleasure.*

> **DUNLAP:** Thank *you*, Brian. And remember, the secret to being a leader is knowing how to follow.

> **VICK:** Oh, barf.

> **DUNLAP:** See, negative energy equals terrible leadership. I'm also available for speaking engagements and private consultations.

NOTE FROM SHAWN: Again, great article, Chief! I learned so much— and can totally see what makes you a strong leader! Congrats!

Scent Dogs:
Ineffective or Just Big Fat Liars?

I would like to amend something I said earlier. I know I said criminal profilers are "total frauds" and "charlatans," and that's true, but I may have given the impression that criminal profilers are the police department's *only* frauds and charlatans, and that's not true. There are definitely bigger frauds and charlatans, and they're called SCENT DOGS.

Let me be clear, I have nothing against dogs—I've seen *Air Bud 3: World Pup* nine and a half times—I just have something against *hiring dogs as police officers*.

Sure, cops like them because chicks think they're cute, but who are these scent dogs really? What do they actually do? And most importantly, can we trust them? As a concerned taxpayer and card-holding member of the Cheesecake of the Month Club, I think we have a right to know, especially since there's plenty of evidence—most of it suppressed by the left-wing media elite—to suggest these puppies aren't exactly who they seem.

EXHIBIT A: Scent dogs don't get paid; they just get bones and belly rubs like every other dog. So what's in it for them? Would you work somewhere if you were getting exactly what you'd be getting if you *weren't* working? I mean, these dogs could go to another job and get the exact same compensation without having to sniff serial killers' underwear. But they don't, which tells me they're either getting *something* for what they're doing or they have an alternative plan they're not telling us.

(By the way, if you were to rub the belly of any other employee, you'd be brought up on harassment charges. So why do dogs—who are given the same level of professional responsibility as other cops—not get identical rights and protections? And don't tell me, "They're dogs; they like to have their bellies rubbed." I *love* having my belly rubbed, but I'm pretty sure it would be against department policy if I asked the deputy commissioner to rub my belly or walked up to the county treasurer and started tickling *her* belly. More importantly, what if some dog *doesn't* like his/her belly rubbed? As any human resources exec will tell you, "If someone *feels* harassed, they're *being* harassed," so the onus is on you not to exhibit harassing behavior. Yet how many scent dogs suffer through the pain and humiliation of having their bellies rubbed because they're too afraid to speak out? And just to be clear, I'm not saying dogs are equal to humans. They're not; they're dogs—if they were in Laos or Carl's Jr., they'd still be considered dinner. What I'm saying is, we put these dogs to work protecting and policing us, then treat them like second-class citizens...*and the dogs don't seem to mind.* Something else is clearly going on; the other foot may not have fallen yet, but it will. Mark my words: *it will.*)

EXHIBIT B: Scent dogs are used because of their supposedly heightened senses of smell. But do they *really* have stronger senses of smell? Evidence would suggest otherwise.

EXHIBIT B.1: I've known fraternity guys, glaucoma patients, and vegans who have spent way more time around drugs than scent dogs, and even *they* can't smell pot from twenty yards away. (To be fair, I once knew a Rasta guy who could smell marijuana from thirty-five yards away; he just couldn't get off the couch to go get it.) So why do we expect an animal with thirty-two more chromosomes than a Kappa Sig to hunt them down? (FYI, science failures—the more chromosomes something has, the less advanced it is. For example, humans have 26 chromosomes; gypsy moths have 62; ferns have 94. Pat Monahan, the lead singer of Train, has 387.)[1]

EXHIBIT B.2: If dogs could actually smell, they wouldn't sniff each other's butts. I mean, I've never been that close to anyone else's ass—human or canine—but I've smelled enough from a distance to know I don't need the up-close experience. If dogs truly had superior smell, I'm pretty sure they'd feel the same way, but the fact that they keep jamming their nostrils up each other's rectums suggests their olfactory receptors may not be top-notch.

EXHIBIT B.3: Having a heightened sense usually means you've lost the abilities of at least one other sense. This is Daredevil 101. When Matt Murdock was blinded, his other senses kicked in to cover the loss. Even Gus gained his own incredible powers of smell when he lost the ability to talk to girls normally. So my question is, if dogs have super senses of smell, what *don't* they have...*and why don't we know about it?*

EXHIBIT C: Every failing sitcom tries to resurrect itself by getting a dog. *Family Ties*, *The Cosby Show*, *Growing Pains*—they all brought on dogs to raise the "cute factor" when the ratings dipped...and they were

---

[1] GUS: This is completely untrue, Shawn. The number of chromosomes has nothing to do with how "advanced" something is. Slime mold, for example, has 12 chromosomes; a rhesus monkey has 42; and a carp has 104.[a]

[a] Says the guy with 967.

all canceled within three seasons. So think it over, folks—are we really going to entrust the safety of our loved ones to the species that couldn't even save *Full House*?[1]

And lastly, the most damning evidence of all: *Cesar Millan has never had a K9 scent dog on the show.* Coincidence? I think not. I mean, if the *dog whisperer* doesn't trust these guys, why should we?[2]

Other Uses for Scent Dogs and K9 Units

I'd like to make another amendment. I didn't mean to imply that police dogs are a total waste of space; it's not like they're the cast of *Basketball Wives*. And just to prove I'm not completely anti-dog (just anti-scent dog), here are some more appropriate uses for professional canines:

- Fur for Lassie's chest wig
- An all-dog remake of *Braveheart*
- Puppy bowling
- Lead vocals for Nickelback
- Designated hitters for the Cleveland Indians
- Meat

CASE STUDY #3

My Faire Lady

You and your sidekick, Ghus (name changed), are standing in line to get tickets for tonight's special screening of *Caddyshack*, the greatest sports movie ever made, when you get a call from your local cop shop requesting assistance with a murder scene at the annual Santa Barbara Renaissance Faire.

---

[1] GUS: Those weren't dogs, Shawn; they were babies.[a]

  [a] Are you sure?[b]

    [b] GUS: Yes. Human babies.[c]

      [c] Weird, I totally remember them as dogs. Oh, well, I think the example still works.

[2] Not verified. I've only seen three episodes of the show.

This shouldn't come as a shock; I can think of plenty of reasons to kill somebody who dresses up like an *Excalibur* extra and runs around all day saying, "prithee, m'lord." But remember, you didn't choose to become a detective; becoming a detective chose you, so you leave Ghus to get the tickets and head for the sixteenth century (just east of the glass eye factory and right behind the landfill).

The victim is Lord Mayor Humphrey Makepeace, the Faire's revered master of ceremonies. Lord Makepeace was discovered this morning behind the jousting stables by Mathias Ludsthorp, the young squire who called the police. Lord Makepeace has clearly been stabbed to death, and only a few feet away lies a bloody rondel dagger, which forensic reports pinpoint as the murder weapon. Cops also discover—hidden in an empty keg of mead—a large gauze bandage, a half-eaten Twix, and a codpiece.

The dagger is traced to Sir Nathaniel Gavell, a knight who believed Makepeace was sleeping with his wife, Lady Gertrude. The case looks open and shut: a beloved Faire leader was murdered by his lover's jealous husband.

Yet you sense something isn't right.

First of all, Gavell was in the fencing ring all morning, surrounded by two hundred witnesses. Secondly, as you chat with the townsfolk, you learn Makepeace wasn't so revered after all. Baron Oswyn Coggshall, the Faire's organizer and producer, had recently accused him of mismanaging funds (right around now, Ghus calls to tell you he bought two aisle seats to the screening). And there was a movement among some of the Rennies to replace Makepeace as mayor with Duchess Millicent Atherton, a longtime Faire favorite.

Other Rennies claim they'd seen Makepeace in a heated argument that morning with a young man, a stranger most assumed was a Dane—short for "mundane," or Faire newbie. (See, this is what they do; they suck you in and make you start talking like them.)

The cops are at a loss and, by this time, drunk on ale, but you're not. How did Makepeace die? And who should the police send to the stocks?

Answer: If you're an astute observer, you've already honed in on the *actual* mystery here: *why would Ghus buy movie tickets on the aisle?*

Especially reserved seats. Isn't the whole point of reserving seats to pick the *best seats possible*? What's the point of watching Bill Murray blow up a golf course on a sixty-two-foot screen with thirty thousand lumens and a custom QSC Digital audio system if you're going to sit on the *aisle*? The whole idea is to be in the middle of the action and not have Rodney Dangerfield look distorted because you're watching him from an 87-degree angle! If I wanted to watch the *side* of the movie, I'd download it and sit in the corner of my living room.[1]

As for the dead guy, he was clearly murdered by Duchess Atherton, who disguised herself as a man, using a codpiece and bandage to hide her lady parts. This was the mysterious stranger Makepeace was arguing with (obvious to anyone who's seen the gender-bender classic *Just One of the Guys*). Atherton then stole Gavell's dagger, stabbed the mayor, and ditched her disguise in the mead barrel.

What still doesn't make sense is why Ghus wouldn't just buy the middle seats and wear an adult diaper. Sure, fifteen years ago there may have been a stigma, but now it's pretty commonplace.

---

[1] GHUS: Okay, look, Shawn—it's a long movie, and you know I have a small bladder. I don't like being trapped in the middle of a row if I have to go to the bathroom.[a]

[a] It's two hours![b]

[b] GHUS: That's three bathroom trips.[c]

[c] Man up, would you?[d]

[d] GHUS: Not to mention, what if there's a fire?[e]

[e] Oh yeah, good point. I guess if there's a fire...*we'll leave the theater!* Have you ever heard of people burning to death because they were in the middle of a movie theater? There are exit signs all over! Besides—it's *Caddyshack*. If a fire's gonna break out, people will be less panicked if they're laughing as they escape.[f]

[f] GHUS: I've told you, Shawn, that has not been scientifically proven. And if you don't like the way I buy movie tickets, buy them yourself next time.[g]

[g] Really? Can I? Thank you! The whole reason I asked you to do it was because I was in the midst of *solving a murder*, but next time I'll take care of the hard stuff on my own.

Chapter Four Quiz

We've done four of these now...Do I really need to explain how these work?

Good. Now do me right.

1 The chief of police does more than just make sure Officer Wigmore doesn't bring chili to the annual bake sale. A chief is also responsible for:

    A. managing the department volleyball team

    B. sewing any torn socks and uniforms

    C. Lobster Thursdays

    D. prioritizing and organizing current cases, as well as all personnel and media matters

    E. the nasty smell coming from the second-floor bathroom

2 A dead body—female, midthirties, Middle Eastern—is found in the foothills just east of town. The corpse has been stripped of its clothing and arranged neatly on a blanket, its hands folded across its chest. To the right lies a small pile of sticks and leaves, and there are several strange markings carved into a nearby tree. Using the principles of criminal profiling, the murderer was probably:

    A. raking the lawn and got interrupted

    B. not great at small talk

    C. stressed about work

    D. hungry

    E. white, male, single, lives with his mother or other immediate family members, frequently dresses in three-piece suits, has a deep-seated propensity for Russian literature

3 It's a Wednesday night, and you're on a stakeout at the Burger Palace when you get a text from your local police department: Code 479. You immediately race to your car, knowing this is the international police code for:

    A. suicide attempt

    B. don't forget to record *Storage Wars*

    C. two-for-one well drinks at McCool's

    D. Steve Perry sighting!

    E. all of the above

    F. none of the above

4 Find the slope of this line: $3x - 3y = 8$.

_____

5 The coroner's finishing the autopsy of a murder victim (female, African American, early twenties) when he announces he's found a contusion of the subcutaneous muscle layer of the right posterior shoulder, as well as a hematoma to the right temporal area of the head and an unremarkable anus. Based on this information, you deduce:

    A. it's dinnertime

    B. this is the work of a serial attacker...and there are more bodies out there

    C. *subcutaneous* is a mid-seventeenth-century word, based on the Latin word *cutis*, or "skin," and the prefix *sub-*, or "under"

    D. high school biology classes are a total waste of time

    E. *Quincy* was a much cooler show than you remember

Answers

1. C—Lobster Thursdays (technically D, but if enough people start pushing for Lobster Thursdays, I'm pretty sure she has to do it)

2. Have you learned *nothing* from me? There's no such thing as "principles of criminal profiling"—it's a fictional dark art, like voodoo or juggling! If you answered anything for this question, subtract two from your total and spend an hour playing *E.T.* on Atari.

3. E and F

4. I'm not really sure. I modified an algebra problem I found on the Internet, but I couldn't verify the answer. If you figure it out, let me know—I may be better at algebra than I thought.

5. C

If You Scored...

5 *Correct Answers:* You got *all* of these things right? You're spending way too much time with employees of your local police department; you should not—I repeat *not*—know this much about cops. It's time to pull back, reprioritize, and focus on your own work.

4 *Correct Answers:* See above paragraph.

3 *Correct Answers:* At least you got *some* wrong. Act now, and maybe there's still hope. Head to Sparky's for Dollar Beer Night and retake this quiz *as soon as you get home*. If you don't do worse, head to Cabo Corral for tequila shooters.

2 *Correct Answers:* Not bad...especially if you missed the coroner thing.

1 *Correct Answer:* You're showing promise. Treat yourself to a shake, don't go near the police station for another week, and consider this an A.

0 *Correct Answers:* You're like the child I never had, mijo. I can't tell you how proud I am...the student has surpassed the master.

Case Closed:
Accusations &
Making Arrests,
or
Spectacular Ways to
Bring Someone Down

Introduction

You know what's great about chapter %? Everything. Crap. Wait. Chapter 5, not chapter %. I think my shift key is busted. Crap. Spill *one* Jamba Juice on your keyboard, and all hell breaks loose.

In any case, dear readers, chapter % is pretty much what you've been waiting for. It's about catching bad guys, crushing skulls, and bringing down perps. In other words, chapter % is about justice. It's about knowing when to deliver the killer breakdown that lands some miscreant behind bars, as well as the delicate process of redacting that very same breakdown because you have, in fact, put the *wrong* miscreant behind bars. That's justice, too, you know. (A justice I, personally, have never had to mete out. Except once. Maybe twice, depending on who you ask.)

Just understand that cleaning up the streets isn't as glamorous as it appears. The proper channels must be coursed. T's must be dotted, and i's must be crossed. And you, Young Jeezy, will have to master the art of cooperation with your local precinct's head detective, which will be one of your greatest challenges, because every crook you bring down is one the head detective *doesn't*. Next thing you know, he's making your life a living hell, whining to your dad, making your girlfriend work late, and just acting generally athwack. It's bad on both sides.

Think of chapter % as everything you need to do to make your detective work stick, because trust me, Lady Justice is not your bitch. One miscalculation can tip that thing she's holding in her hand[1] and put some dangerous criminal back on the streets, and then it's only a matter of time before he or she finds you. Scared? Don't be. Detectives aren't scared of anything. Just read chapter %. It may save your life.

---

[1] GUS: It's called a *scale*, Shawn, and she's weighing competing claims with it. She's also got a sword in her other hand, which represents the court's coercive power. Her blindfold represents impartiality.[a]

[a] *No one* cares, Gus.

Confronting Criminals

Congratulations! I'm assuming you're reading this because your hard work has paid off, you've followed the clues, and you now find yourself face-to-face with a real-life, honest-to-goodness *criminal*. In other words, mazel tov, my friend—welcome to the show!

However, this is probably not the best time to actually be *reading* the section titled "Confronting Criminals." Ideally, you would've read this yesterday or last week, so you could've had time to prepare for this moment. But since you're here, confronting an actual criminal, let's talk about it.

Here's the thing to remember about criminals—they're more scared than you are. That's why they're pointing a gun at your face. If they weren't scared of you, they'd just leave. Or shoot you. (To be honest, I've never understood why more criminals don't just shoot the people confronting them. I actually think it reveals a severe mental deficiency in America's criminals. It's like, *Dude, you're already busted. You're about to be arrested. If you don't shoot now, you're not getting another chance.*)

Of course, I'm not a criminologist. Sure, I've stared down my share of serial killers, but I probably don't have any real business advising you on how to do it. I usually just think about baseball and wait for the cops to show up.

So rather than wasting your time with a bunch of nonsense about keeping a level head and not making any sudden moves, here's the advice of some of SBPD's finest, and Gus, on how to confront and arrest criminals.

1 **LASSIE** Proven fact: when it comes to being confronted by law enforcement, there are two types of criminals—those that want to kill you and those that want to maim you. As a detective, you're rarely going to have the luxury of distinguishing between the two; therefore, it will be imperative you speak in the only language criminals understand: brute force.

Now this is in no way meant to suggest I advocate police brutality or excessive use of force. I most certainly do not. That kind of crap is for amateurs, the very amateurs who give legit cops a bad name. As far as I'm concerned, a good collar requires a bit more nuance, because everybody knows there is no glory in delivering someone in a body bag. A real detective looks his perps in the eye so they know exactly who it is that brought them down. This is the order of things.

That said, a dead criminal is better than no criminal, so do what you have to do.

Above: See, Lassie? You can *arrest someone and look sexy at the same time.*

2 **JULIET O'HARA** I know this will sound weird, but I've never liked arresting people. Sure, the perp may be guilty, but no one's genetically programmed to become a cat burglar, or a mass murderer, or a con artist. We become these things because we make *choices*.

We choose to skip our daughter's third-grade dance recital so we can meet some "business partners" in Monte Carlo; we decide to join some "colleagues" in the Everglades instead of going on the family trip to Disney World; we opt to attend a "special conference" in Alaska rather than watch our kid graduate from college.

So when I make an arrest, it's not just the target of an investigation I see before me. It's all the people their choices have affected: the little girl who doesn't understand why her daddy didn't come home tonight, the worried wife pacing before the window, and the lonely teenager just wanting her dad to come home and notice her. When I put the handcuffs on someone, *these* are the people I'm really handcuffing, because these are the people suddenly shackled to a life they didn't choose.

That's why I hate making arrests. Putting away bad guys is easy; thinking about those they leave behind isn't.[1]

3 **GUS** When confronting criminals, I often utilize the scream-and-run method, a carefully executed psychological technique that tricks the criminals into thinking they're in control of the situation.

Basically, it works like this: the criminal pulls a gun or knife; I scream and run. This convinces them they're masterminding the situation, when in reality, *I'm* masterminding the situation, because *I'm* the one who chose to scream and run. I then lead them directly into the grasp of the police or SWAT team or whoever's waiting outside. If there's no police or SWAT team waiting outside, I lead them to my car, where I quickly lock the doors and drive to the police station, delivering the criminals right to the cops' front door. Even if the criminals don't follow me, I'm able to give the authorities such an accurate description that they can then make an official arrest.

4 **CHIEF VICK** There are three keys to a successful arrest: protocol, protocol, and protocol. While every situation is different and officers must be free to think on their feet, it's following protocol that keeps criminals from getting off on technicalities.

---

[1] Uh...wow. That was really deep, Jules. I was just hoping you could give some quick advice about how to hold a gun, read Miranda rights, etc.[a]

[a] JULIET: Oh. Sure. Hold your gun in your shooting hand, keeping your thumb straight so it doesn't get in the way of your support hand. Also, make sure there are no spaces between the fingers of your support—this makes it harder to fire repeatedly. And memorize the Miranda rights word for word; even though you can legally paraphrase, it's a lot easier to say them the same each time. How's that?[b]

[b] Perfect, thanks.

This is especially important in a department like ours, where we frequently hire outside consultants such as psychics and profilers. The more breaches of protocol, the more a department leaves itself legally vulnerable.

In the last year alone, we've had consultants recite the Miranda rights in pig latin,[1] put suspects through a "spanking tunnel,"[2] and ask a perp if he preferred his handcuffs to be French or turnback.[3]

Thus, as chief of a large metropolitan police department in an increasingly litigious society, following protocol has become more and more important. Frankly, if our freelancers didn't have such a remarkable success rate, I'd probably stop using them. In fact, if any of them are reading this, I'd like to say, from this point forward, "Whoop, there it is" is not a legal term, and being unable to do the "Lean wit It, Rock wit It" dance is not sufficient grounds to make a citizen's arrest.

How to Deliver a Killer Breakdown

I thought you might like to know that everything you think you know about breakdowns is wrong. In fact, you might not even know what a "breakdown" is. Well, I'll tell you—it's a highly inside-detectiving term for that moment when the detective catches the bad guy and explains (to the bad guy himself) how he pulled off his crimes.

As a consumer of media, I imagine at least most of the time, when you see a TV detective dress down some scofflaw, you're sitting there thinking, *Why doesn't this dude just run? Or shoot the detective? What criminal stands around while someone explains to him what he already knows? This would never happen!* It's a valid point. It's also 1,000 percent *wrong*.

In the real world, this is exactly how detectives do it. Every time. Furthermore, the breakdown is my nominee for most overlooked component of kick-ass detectivery and a crucial element to your success.

---

[1] In my defense, certain working-class neighborhoods of Switzerland *do* speak Mattenenglisch, a dialectical version of pig latin.

[2] The Mossad has used this technique for years.

[3] In Gus's defense, the perp *was* improperly wearing silk knot cuff links, so it seemed like a reasonable question.

A breakdown is like a movie pitch in reverse. It's the beat-by-beat story of a movie, only told after everyone has seen it. Throw down some dramatic pauses. Change up the tone of your voice, don't scrimp on the body language, and you'll have them hooked. This is why the criminals don't run away when I'm breaking their business. They're spellbound, their feet bound to the ground by the glue of their own vanity, because someone is taking the time to point out their brilliant plan. It's like having your own *E! True Hollywood Story.*

This means the burden is on you, Honorable Sleuth, to make sure your breakdown (sometimes called a *crime pitch*) is (A) accurate and (B) delivered in a gripping, confounding, compelling, and utterly mind-blowing manner. In this way, you keep cops *and* crooks interested, and this is how perps are ultimately delivered. Let me emphasize again the importance of keeping your facts straight. The last thing you want is to be corrected by a criminal in front of your friends and coworkers, and if you can't keep things moving, people are likely to fall asleep or shoot each other.

So let's take a look at some breakdowns and analyze what works and what doesn't.

A Good Breakdown

(The following is an exact transcript of the breakdown I delivered while capturing famed hand model Bill Lucero for the murder of rival hand model Arnold Putman.[1])

> **ME**
> Nice try, Lucero. The poison, the photos, the faint smell of body lotion... only one thing didn't fit, the lines on Putman's wrists. Were they some kind of rash or—
>
> *(Twitching and convulsing as I receive a psychic vision)*
> Wait! I'm seeing something! A man...oh, God, it's you...You have a... a saw...You're cutting something...No...no!...You're cutting—*you're cutting off Putman's hands! That's* what you wanted, isn't it, Lucero?... You didn't just want Putman dead; you wanted Putman's most valuable asset. His hands!

---

[1] By *exact transcript,* I mean, "It happened eight months ago, so it's probably not all that exact."

(Turning to Lassie)
Arrest him, Lassie. And check his computer. You'll find several Google searches for "How to Remove Someone's Hand Skin and Put It Over Your Own to Make Your Hands Look Younger and Prettier." Also, for "Naked Paula Deen."

As I'm sure you've noticed, there are several things that make this breakdown brilliant.

1. It's short.
2. It's directed toward the criminal element, Lucero, marginalizing the cops.
3. It recaps the major clues of the case without spending a lot of time explaining them.
4. It highlights the fact that I saw the most important clue of all *and the cops didn't.*
5. It has a psychic vision, which makes any breakdown extra cool. (You may not have the advantage of receiving messages from another dimension, but don't let that stop you. After all, it didn't take psychic powers for me to see the marks on Putman's wrists; it just took psychic powers for me to know how they got there. So if you don't have psychic powers— well, truthfully, your job's going to be a lot harder. Blame your parents.)
6. Even after the psychic vision has literally *shown* me the answer, I connect all the dots for anyone slow on the uptake.
7. I always try to give the cops a solid piece of evidence, like Lucero's computer, to help close the case. (Most cops don't believe in psychic visions, which is ridiculous. Did Colm Feore need "evidence" that Riddick was going to destroy the Necromongers? No, someone had a vision, so he went out and slaughtered everyone—a perfectly reasonable response if someone tells you you're going to get your ass kicked. But today's cops want evidence. So I give it to them. It just makes me look smarter in the end.)

A Bad Breakdown

Perhaps most notable in the canon of legendarily sucky breakdowns is this little scatwad from Brian De Palma's classic *The Untouchables*. The fact that Movie Eliot Ness still managed to take down Movie Al Capone after this pathetic display baffles me. And I'm not easily baffled.

(NOTE: This is from the original script, not the version that was ultimately shot.)

ELIOT NESS
It's the end of the line for you, Al Capone. We've been chasing you all over Chicago, which, frankly, isn't that hard because this place has amazing public transportation...but we finally got you. And we know you did all that bad stuff, like murdering people and making moonshine and burning down the retired clown home on Belmont. And now you're gonna pay. Not for those particular crimes, because we couldn't find any actual evidence linking them to you, but for something just as bad: tax evasion! That's right...We know you shifted all those numbers around. Very clever...the way you carried the two and divided your assets by the square root of seven, then folded the interest from your kid's 529 into a thirty-year fixed rate on your second home. I couldn't follow it all myself...but we have experts who said it was very impressive. I mean, totally illegal, but still impressive. So yeah, you're under arrest.

There are two things wrong with this breakdown.

1. It's long.
2. It blows chunks.

Here are two more, just for good measure.

Another Good Breakdown

Delivered last month to world-famous zoologist Stanley Porter. Guilty.

ME
It's over, Porter. We traced the flea collar to Baxter Pets, the only store in town that carries cockroaches. Weird choice for a pet store, right? Unless, of course, that store carries animals that *eat cockroaches*, like ferrets. But ferrets are illegal in California, so why would a store carry them?...Unless it was dealing in illegal pets...like ferrets and, say, tigers. *Tigers whose fur matched the fibers found on your jacket.* That's right, Porter—boom-shaka-laka—you're busted!

If you're not weeping just reading that, it's a cold heart beating within your chest.

Another Bad Breakdown

From the breakdown I used while busting elusive drug kingpin Lincoln "the Dice" Webster.

> **ME**
> What do you think you're doing? Twisted Sister? What kind of a man desecrates a defenseless textbook? I've got a good mind to slap your fat face! You are destroying your life with that—that—that garbage! All right, Mr. Sister, I want you to tell me...No, better yet, stand up and tell the class, *"What do you want to do with your life?"*

I suppose you might be wondering why this is in the bad breakdown category. And in fact, you're not totally mistaken. It's actually pretty good. Direct. Strongly worded with a slight mocking tone that puts the criminal on the defensive. However, this breakdown only works if the criminal's holding a textbook, so its functionality is extremely limited. Also, it has nothing to do with the crime.

Hopefully, this little primer has edified you in some way, or at least reminded you how awesome Twisted Sister's "We're Not Gonna Take It" video is.[1]

---

[1] BUZZ McNAB: Great piece, Shawn! Seriously, loved it. Just one thing, and I don't mean to correct you or nitpick in your own book, but since you asked me to edit this segment, I figure it's okay. That's actually the opening from "I Wanna Rock," not "We're Not Gonna Take It." It's an easy mistake, since Mark Metcalf plays the teacher in one and the father in the other, but the opening of "We're Not Gonna Take It" goes like this: "All right, mister, what do you think you're doing? You call this a room? This is a pigsty! I want you to straighten up this area now—you are a disgusting slob! Stand up straight, tuck in that shirt, adjust that belt buckle, tie those shoes!" (Spotting a Twisted Sister poster) "Twisted Sister? What is *that*? Wipe that smile off your face. Do you understand? What is that, a Twisted Sister pin—on your uniform? What kind of a man are you?! You're worthless and weak! You do nothing; you are nothing; you sit in here all day and play that sick, repulsive, electric twanger! I carried an M16 and you—you carry that—that—that guitar! Who are you? Where do you come from? Are you listening to me? What do you wanna do with your life?"

Keep in mind, delivering a killer breakdown, like painting the Sistine Chapel or sculpting a woman with no arms, is an art, and art takes time to perfect. You probably won't get it right the first time, and the person against whom you've leveled charges might go free. I know, some of the subjects of my early failed breakdowns are still at large. But Malcolm Gladwell says it takes ten thousand hours to become an expert and so I take solace. So should you. If after ten thousand hours of thinking about breakdowns, you're still not nailing it, you're probably just a crappy detective and should go back to trimming trees or working at the Gap.

How to Know If a Suspect Is Guilty

by Carlton Lassiter

I believe in our court system, but sometimes the court system fails: O.J. Simpson, the Scopes trial, Watergate. We all know the Bill of Rights says you can't try someone twice for the same crime, but that doesn't mean they didn't do it. And a good cop always knows. You want to know if the perp you just interrogated or arrested is guilty? Here are some telltale signs they did it:

- They swear they didn't do it.
- They ask for a lawyer.
- They cry.
- They tell you they "couldn't have done it" and explain why.
- They plead the Fifth, the only stupid amendment.
- They scream, "I know my rights!"
- They ask for their one phone call.

Pep Up Your Breakdown: Use a Soundtrack!

Simple fact: music makes everything better. Ever watch *The Shawshank Redemption* without the soundtrack? It's like listening to Chris Matthews talk with his mouth full, which is pretty much like listening to Chris Matthews talk *without* his mouth full. On the other hand, put on *Fried Green Tomatoes*, turn off the sound, and crank *Stone Cold Rhymin'* by Young M.C., you suddenly have a decent movie.

In other words, music makes or breaks just about anything. So if you can take a boom box or stereo to your breakdowns, it almost always pays off. (Reminder: you'll also need a sidekick or assistant to press play and possibly to switch songs at the appropriate time.)

The key, of course, is to match the music to the type of criminal you're busting. You obviously wouldn't play Roxette while taking down a jewel thief, just as you wouldn't use *Standing Hampton* to bust someone for insider trading. Personally, I recommend:

- Pat Benatar—kidnappers, graffiti artists, Ponzi schemers
- The Ramones—mass murderers, shoplifters, city councilmen
- Portishead—pickpockets, animal pornographers
- Dead Milkmen—people who park in handicap spots without a placard
- The The—serial killers, counterfeiters, anyone calling themselves a "real-life superhero"
- Elvis Costello (circa 1978)—rapists, smugglers, the guy who made *Tree of Life*
- The Dixie Chicks—cannibals, tax evaders
- The Beach Boys (post–Brian Wilson)—meth cooks, all the parents from *Toddlers & Tiaras* or *Dance Moms*

(SPECIAL NOTE: I've also heard if you start Dark Side of the Moon *as you begin your breakdown, the cops come in just as Roger Waters sings, "The lunatic is in my head." I don't know how it works, but it supposedly does it every time.)*

What *Should* Be in the Miranda Rights

Let me explain why the Miranda rights came into being.

I never met this Miranda chick, but I'm guessing she's one of those skinny girls who just babbles on about her cats and how some guy won't text her back and why she loves *Dancing with the Stars*, and some cop finally just chucked her in the back of a squad car to shut her up. But then her parents, who probably come from money and hang out at places like the Harrington Club, sued the police, and the judge decided you can't arrest someone for being an irritating talker without first informing them that they have the "right to remain silent."

So fine, whatever...it's not a law that'll ever apply to me, but I get it.

Here's the bigger issue. Miranda rights are designed to protect people getting arrested, but by focusing on this "right to remain silent" issue, we're forgetting even more important rights. Not that I'm advocating for arrested people, but if we're gonna give them rights, why not make sure they have some rights that are actually useful?

For instance, if you're arrested, you should have the right...

■ To a public defender who didn't go to the University of Phoenix. (To be fair, no halfway decent lawyer *wants* to be a public defender—but that's beside the point; you should have the right to be represented by someone who knows what an actual "tort" is. Or an actual "school.")

■ To run home and set your TiVo, or at least be able to watch *Bad Girls Club* in the joint. (They can't legally make you miss your stories.)

■ To wear something more slimming than horizontal black-and-white stripes or a shapeless orange jumpsuit. (I've been lobbying for years to let prisoners wear Hare Krishna robes. They're the same color as jumpsuits, but breathe so much easier.)

■ To nutritious, balanced meals as long as you're in the clink. Remind the cops of *Gonzales vs. Connecticut*, the groundbreaking 1997 decision that ruled all meals served in jail must include at least one Heartpounder burger from the Larder, two bowls of Banana Nut Crunch, a medium Cap'n Torry's Swirly Fries, a side of zing-zing sauce, three Taco Bell gorditas, and a bottle of Gatorade Rain Lime.

■ To walk around jail in a Hannibal Lecter mask if it keeps you from being somebody's bitch. (Personally, I think walking around *town* in a Hannibal Lecter mask would send a nice signal, but it's especially helpful in jail.)

■ *NOT* to remain silent. In other words, say stuff and let the cops *try* to use it against you. Such as, "Anyone up for a head massage? I have fingers like silk." Or, "Hey, settle a bet for me. Who do you think is hotter—Kiefer Sutherland or Gordon Ramsay?" Or, "Shawty wanna thug, bottles in the club, shawty wanna hump, and oh, I like to touch ya lovely lady lumps."

A Word about Equal Treatment under the Law: A Treatise

by Carlton Lassiter

I would like to clarify some facts regarding a confrontation you may have heard about last Friday night at the Pine Ridge Ranch & Lodge.

I was with my lovely wife, Marlowe Viccellio, attending her family reunion in the Sequoia Room. I had gone to the bar to get a lemon drop martini when I noticed the perp arguing with my wife's sister, Gwen, in the corner. Things looked heated, but I refrained from intervening until the perp grabbed Gwen's arm, yanking her toward the floor. I then approached and asked if everything was okay.

Above: The Pine Ridge Ranch & Lodge, home of America's least qualified security team

I suggested the perp get some air, but he demanded I leave them alone.

I did *not*, contrary to rumors, pull my gun until *after* the perp struck me in the face, at which point I drew my weapon, ordered him to the floor, and secured him in a figure-four armlock.

What happened next is—in my opinion—illustrative of how the public's endemic disrespect for law enforcement hampers police officers and puts innocent citizens in jeopardy.

Instead of apprehending the *perp*, security arrived and escorted *me* off the property. No arrests were made, so Gwen couldn't press charges, but she made it clear she wouldn't have anyway, which sheds light on the unfortunate reality that many people today are simply too scared to take a stand against criminal behavior. Maybe that's why we have the highest crime rate in the world (according to certain websites that justify this argument).

Incidentally, there is one thing you may have heard that is *not* a rumor. Yes, the perp was my wife's four-year-old nephew, Lyle, although I don't really understand how that makes any difference. Sure, maybe I did pull a gun on a four-year-old, but this is a distraction to the real tragedy of the iniquity of treatment under the law. An offender is an offender, whether he's a thrice-imprisoned, hardened criminal or just out of diapers. Just like you can't *kind of* break the law, you also can't cut lawbreakers any slack. I don't care if they still suck their thumb.

It's worthy to note here that the safety was never off on my weapon.

And while my lovely, beautiful lady love Marlowe was more than a little ticked off, let's just remember that this was an act of violence, which is in direct violation of my own zero-tolerance policy against such acts, for which I've been sworn to uphold and for which I've been twice decorated.

In other words, the kid needed a lesson. If people don't learn to respect the law as children, they're sure as hell going to learn sometime, and that sometime will probably be after they've committed their first felony. This much I know is true. Mark my words, as I write this, there's a kid out there screaming at his mom in some convenience store. Fast-forward six years, and you'll find that same kid holding up that convenience store, probably wearing a skin coat he made from some prostitute two hours before. I've seen it a million times. (Okay, twice.)

This is my point: spare the rod, spoil the child. And by *spoil*, I mean, "turn him into a bloodthirsty psychopath."

So do I regret my use of force against the perp? *Absolutely not.* I hope both he and his mother learned a valuable lesson.

I also think my amazing, lovely, and deeply understanding wife, Marlowe Viccellio, should see this is evidence of my paternal instincts and that sending her two dozen long-stem roses should allow me back in the house.

A Note from Henry Spencer

I can't believe I'm saying this, but I agree, in part, with Detective Lassiter. Today's children have been coddled, which is why they grow up to be undisciplined adults that can't hold a normal job or return their father's electric screwdriver when they borrow it.

A Word from Mr. Yang

(NOTE FROM SHAWN: First of all, let it be known that I did not invite raging serial killer/best-selling author Mr. Yang to submit an entry for this book. But you know how the literary world is—writers talk. And Yang apparently heard from Mitch Albom who heard from Toni Morrison who heard from Jonathan Franzen that I was working on "something big," so Yang wrote me asking if she could participate. I said no (A) because she's a serial killer and (B) because I wasn't that impressed with her first book, From Serial Dater to Serial Killer: How Murder Kept Me Skinny, *although I hear her second,* Carving and Craving: A Dieter's Guide to the Art of Dismemberment, *is much better. So after much consideration and several annoying letters from Yang, my editor and I acquiesced. We figure she's behind bars, heavily medicated, and hasn't killed anyone in months. Plus, her potatoes are pretty damn good.)*

Mr. Yang's Twice-Baked Potato Recipe, by Mr. Yang

1 large russet potato
Olive oil
1 strip bacon
1/8 cup sour cream
1/8 cup milk
1/2 tablespoon butter
1/4 tablespoon cream
Chopped scallions
Nutmeg
Salt
Pepper
1/4 cup cheddar cheese, grated

1. Preheat the oven to 400° F.
2. Wash the potato so it's free of dirt and filth, then poke it over and over and over and over and over with a fork. (This is so steam can escape. Otherwise, it just builds and builds until the potato can't take it anymore, exploding in a fury of steam and hate and anger.)
3. Now, rub some olive oil into the potato, letting your hands slide over its skin like it's the creamy flesh of a young brown-haired psychic with the sexiest hint of facial stubble. Massage the oil into each bump and crevice. Caress every pore. Smell every curve. Then place the potato in the oven and bake for 1 hour and 15 minutes.
4. As the potato is cooking, fry the bacon and set aside.
5. When the potato is done, hold it in an oven mitt as you use a knife to slice slowly, gently, through its moist, tender meat. You shouldn't have to push too hard; the potato will be soft and giving, welcoming your blade inside it. Cut the potato the long way to make a coffin shape, removing and setting aside an oval-shaped lid.
6. Next, scoop out the potato. You can use a spoon…or, if you prefer, your hands. There's something exhilarating, even sensual, about having your hands inside another living thing, even if that living thing is no longer living.

7. Take the scooped-out potato remains and place them in a bowl with the sour cream, milk, butter, and cream. Use a potato masher to mash the ingredients together until they are one. Mash mash mash. Mash mash mash mash mash mash mash. Let the ingredients intermingle into a single, gooey blend. Mash mash mash mash mash mash mash mash mash. (But not too much, or the mixture will turn pasty.)

8. Crumble up most of the bacon and mix it, along with some of the scallions, into the potato mixture. Add nutmeg, salt, and pepper to taste; then spoon the potato mixture back into the potato coffin. (This is my favorite part. I like imagining what it feels like to be the potato—your insides removed, transformed into something else, unrecognizable, then placed back into your body. It gets me hungry just thinking about it.) Sprinkle the cheese, as well as the remaining bacon and scallions, on top of the potato; then place it on a baking sheet.

9. Slather the sliced-off potato top with olive oil, stroking tenderly until the entire thing is covered. Place it on the baking sheet next to the potato, two parts of a single, beautiful whole.

10. Place the cookie sheet into the oven, letting the potato and its top bake together for 15–20 minutes. Serve immediately.

Serves: 1

How I Would've Solved Famous Cold Cases

It's no secret there are a million unsolved mysteries floating around out there. Maybe two million. Jack the Ripper, JonBenét Ramsey, even Nicole Brown Simpson. Yet what's even more mind-boggling is how many *solvable* unsolved mysteries are floating around out there.

Now, look, I get it. Cops are overworked, underpaid, and half their day is taken up with ridiculous paperwork like warrants and booking forms. But come on, most crimes are solvable with some basic common sense. (Granted, I say that as someone whose common sense includes supernatural messages from beyond, but still...)

If I had time, I'd dedicate myself to closing all the cold cases out there (even if only to meet Kathryn Morris, who's way sexier than Marg Helgenberger any day of the week), but I don't have time, and the *polizei* are never going to learn anything if I keep doing everything for them.

So I won't solve the stuff for you, cops, but I'll point you in the right direction on four cases you should be able to solve in your sleep (which takes up 90 percent of your workday anyway).

■ **JIMMY HOFFA** Why not just call Hoffa's cell phone and listen for the ring? If that doesn't work, try to convince everyone involved that he doesn't exist (like Van Halen did when, after replacing Michael Anthony with Wolfgang, they took down all Mikey's pictures off their website, including old album cover photos. Come on, guys—seriously? He was in the band for *thirty-five years*! You don't have to like him anymore, but do you really think you're fooling anyone?).

■ **D. B. COOPER** Get in a plane. Fly the same route as D. B. Cooper. Jump out where he jumped out. See where he landed. I don't understand why no one has done this already. (Actually, I do understand, because every time you look at a ticket on Orbitz, the price goes up. It's like they're watching you. So I'm sure a million cops have *wanted* to do this, but when they go to buy a ticket, it's no longer cost-effective.)

■ **THE LINDBERGH BABY** I'd wait a few years before trying to crack this. A baby is small, and if you wait till he's seven or eight, he'll be a lot bigger and easier to find.[1]

---

[1] GUS: They already found the Lindbergh baby, Shawn.[a]

  [a] Really? You'd think newspapers would be all over that.[b]

    [b] GUS: It was over eighty years ago.[c]

      [c] Huh. I've never seen a single interview with him.[d]

        [d] GUS: He was dead.[e]

          [e] That sucks. Still, that seems like something they should be reporting on.

■ **THE ZODIAC KILLER** Killing four people is bad, but if you've ever read the Zodiac's letters, you know that the real butchering was to the English language.

I'm guessing English was not this guy's first language, or if it was, the San Francisco school system has some explaining to do. However, that's also the key to solving this case. (A) The guy calls himself the Zodiac, and (B) he has terrible English, suggesting he's either not from this country or a substitute ESL teacher. So what other culture speaks broken English and has their own zodiac...and coincidentally (or not) has a large San Francisco population?

That's right, the Chinese.

In other words, this guy's not just the Zodiac Killer, he's the *Chinese* Zodiac Killer.[1] So you wanna find the Zodiac Killer? Start looking for Chinese guys who don't speak great English. (Another clue in support of this is most of the Zodiac's victims were shot, which makes sense, since most Chinese dudes are small and probably couldn't manhandle their victims. In fact, one of the only people the Zodiac ever stabbed...*survived*.)[2]

---

[1] Keep in mind, no one thinks of themselves in terms of their ethnicity. To a Chinese guy, the Chinese zodiac is just the zodiac, not the Chinese zodiac, so he'd have no reason to say, "I'm the *Chinese* Zodiac Killer." Just like Gus thinks of himself as Gus, not Black Gus.[a]

[a] GUS: Actually, Shawn, Black Gus is Tap Man's evil alter ego who comes forth whenever someone plays *Happy Feet*, the worst animated *and* worst tap film of all time. He can only be destroyed by the power of Gregory Hines's voice.

[2] GUS: Shawn, you realize how racist this is, right? You're basically suggesting that a deranged serial killer was Chinese simply because he (a) spoke broken English (which does not mean he's Chinese) and (b) didn't stab many people, so he must be too small (again, no correlation).[a]

[a] Oh, sure, when *I* say it, it's "racist." When Declan Rand says it, it's "brilliant profiling." I wouldn't expect you to understand, Black Gus.

Taken from *The Santa Barbara Mirror* (March 14, 2008)

FILM REVIEW:

American Cop: A Study in Cinematic and Crime-Solving Brilliance

by Kelly Drinan, film critic ★★★★☆

First-time director Lauren Lassiter's award-winning documentary, *American Cop*, is not only an astounding piece of filmmaking, it takes audiences deep into the clockworks of an actual police investigation.

The film follows Carlton Lassiter, the director's older brother and head detective for the Santa Barbara Police Department, as he attempts to crack the case of a framed polar bear, all the while giving his sister and her film crew unprecedented access to the detective's process.

Above: American Cop, *Golden Buffalo winner.*

Particularly revealing is Detective Lassiter's reliance on SBPD's resident psychic, Shawn Spencer, a private detective with his own firm, Psych. Detective Lassiter may be the one who puts the pieces of the case together, but it's the rascally Spencer who actually provides the pieces themselves. In fact, the real thrill of the movie isn't watching Lassiter's detective prowess, it's watching Spencer bound effortlessly from psychic vision to psychic vision. Together, these two make a captivating team: Lassiter as the face of the operation, Spencer as the brains behind it.

It's easy to see why *American Cop* has already won Best Documentary at the Topeka Film Festival, Top Doc at the Red Oaks Movie Marathon, and the Golden Buffalo at Boise's Hollywood Ho-Down. But in this reviewer's opinion, this film should be on the Must Watch list of every film class and police department in America.

DIRECTOR. . . . . Lauren Lassiter
WRITER . . . . Lauren Lassiter
PRODUCER . . . . Lauren Lassiter
EXECUTIVE PRODUCER . . . . Lauren Lassiter
ASSOCIATE PRODUCER . . . . Lauren Lassiter
DIRECTOR OF PHOTOGRAPHY . . . . Lauren Lassiter
EDITOR. . . . . Lauren Lassiter
MUSIC . . . . Lauren Lassiter

PG-13 rating, 116 minutes

Letter to the Editor (March 15, 2008)

Dear editor,

As a nearly twenty-year veteran of the SBPD, I would like to comment on the steaming pile of crap your "film critic," Kelly Drinan, published last Tuesday.

First of all, I have never in my life relied on a "psychic," just as I have never relied on Santa Claus or the Tooth Fairy…*mainly because none of them exist.*

Secondly, there is no "teamwork" or "brotherhood" between Shawn Spencer and myself. Yes, he has contributed to cases, but only because, as a civilian, he's allowed to circumvent laws and act like a complete jackass in ways actual detectives are not. Also, my line, "He's the kind of man I'd like to be someday," was taken completely out of context. I was referring to Clint Eastwood, not Shawn Spencer, who's not even someone I would classify as a man.

If this is the type of criticism that passes as a "film review" at *The Santa Barbara Mirror*, I strongly suggest rethinking your definitions of the words *film* and *review*.

Please cancel my subscription immediately.

Carlton Lassiter

Head Detective

Santa Barbara Police Department

Letter to the Editor (March 16, 2008)

Dear editor,

While I agree Lauren Lassiter's *American Cop* bravely exposes the truth behind the SBPD's unorthodox crime-solving techniques, it also commits one fatal flaw: it completely neglects psychic Shawn Spencer's brilliant partner. Sure, psychic visions are cool, but does Spencer have the scientific knowledge to solve cases involving rare chemical compounds like isopropylbenzene or bongkrek acid? Does he have evolutionarily advanced olfaction capable of detecting rhubarb pie from over forty-three yards away? He probably doesn't even balance his own checkbook.

I'm not writing to criticize Ms. Drinan's review. I'm just saying I'd rather watch a movie about the hardworking dude who does the heavy lifting than a psychic who can't even replace the toilet paper when he uses the last roll.

Sincerely,

Britton Gaster

Concerned Citizen

Letter to the Editor (March 17, 2008)

Dear editor,

I would like to thank Kelly Drinan for her excellent review of Lauren Lassiter's groundbreaking new movie, *American Cop*. Drinan's observations were dead-on, even if she didn't bother to mention the cloying performance of former detective Henry Spencer.

I would also like to respond to yesterday's Letter to the Editor from Britton Gaster: Britton, you're right.

I *should* give some recognition to my partner, which is why I would like to take this moment to thank my luminous and ever-present partner, Hercules Pendergast.

Also, please cancel my subscription. I love your paper, but I can get it free online.

Sincerely,
Shawn Spencer
Private Detective *and* Private Dancer

Casting Call

Crime solving is one of the sexiest, most glamorous professions in the world, just after supermodeling and designing roller coasters. This is why there's such a long list of real-life detectives who have had their lives turned into movies: Donnie Brasco; Father Richard Moore, portrayed by Tom Wilkinson in *The Exorcism of Emily Rose*; 50 Cent, played by 50 Cent in *Get Rich or Die Tryin'*.

But what do they all have in common?...*Their movie selves were all totally miscast*.

So my advice, if you're going to take this detective thing seriously, start thinking *now* about who will play you and your associates in the biopic about your life. Imagine how you'll feel, after a lifetime of community service and death defiance, when Deadline.com reports you'll be played by the horse from *War Horse* in an all-equine interpretation of your life story. Or worse yet, one of those kids from *Glee*. Or Cate Blanchett dressed as the ghost of Heath Ledger dressed as Bob Dylan. There are ten thousand ways your movie can go off the rails. I'm not going to let it happen to me.

Here is a casting list for my biopic, *The Bourne Retaliation: The Shawn Spencer Story* (written by either Joe Eszterhas in the '90s, Diablo Cody [with a polish by Sylvester Stallone], or the late Billy Wilder).

Shawn Spencer (me)

← CHRISTIAN BALE
I'll say this and I'll say this once: f'ing hot.

DON CHEADLE →
Who *wouldn't* want to be played by Don Cheadle?

SHAWN SPENCER
I'm probably most qualified, although I'll be a bit nervous if I have to audition behind Cheadle.

Burton Guster

MICHAEL WINSLOW
The coolest black guy around…and last time I checked, he wasn't busy with any more Police Academy movies.

GWYNETH PALTROW IN *IRON MAN*
They both share that same intellectual sexiness.

Juliet O'Hara

JULIET O'HARA →
Because no professional actress is beautiful enough to capture her radiance…or talented enough to capture her complexities.[1]

Carlton Lassiter

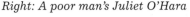

← ROWAN ATKINSON
For the first three months I knew him, I thought Lassie *was* Rowan Atkinson.

Chief

HAILEE STEINFELD FROM *TRUE GRIT* →
Yes, she's only three years old, but this girl could totally run a police department.

Dad (Henry Spencer)

CRAIG T. NELSON
Balding, full of gravitas, and recognizable to millions of fans of his beloved '80s TV show… it just seems like the right fit.

BILLY IDOL
How cool would it be to have Billy Idol as your *dad*?

---

[1] *Bam!* That, Gus, is how you compliment a woman, not by staring at her creepily and asking if she wants to see your thimble collection.[a]

[a] JULIET: Nice try, Shawn. Why didn't you just put Meryl Streep like I asked you to?

Right: A poor man's Juliet O'Hara

Blowing Off Steam: Wicking Off
by Santa Barbara SWAT
Commander Cameron Duntz

For our final installment of "Blowing Off Steam," a three-part investigative report on the art and science of relaxation, I'm proud to introduce one of Santa Barbara's most esteemed crime fighters, Lead Hostage Negotiator Commander Cameron Duntz.[*]

[*] DUNTZ: Actually, Spencer, it's Luntz. With an L.[a]

[a] OMG, I am so sorry. Thank you for catching that, Commander Spuntz. This is why I use outside editors.

There are few jobs as stressful as Hostage Negotiator. Brain surgeon is pretty stressful. And fighter pilot. But beyond that, few jobs create more anxiety than Hostage Negotiator. I'm not saying your job, whatever it is—subway operator, welder, carpet installer—isn't stressful; I'm just saying that as a man who regularly talks homicidal maniacs out of blowing people up, I've had my share of pressure.

The trick, of course, is to keep a cool head and a calm demeanor. One false move, one overzealous step, and you're picking cranial matter out of your Kevlar. Which I've done before.

So as a leading expert in the world's third most stressful job, I need to be as vigilant *off* the field as I am *on* the field. As my father used to say, and his father before him, "If you can't *relax*, you can't *kick* ass."

Which is why, when it comes to heavy-duty relaxation, I turn to candlewicking.

Now, I know what you're thinking: candlewicking isn't "legitimate" embroidery. It's too rustic, too plebeian; it lacks the intricate precision of appliqué or needlepoint. But as an eleven-year member of the National Candlewicking Alliance, I can assure you, you're wrong. *Dead wrong.*

Below are three of my favorite candlewicking patterns. Give them a try… I suspect you'll rethink your preconceived notions about America's greatest nineteenth-century handicraft.

Colonial Knot Pattern No. 312

A wonderful traditional colonial knot pattern I designed shortly after the 2011 Fillmore Library Massacre. I suggest using a No. 1 milliner's needle. Also, be sure to wash your hands of any GSR (Gun Shot Residue) before you begin work, as even tiny lead and barium particles can stain and weaken the cotton fibers of your embroidery floss.

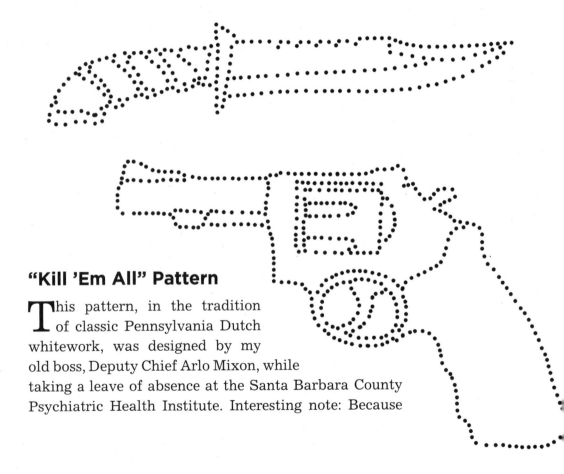

"Kill 'Em All" Pattern

This pattern, in the tradition of classic Pennsylvania Dutch whitework, was designed by my old boss, Deputy Chief Arlo Mixon, while taking a leave of absence at the Santa Barbara County Psychiatric Health Institute. Interesting note: Because

Mixon wasn't allowed access to sharp objects or thread while inside, he learned to candlewick using only fingernail clippings and human hair. Try it! I've used this exact method several times, including on the slipcovers I gave as department Christmas presents last year.

"Tranquil Stream" Pattern

This pattern is obviously *not* a tranquil stream, but it's so calming it *reminds* me of a tranquil stream, kind of like target practice and DFM (Deadly Force Maneuvers) training. I especially like doing the French knots along the nozzle. Be sure to use a thicker linen with this pattern so it's easy to wash out blood or other organic fluids. ALSO, HIGHLY RECOMMENDED: For maximum relaxation, I suggest working on this pattern with a glass of 1982 Château Le Pin and the soundtrack to *Full Metal Jacket*.

CASE STUDY #4

No Room at the Inn

You're sitting at home on a crisp Sunday afternoon, planning a San Diego road trip with your girlfriend, Ariannah (name changed), to see Huey Lewis and the News. You're about to book a room online at the Cozy Nook Inn, Ariannah's favorite bed-and-breakfast, when the phone rings.

It's your dad. He wants to borrow your power drill. You explain you don't own a power drill, that's why you always use his, and he says, "Yeah, and you still have it. That's why I need it. Bring it over." You tell him you can't bring it over, you're waiting for a *Three's Company* marathon to start, but he's welcome to come over and get it. He hangs up, which you find unnecessarily rude.

You turn back to Ariannah, who now says, "I don't know, maybe we shouldn't stay overnight."

To which you say, "Fine with me, but I thought you wanted to?"

"I did," she says, "it's just so expensive. Maybe we should drive back after the concert."

"Okay," you say and start to turn off the computer.

"I mean, do *you* want to stay overnight?" she asks.

"I'm fine either way."

She stares. "Well, will you be mad if we don't stay over?"

"No, not at all."

"I mean, it'd be fun, right? Staying in a hotel together?"

"Totally."

"I just wonder if we should save our money, that's all. Be smart."

"Well, we don't have to stay in the most expensive place."

"So now you *do* want to stay overnight?"

"I'm just saying—we *can*. We don't have to. Whatever you want."

"Well, are you going to be mad if we spend the night? You don't seem like you want to."

"I'm fine either way. You just need to tell me what you want. Do you want me to book a room? I'm happy to book a room."

"I don't know—that's what I'm trying to talk about. Don't get mad at me."

"I'm not mad. I'm just waiting for an answer."

"Well, you won't tell me what you want to do!"

"I've told you a million times! It'd be fun to stay over, but I'm fine driving home. Whatever you want!"

"Well, I can't think when you're yelling at me!"

"Who's yelling?"

Her bottom lip opens and her eyes go wide. You've seen this look before, and it's never good.

"I can't...I can't talk about this anymore," she says. "If you don't want to go away with me, just say so!"

She storms out, the bathroom door slamming behind her.

Now, obviously, a detective of lesser intuition would be stymied by this bizarre behavior. But not you, you're a master code breaker of human behavior. So tell me, grasshopper, what the hell happened here?

Answer: Because this is your final case study and a true test of your detective powers, I've chosen not to publish the answer here. Instead, you can e-mail your answers—preferably before next Saturday—to pineapplelover@prodigy.com. Also, if you have any recommendations for a romantic but not overly expensive San Diego hotel, that'd be great.

Chapter % Quiz

For the record, I had written a long, eloquent intro to this quiz, talking about how this was the last section, you'd reached the end of the road, I was proud you'd made it this far.

And then someone who shall remain nameless, but has a medium build, dark-complected skin, and a preternaturally shiny head, spilled a Butterfinger milk shake across my keyboard...only a few hours after I'd already spilled a Jamba Juice across the damn thing.[1]

So not only did I have to shut everything down without saving, I had to drive across town, convince the manager of the computer store to let me in before it closed, and beg them to clean everything out as soon as possible.

By the time I got back, the frozen pizza I'd taken out of the freezer was thawed, I'd missed the first half of *Bloodsport* on Reelz, and—quite frankly—I was in no mood to rewrite the whole freaking intro.

Besides, when you write something that brilliant, you can't just conjure it up again. It happens once; it's gone—lightning in a bottle.

So here's your quiz. It's the last one. Blah blah blah.

1 You are cornered by a knife-wielding serial killer intent on cutting your throat. What is the secret password/phrase that tells all serial killers to stand down?

       A. "Do you really want this on your permanent record?"

       B. "Let's dance, sucker."

       C. "Spumoni."

       D. "You can't handle the truth!"

---

[1] GUS: First of all, Shawn, it wasn't my milk shake.[a] Second of all, I'm not the one who set the milk shake on the arm of the chair. Why would you do that? It has no stability, and you knew you were going to sit there with your computer.

   [a] Not sure why/how this is relevant. It doesn't matter whose milk shake it is. What matters is who spilled it.

E. "For the love of God, don't do this...I'll never tell, I swear...I have a family...Tell me what you want; I'll do anything... please...ohGodohGodohGodohGod..."

2 Which of the following is not legally allowed when making a citizen's arrest?

    A. taking the perp's last Cheez-It

    B. asking them to listen to your beat poetry version of "Darling Nikki"

    C. Tasering their groin, yelling, "This one's for Biggie!"

    D. dating their girlfriend immediately after the arrest

    E. making him play Jacqueline Bisset in your shot-for-shot remake of *Wild Orchid*

3 Use the four principles of Taoism (Tao, De, Wu Wei, and Pei) to illustrate how *Street Fighter X Tekken* is an eschatological commentary on post-Soviet Chechnya.

4 Being a successful detective means having knowledge of past crimes and cases. Below are some people famous for committing crimes—as well as some who didn't commit crimes at all. Match each name with the action or crime that made that person famous.

    A. Jamie   a. Never backed down

    B. Janie   b. Has got a gun

    C. Jayne   c. Is a total slut, banging some guy in a Ford Cortina

    D. Janie Jones

    E. Gina   d. Is crying

                  e. It's a shame what happened to her.

5 Mr. Stubbins, my old seventh-grade science teacher, kept a two-headed animal in a jar in his classroom. That animal was:

    A. a pig

    B. the same animal Mrs. Schweiger saw rooting through her garden at night

    C. nicknamed "Commodore Stubbles"

    D. eaten by Travis Oaxaca on a dare

    E. the second runner-up in the 1993 Santa Barbara Beauty Pageant

Answers

1. Honestly, if you're being cornered by a knife-wielding serial killer, say whatever you can to get out of there. Answer A is a good choice, with E as a runner-up. If those don't work, you're on your own.

2. C, obviously. It's illegal to Taser someone's genitals in forty-nine states. Having said that, the fact that you're making a shot-for-shot remake of *Wild Orchid* is way more disturbing.

3. Because this one's not multiple-choice, I won't actually count it, but the key is to examine the characters of Ryu and Balrog.

4. A—d
   B—b
   C—e (although she now has a ballad, so it's not *that* much of a shame)
   D—c
   E—a

5. A and C—it was a pig *and* nicknamed "Commodore Stubbles."

Scoring

I'll be honest...I feel a lot better about the whole milk shake incident now that I've calmed down and had something to eat. (I found some leftover saag paneer in the fridge.) I can even see how leaving the milk shake on the arm of the chair wasn't the best idea, although it doesn't take a ton of awareness to watch where you're putting your elbow. I'm also at the very end of *Bloodsport*, right at the part where Chong Li throws the quicklime. So go ahead and score yourself however you think is appropriate; you've read the whole book now—it's not like I know that much more than you.

Epilogue

Well, *mon canard*, congratulations—you've made it. You are now officially a detective. Although to be fair, I told you that in the first chapter. But now you're something infinitely more powerful: *a detective who's read this book*. And that's a claim most other assassintruders can't make.

Anyway, there aren't words to tell you how proud I am.

Actually, there *are* words, but I'm running late for a date with Jules, and she's already pissed because I blew off dinner with her aunt Tuesday night so Gus and I could go to the WWE Raw Supershow. So do a quick Google search for Barbara Kingsolver's 2008 Duke University commencement address and read that. She pretty much stole everything she wanted to say from me anyway. (We've never actually met, but her speech sounds eerily similar—like, *exact*—to a speech I gave at the 1998 homecoming pep rally. Coincidence? You tell me.)

If you don't have time to do that, then at least take to heart this quote from Genghis Khan. I keep it above my bed and read it every morning; it's gotten me through some incredibly tough times. I hope it inspires you as it's inspired me.

> "A man's greatest work is to break his enemies, to drive
> them before him, to take from them all the things that have
> been theirs, to hear the weeping of those who cherished them."

Kick some ass out there, amigo. Also, never call me.

Afterword

One last thing: if you ever get a chance to have dinner at the Redwood Bistro, I *highly* recommend the pan-roasted sea bass with red peppers. Amazing. But switch out the cauliflower au gratin for the Brussels sprouts with bacon. They don't usually make substitutions, but ask for the chef, Bernard, and tell him you know me.

After-Afterword

I almost forgot; if you talk to Bernard at the Redwood, use the name Chester Stockenfield.

DO NOT—repeat, DO NOT—use the name Shawn Spencer. It's a long story, but trust me on this.

Acknowledgments

This book has been a dream of mine since at least the last half of last year, and without the dedicated assistance of those around me, you would probably be reading something crappy and lowbrow like Harry Potter or *The New York Times* crossword. I am engorged with gratitude to the following:

To my best black friend Gus, who repeatedly managed to secure research materials for me at the local library, but then stopped after incurring $1.70 in late fees, which he's now formally protesting. I say that's what happens when you return books to the bin in the parking lot the afternoon before a holiday. No one is going to walk out there, collect, and check in those books, dude. They're watching the clock. Those poor people want to go home and start enjoying their day off, for Saint Crispin's sake! They work in a library!

To my close personal friend, thrice-decorated Head Detective Carlton Lassiter of the Santa Barbara Police Department, who provided valuable technical consultation in matters related to real police work. His marionette-like gait, reptilian profile, and utter refusal to recognize my superiority couldn't have provided a better example for how *not* to be an effective crime fighter.

To my father, Henry Spencer, who offered very little by way of actual assistance, but who will probably give me a ton of crap if I don't at least mention him here.

And to Juliet. For everything else. You radiate and glimmer, like an exquisite abalone.[1]

---

[1] JULIET: Shawn, did you just compare me to *a sea snail*?[a]
   [a] A sea snail that has one of the most advanced suits of body armor in the entire animal kingdom. I also called you "exquisite."

Photography and Illustration Credits